BRINDLE

BOOKS

http://www.brindlebooks.co.uk

WELLINGTON'S DRAGOON 1:

TO THE DOURO

BY

DAVID J. BLACKMORE

Acknowledgements

The first people I have to thank are the members of the writing group in Howden. It is because of them, their encouragement and their advice, that this book got written. Our monthly meetings are always stimulating and fun, and sometimes challenging. Such as the challenge to write the opening paragraph of a novel, which eventually led to this book series. Thanks are also due to Gillian Caldicott for reading everything, and seeing the wood for the trees, as well as my typos.

I have been re-enacting cavalry of various types for a long time, most recently B Troop, 16th Light Dragoons. It was with them that I learnt some of the realities of being a Light Dragoon, like the correct way to handle a 1796 Light Cavalry Sabre, and how to wheel by threes. It was with them that I took part in Waterloo 200, and charged across the original battlefield through the standing corn. Without those experiences this book would not have been written. My thanks to you all, and to all I have ridden with over the years.

I am fortunate to be able to ride two or three times a week, frequently on Johnny, who is a real horse, and on many other excellent horses. I am grateful to Mark Atkinson of Atkinson Action Horses who makes all that possible, from whom I have learnt so much about horses and riding, and who continues to make a me a better rider than I was last week. There is no better pastime than being out on a good horse, whatever the weather.

Finally, of course, I must thank Neil Hinchliffe for introducing me to Richard Hinchliffe of Brindle Books, and Richard for taking up my offering.

Introduction

The 'Wellington's Dragoon' series relates the adventures of a young officer, Michael Roberts, of the 16th Light Dragoons during the war against Napoleon in Portugal and Spain, and in the final campaign of Waterloo.

The 16th Light Dragoons is a real regiment, the only one to serve under Sir Arthur Wellesley, later the Duke of Wellington, from when he took command in April 1809, all the way through the Peninsular War to its end in 1814, and again in the Waterloo Campaign of 1815. Michael Roberts, is a complete invention, as is Emyr Lloyd and many, but not all, of the NCOs and dragoons of the regiment. All the other officers that appear served in the Regiment. William Tomkinson left us one of the finest diaries of a cavalry officer from the period.

Many of the other characters you will meet in the series were real people, and many of the events are also real, including the crossing of the Douro using wine barges that is the pivotal action of this book. How those barges came to be there has never been explained, until now.

I hope that I have done justice to everyone, and every event, real and imagined, if not, the fault is mine.

You may be struck by the spelling of Buonaparte. That is the early spelling of Napoleon's family name, he changed it to try to appear more French, but the early spelling remained in common usage in a slightly derogatory manner. Given Michael's family history, it seemed appropriate to use it.

Finally, as you will see, Emyr Lloyd's speech is peppered with Welsh. "Diolch" is thanks, "diolch yn fawr" is thank you very much, "chwarae teg" literally translates as fair play, and is used in the sense of 'fair enough.' The rest the reader can probably guess.

Chapter 1

In the distance he heard cannon fire, and knew, without needing to see, that one of His Majesty's Ships was entering the Carrick Roads and exchanging salutes with the guns at Pendennis Castle. It was an unwelcome reminder of the war, but Michael Roberts strolled on, carelessly, along Falmouth's narrow Market Street and passed by the Parish Church. The latest news was not good, with a French army reported to be marching on Portugal. He and his parents had been forced to flee Lisbon six years before, only able to return a year later with the Treaty of Amiens, short lived though it was. And now it was happening all over again. Well, he thought, there was nothing he could do about any of it.

A gust of a chill November wind plucked at the stylish top hat that sat rakishly on his head, and his hand flew up to secure it, while his open topcoat billowed open, revealing a young man of middling height, with a build that was muscled, but lean. Under the hat, thick, dark brown hair framed his unfashionably tanned face, with its brown eyes, hinting at an exotic background. Well dressed in a blue tailcoat, white pantaloons, polished top boots and a crisp, white neckcloth, he was a well known figure in the town.

A moment later he was pushing his way through the doors of Wynn's Hotel. It was still only late afternoon, but he hoped he might find a familiar face and a game or two of billiards to pass the time. The main public room was empty save for two figures at a table in the corner. As his eyes adjusted to the gloom he made out Captain Porteous, captain of one of the packet ships that sailed regularly between Falmouth and Lisbon. He knew the sailing times as well as anyone in Falmouth and realised that the captain must have just returned from Lisbon. He didn't know the other man, but walked over anyway. As he neared the table he was aware of Porteous' companion scrutinising him carefully.

"Captain Porteous," Michael began, "excuse me for interrupting. You're just in from Lisbon?"

Porteous smiled at him, "Yes, indeed, Mr Roberts, and we had a fast run, only thirteen days." The smile changed to a frown. "But I doubt I'll be going back for a while. The Walsingham should be there about now, but the rumour was that the French were demanding the ports be closed to British vessels." Porteous smiled again, "I did see your father, Michael, he was well, and told me your mother was, as well. From what he told me they should have left Lisbon by now, sailing on the Venus."

Michael beamed at this news. "That is splendid news, captain, thank you."

"My pleasure," replied the captain, "they should be back here by the end of the month, early December at the latest."

"Well, thank you, again, captain," said Michael. "I won't intrude on you anymore." He glanced at Porteous' companion who was watching Michael intently. Nodding at both men, Michael left them, and made his way to the billiard room, calling for a glass of claret as he went.

The billiard room was empty, and Michael set about a few practice shots while he sipped his wine and waited to see if anyone joined him. A quarter of an hour later he had almost finished his wine and was thinking of giving up and going home when the door opened. To Michael's surprise it wasn't one of the billiard room's usual patrons who entered, but the man who had been sitting with Captain Porteous. He was well dressed, in his thirties, with a large domed forehead and receding hair. His expression was slightly questioning, an effect aided by piercing, pale grey eyes. He was followed by one of the hotel's waiters bearing a tray with two glasses of claret on it.

"Mr Roberts, forgive my forwardness, but perhaps you would be good enough to take a glass of wine with me?" As he spoke the waiter placed the tray on a side table and left, closing the door behind him.

Somewhat taken aback, Michael replied. "I fear you have the advantage of me, sir."

"Yes, yes, I suppose I do." The man paused for a moment as if thinking. "I could have asked Captain Porteous to introduce me, but, no matter, and, in any case, he has just left the hotel. The name is Musgrave, Thomas Musgrave."

"Well, Mr Musgrave, if you are known to the captain, that is good enough for me." Michael walked to the table, and both men took a glass. "Your health, sir."

"And yours, Mr Roberts." They both took a sip, and then, to Michael's astonishment, Musgrave continued in fluent Portuguese. "I gathered from your exchange with Porteous that your parents are, or were, in Lisbon. I took liberty of enquiring of the good captain a little about you."

"Really?" replied a mystified Michael, slipping easily into familiar Portuguese.

"Yes. I find it useful to know of people like your good self, with a good knowledge of foreign places, and a command of a language. In my business I never know when I might need to call on such."

"And, might I ask, sir, what that business is?"

"Ah, I am associated with the Post Office, which is how I know Porteous. And you, if I might ask, what are you occupying yourself with?" Musgrave's eyes seemed to say, 'the truth now, I shall know if you tell me anything else.'

Michael paused, wondering how to answer, when the honest reply would be 'nothing'. "To tell truth, Mr Musgrave, very little. I keep hoping to return to Lisbon, it is where I consider my home to be."

"I see." Musgrave looked thoughtfully at Michael. "I understand that you were born in Lisbon, grew up there. You speak the language like a native."

"Indeed, I was, and your Portuguese is also excellent, Mr Musgrave," Michael interrupted. "You must have spent some time there yourself?"

"Yes, I did, some little time ago. But, tell me, as you were born and raised there, do you consider yourself Portuguese or British?"

Michael bridled at the question. "Sir, you are presumptuous."

"I beg your pardon, Mr Roberts," Musgrave smiled apologetically, and raised his hands, palms outwards towards Michael. "I meant no offence; I am simply curious."

Michael nodded his acceptance of the apology, "Then none taken, Mr Musgrave, but you may take it that I consider myself thoroughly British."

Musgrave nodded, thoughtfully. "Then I will ask you to forgive one more presumption? You, perhaps, feel a connection to Portugal, you would help her, if it were possible?"

"Of course I would." Michael's answer came back sharply. "I love Portugal, I grew up there. I have friends there." Musgrave was beginning to irritate him.

"Yes, yes, of course." Musgrave looked pleased at Michael's response. "...and have you given any thought as to how you might help Portugal?"

"No, Mr Musgrave, I have not, nor do I see how I could be of any possible assistance here in Falmouth."

"Perhaps if you returned to Portugal?"

"Perhaps, but I see little prospect of that, with a French army marching on Lisbon."

"Indeed, Mr Roberts, indeed, but one must keep an open mind on these matters." Musgrave consulted his watch. "Now, however, I must ask you to forgive me again. I have an appointment that I cannot afford to be late for." Musgrave turned to the door and had half opened it when he paused and looked back at Michael. "Perhaps we shall meet again, Mr Roberts? In the meantime, I wish you well, and a safe homecoming for your parents. Good day to you." And with that he was gone.

Michael stared at the closed door. He took a drink of his wine and realised that Musgrave had barely touched his. He ran the conversation through in his head. He was mystified, and a little irritated by the sense of having been interviewed and assessed. He would ask Porteous about him the next time they met. Then the door opened again, and two of Michael's friends came in. He won a game and a guinea, and tried to put the strange Mr Musgrave from his mind.

Two hours later Michael was walking through the dark November evening back to his uncle's house where he had been living since leaving Lisbon. The south easterly wind blowing along the street was now in his face, bringing with it the smell of the open sea, and he buttoned up his top coat as he walked along. He liked Falmouth, but it wasn't Lisbon. The weather was colder and damper in the winter, not so hot in the summer. He loved the hunting he managed two or three days a week. The fortnightly balls at Wynn's Assembly Rooms were pleasurable, and he never wanted for a dancing partner. He was considered, by the eligible young ladies of Falmouth, to be quite handsome, but in this town with its many places of worship, and large congregations, their parents and guardians considered him to be dangerous. Consequently he missed Roberta. He had a few friends to dine with and play billiards with. He kept himself amused. Still, he missed Lisbon, his parents, their home, the wine and the food, his friends. He wondered if Roberta missed him.

His uncle was a lawyer, and, unfortunately, kept trying to persuade Michael to become a lawyer as well. He could not understand Michael's reluctance to enter a safe and profitable profession, and become his partner, eventually taking over the practice. At times, the atmosphere between them was somewhat strained. He wished his parents safely in Falmouth. He wished the war was over so that he could go home.

Around the corner by the church the wind became fresher still and he quickened his pace, hurrying on to his uncle's home. He came in sight of the fine red brick house with its three floors and bow windows, and reaching it a minute later, Michael bounded up the steps, pushed through the door and quickly closed it behind him, against the strengthening wind.

To the right, the door to his uncle's study, where he conducted his business as a lawyer, stood slightly ajar, and he heard his uncle call out, "Michael, is that you?"

"Yes, uncle, just a moment," Michael replied as he removed his hat and coat.

Inside the room his uncle Jocelyn looked up from a letter he was holding. "It's from your father," he said. "Captain Porteous delivered it personally, about an hour ago."

"Oh? I saw Porteous in Wynn's, not two hours ago, he said he'd had a good run, and that he saw father in Lisbon, he said nothing to me about a letter, but he was in company."

"I imagine he was being discreet; he shouldn't carry private mail." Jocelyn passed the letter to Michael, who quickly read the short note.

'Lisbon, 17th October, 1807

Dear Brother, forgive the brevity of this letter, but the Falmouth Packet sails soon and I must ensure this letter is on it. There is news that the French are marching on Lisbon. Baron Quintela has urged us to leave for England as soon as possible. I have liquidated what assets I can, and I am sending something for you. I shall carry with us what I can of our wealth, perhaps half, but to spread the risk I shall leave the rest in Lisbon, under the protection of Augusto, and I enclose a duplicate key to the strong box. We hope to sail on the 21st on the Venus, in convoy with HMS Lavinia. We should make Falmouth towards the end of November.

Susan sends her love to you and Michael, your affectionate brother, Edward.'

Michael looked at his uncle who said "Porteous was able to tell me that Edward and Susan are well, although he only saw your father."

"Yes, he told me the same, and about their plans to sail on the Venus."

Jocelyn paused for a moment. "There was also this." He indicated a small box, its lid off, lying on the desk. It was no larger than a pack of cards, the paper wrapping and the string, generously sealed with red wax, lying discarded. On the paper he saw his uncle's name, but no address, written in what he recognised as his father's hand. In the box was a key, on a silver chain, and a small, velvet bag, drawn closed with a red ribbon.

Jocelyn spoke quietly, "Tip the contents of the bag into the box. Carefully now."

Michael gave his uncle a puzzled glance, then he lifted out the key, placed it on the desk, and picked up the bag. It felt as if there were small bits of gravel in it. He loosened the ribbon and very carefully tipped the bag into the box. What came out was a cascade of small, rough, glass-like stones. "Are those…?"

"Yes, Michael. They're uncut diamonds."

The two men were quiet for a moment, staring at the pile of stones. Jocelyn said, "These can go in my strong box, and I think it best if we tell no one about them. Apart from that there would seem to be very little that we can do except await the arrival of your father and mother."

Michael nodded his agreement.

Jocelyn carefully poured the stones back into the pouch, and placed it and the key in their little box. "If you will wait a moment, I shall go and secure these in the box in my bedroom."

While he was gone, Michael took the opportunity to read again the letter from his father. Baron Quintela traded in many things, including diamonds from Brazil. Michael knew that the Baron and his father got on well, and that there was a strong, mutual respect between them. The Baron was happy for Edward Roberts to trade in his own name in what was, in a small way, almost a partnership. It was little surprise, then, that his father should have diamonds in his possession.

Jocelyn returned a few moments later. "That's those safely away," he said, as Michael handed the letter back to him. Then he asked, "Now, tell me, Michael, who is Augusto?"

"I am afraid that I have absolutely no idea," Michael replied.

"Oh!" Jocelyn was taken aback by Michael's answer. "Some business acquaintance of Edward's perhaps? It is two years since you have been in Lisbon."

"True, uncle, but it would have to be someone close to my father for him to entrust them with, well, I don't know, I don't know what property he has, exactly. There is the house, presumably there are trade goods, perhaps money in the bank."

"Indeed, indeed," Jocelyn paused. "However, I am sure your father will explain when he arrives. I think we can expect them at the end of the month, as your father said, or early December at the latest, depending on the weather. We must be patient, Michael, patient. There is nothing else we can do."

"No, indeed not, uncle."

"And now," Jocelyn smiled at Michael, "I am expecting a client, so if you will excuse me? And then we shall have a little supper in an hour."

"Yes, of course, uncle." Michael left the study and walked to the back of the house and into the kitchen, where Mrs Trevellick, his uncle's housekeeper, was preparing food, helped by the maid, Jenny. "Mrs Trevellick, do you think I might have a cup of coffee? I shall be in the parlour."

"Oh, Mr Michael, of course you can, sir. No word from your parents?"

"No, I am afraid not, nothing at all. Captain Porteous has called to say he had seen my father in Lisbon, and that they were making arrangements to come to England."

A few minutes later Michael was comfortably settled in front of the fire, coffee to hand, and the previous Saturday's Gazette. He would hunt on Saturday, as for the intervening two days, he was sure he would pass the time. The recollection of Musgrave's question about how he occupied himself came to Michael. Briefly an unsettling feeling of dissatisfaction with his answer rose in him. He crushed it ruthlessly.

The following Monday, by pure chance, Michael met Captain Porteous in the street. "Captain Porteous, I am glad to see you, sir. I must thank you for the assistance you gave my father."

"Oh, think nothing of it Mr Roberts, it was a small favour, one best not mentioned." Porteous smiled and tapped the side of his nose.

"Of course not, Captain," Michael smiled and nodded his agreement, "but might I enquire a little about Mr Musgrave?"

Porteous looked puzzled. "Who? Musgrave? I am afraid I know no one of that name."

"But he was talking to you when I saw you in Wynn's, last Wednesday, the day you made your visit to my uncle."

"Him? Was that his name? I am sorry Mr Roberts; I'd never seen the gentleman before. He came up to me in Wynn's and was asking me about passengers on the packet. Said he was expecting someone, but we had no passengers on that run. Then he asked if he could join me and was asking about how things were in Lisbon."

Michael was more than a little confused. "He didn't ask you about me, or my parents?"

"No, he didn't mention you or them."

Michael was completely bemused. "I beg your pardon, Captain, I must be confused with someone else. No matter, and thank you again."

They bade each other good day and Porteous walked off towards the harbour. Michael walked slowly home, deep in thought. How on Earth could Musgrave have known about his parents, and his own history?

Almost eight weeks later Michael and Jocelyn were sitting in the candlelit gloom of his uncle's dining room. Trevellick, his uncle's manservant, and Jenny, the maid, had cleared the table after dinner, and left the two men with a bottle of port. A healthy fire warmed the room, but outside it was dark, and a cold rain was lashing at the window. It was Christmas Eve.

Jocelyn broke the silence that was as gloomy as the night. "I think, Michael, that we must face up to it. The Venus has not been seen since the Lavinia parted company with the fleet from Oporto. All the other ships in the fleet are now accounted for. I am afraid that they are lost to us."

Michael stared into his glass of port. "Yes, uncle, and I am sure you are right, but it is difficult just to give up hope without any certainty. Perhaps they were forced into a port in northern Spain, or taken by the French?"

They sat in silence for a moment before Jocelyn replied. "Yes, it is difficult, I know, but there has been no word at all. If the Venus had made land somewhere, even if she was wrecked or captured, I would have expected to hear something, and yet there has been nothing, nothing at all."

"And what am I to do if they are lost?" Michael asked with a touch of petulance. "I cannot inherit my father's property until he is declared dead, and when might that be? And what property? If the Venus has indeed been lost, then everything my parents had with them is lost, and as to any property in Lisbon, I know of no one called Augusto, no one!"

Jocelyn sighed at Michael's tone, but maintained his patience. If Edward was lost, then he was going to have to have a serious conversation with Michael about his future. He did not relish the prospect, but Michael could not continue to lead a life of indolent leisure. "Indeed," said Jocelyn, "and at present there is no way to communicate with Quintela and seek his help."

Silence fell once more, and Michael felt wretched. He hadn't seen his parents for nearly three years, not since he had been sent to England after the war with Spain broke out in late '04. The regular packet service between Falmouth and Lisbon had meant that hardly a month went by without a letter from his mother, and sometimes his father. His mother's letters he shared with her father, a clergyman with a rural parish four hours ride from Falmouth. Now it seemed that there would be no more letters, and he would never see them again.

Jocelyn spoke quietly. "As, of course, you know, it is almost another two years before you are twenty one, and your father gave me authority to act as your guardian while you are here."

"Yes, uncle."

Relieved at Michael's calmer tone, Jocelyn took a sip of his port before speaking again. "I also hold your father's will. It is straightforward; everything is left to you. Of course, there was provision for your mother, but that is now of no matter. He also gave me a power of attorney to act on his behalf in all matters relating to his affairs." He paused, and glanced at Michael before continuing. "Consequently, I should tell you that I have taken steps about the diamonds."

At that Michael looked at him sharply. "Have you?"

"Yes." Jocelyn took another drink. "I have sold them."

"What? What were they worth?"

"A little over five thousand pounds."

"Five thousand pounds?" Michael was shocked at the sum.

"As you know," Jocelyn continued, "I have connections, friends even, amongst the Jewish community in the town. I helped them obtain the land for their new synagogue. They know Jews in the London diamond trade, and one happened to be visiting relations here. I was able to get a valuation, discreetly, of course. Then the dealer offered to buy them, and I accepted."

"Can you trust this man?"

Jocelyn looked hard at his nephew, and spoke very distinctly, "I trust his relation completely."

"Forgive me, please, uncle. This is something of a surprise. Where are the diamonds now?"

"London, I imagine, and the five thousand pounds has been deposited with Praed's in London, and can be drawn upon at the Cornish Naval. And you must forgive me for acting without consulting you, but I considered it the best course of action. Money in the bank is safer than a small pouch of pebbles."

"Uncle, they were my father's stones, he gave you authority over them; he addressed them to you. Let the money sit there until, well, I don't know. As you say, it is almost two years before I come of age, but unless my father is declared dead I won't inherit, and you will continue to manage his affairs in England."

"There is a better use for the money, Michael. It is more than enough to cover the costs of you training to become a lawyer."

Michael swallowed the sharp retort that came to his tongue, and sat silent for a moment. If his father was dead, what choice did he have, with his uncle as his guardian? "Indeed, uncle, and I know how much that would please you. Perhaps we might discuss it after our visit tomorrow?"

In the morning they were to ride over to visit Michael's grandfather, and stay for a few days. He had been a chaplain to a cavalry regiment, and had a somewhat more robust view of life than most of the clergy and ministers of Falmouth, with his liking for horses, hounds and hunting. On Boxing Day Michael and Jocelyn planned to join the local hunt.

"Certainly we can, and thank you, Michael, I am glad you feel that way." Jocelyn was relieved, and decided to let the matter lie for the moment, reaching for the port bottle, and topping up the glasses. "There's only three dozen of that port left in the cellar. If the French take Portugal I don't know where we shall get any more."

The conversation readily turned to a discussion of the political situation, the question of where to get more port, and the weather prospects for the next few days.

Later that night they attended Midnight Mass and lit candles for Edward and Susan Roberts.

Any concerns about the weather were proven unfounded when Christmas day dawned bright and frosty. By eight-thirty Michael and Jocelyn were mounted, and riding out of town, followed by Choak, Jocelyn's groom, leading two fine hunters. At first the going was difficult, the ground frozen and slippery, but clear blue skies meant that what little heat there was in the sun soon softened the ground and they began to make good progress.

After a couple of hours they stopped at a small inn and had a tankard of mulled cider that warmed them through as they stood in front of a roaring log fire. Choak joined them after taking care of the horses. On occasions like this the boundary between master and servant became blurred, such was the fellowship of horsemen. Michael liked it, he enjoyed the easy conversation about the horses and the prospects for tomorrow's hunt. Horses seemed to him to be a great leveller, sometimes literally!

Shortly after midday they arrived at the vicarage, built of grey stone, surrounded by low, moss covered walls, sitting next to a grey stone church with a squat tower, the churchyard full of grey headstones within its own wall. It nestled on the edge of a small village not far from Helston, pretty enough in summer when the trees were in leaf, but now it struggled to look anything but bleak in the weak sunlight. However, the greeting that awaited them was anything but grey and bleak. As they clattered up, the door of the vicarage swung wide and the Reverend John Isles strode out, giving the lie to his seventy years. He was followed by his housekeeper and the maid, while around the corner came his groom. "Michael, Jocelyn, so good to see you, come on now, off those horses and come inside. Good to see you as well, Choak, Scobell will help you with the horses, the stables are ready, and Mrs Menwynick has something hot for you in the kitchen."

Within minutes Michael, Jocelyn and John Isles were in the parlour with a glass of mulled wine each. After the initial euphoria of greeting the mood turned sombre. "I have to ask," said the Reverend, "is there any news?"

"No, John, I am afraid not. None at all," Jocelyn replied.

The Reverend sipped his wine thoughtfully. "Then I fear that we must reconcile ourselves to the loss of our beloved relatives, and take what solace we can in the certain knowledge that they are with God." He took another sip of his wine before continuing. "It is right that we think of those who we have lost, but not only in sadness, rather also in joy at the lives they shared with us. It is right that we should mourn, but we must also look to the future. We three are now all of our family, and it is good that we are gathered together on this Holy Day. And it is in joy that we should celebrate this day of all days, and I am sure, as sure as I am of Christ's love, that Susan and Edward would wish us the joy of the season."

He paused as Michael nodded at his words and Jocelyn spoke. "Amen, John, you are right there. And I can almost hear your Susan telling us to cheer up." He smiled sadly.

Michael stared at the floor, grappling with his feelings of loss, of being lost, and the truth in his grandfather's words.

The Reverend Isles put a kindly hand on Michael's shoulder. "Now, Michael, I know Mrs Menwynick and Mrs Scobell have been labouring for days, and were up this morning before all, and should be preparing a most sumptuous dinner for us. We must not disappoint them with long faces! And today we shall all dine together, masters and servants without distinction, and give thanks for the mercies that we have. So, come, drink up, and be of good cheer!"

Michael and Jocelyn could not help but smile at the Reverend as he banished, for the moment, all sadness and melancholy, and they drained their glasses with him. "Now," the Reverend continued, "dinner will be at six prompt, but there is a cold collation in the dining room to tide us over, and then we shall take a brisk walk to work up an appetite, I think we will need it."

Chapter 2

That Christmas dinner was one that Michael would often look back on, and always the memory would bring a smile. His grandfather sat at the head of the table, Jocelyn to his right, Michael to his left, then Choak and Scobell opposite each other, Mrs Menwynick at the other end, when she was not rushing to and from the kitchen. She was flanked by the maid, Amy, and Mrs Scobell. A piping hot beef and vegetable soup was followed by a huge goose, venison, roast beef, with vegetables and gravy, after which came a game pie, and then the plum pudding. Naturally, all this was washed down with good local ale and fine French claret.

When the table was cleared, Mrs Menwynick, Amy and Mrs Scobell retired to the kitchen, from whence a lot of clattering and occasional laughter could be heard. Choak and Scobell disappeared to the stables to feed the horses, and check that all was ready for the morrow. Michael, Jocelyn and the Reverend were left with the cheese, and a bottle of port. Eventually the bottle was empty, and the conversation turned into a satisfied, comfortable silence while the three men sipped the last of their port.

"Well, now," said Jocelyn, "that, John, must be one of the best Christmas dinners I have ever enjoyed."

"Indeed, grandfather, it was a rare feast," added Michael.

"Thank you, both, thank you. But now I see it is eleven o'clock, and we must make an early start if we are to get to the meet on time. It is a good hour's hack from here, so we should be ready to leave by eight."

"Grandfather, do you intend to go to the meet tomorrow?" Michael asked.

"Indeed I do, who knows, it might be my last chance to ride out with you both on Boxing Day."

"Now, come, sir…" Jocelyn started to protest at the thought.

"No, no, Jocelyn, calm yourself, please. I have every intention to ride for many years yet, including, the Good Lord willing, on Boxing Day, but I shall no longer be following the hounds. No, tomorrow I shall stay with the ladies in their coaches. They do like to press refreshments on me," he chuckled. "And now," he said, rising from the table, "I shall bid you both goodnight." With that he took up a candle stick and left the room.

Jocelyn shook his head and finished his port. "A remarkable man, your grandfather, quite remarkable. Well, goodnight to you Nephew, and Merry Christmas!" With that he took another candlestick and followed the Reverend out of the room.

Michael sat by the light of the remaining few candles and the flickering fire. He sipped his port and stared reflectively into the glowing embers. His grandfather's words on their arrival were true. He was not yet reconciled to the loss of his parents, nor, if he was honest, had he entirely given up hope. Yet he could not mourn for ever. In the last few weeks he had come to feel that he had to do something with his life, something meaningful.

The changes in his circumstances had made him examine his position, and he had seen an idle man, achieving nothing, a man with no aspirations, no expectations beyond the next game of billiards, or the next day's hunting. And they were no longer enough. He could no longer crush the increasing sense of dissatisfaction and frustration with the prospect of mere pastimes and entertainments. He needed more.

As he saw it, he was a penniless orphan, well, perhaps not penniless, but far from financially secure, and he was now entirely dependent on his uncle. His father, he knew, had periodically arranged transfers of money to his uncle, not that his uncle was not comfortably off himself, his law practice was successful. But his own sense of what was right would not allow him to continue to be dependent on him, particularly if that meant entering the legal profession.

He was, despite his uncle's pressure and his apparent acquiescence to the idea, quite sure about that. His Latin was simply inadequate, his penmanship, or lack of it, would also seem to an obstacle. Let alone the fact that the idea of a life shackled to a desk and dusty law books, and forever in Falmouth, was a complete anathema to him. About the only skill or ability he had was as a horseman. There had to be something else, there just had to be, but he was running out of time.

The door to the dining room opened and Mrs Menwynick came in. "Oh, Mr Michael, I'm sorry sir, I didn't realise you were still here." She made to withdraw.

"No, no, Mrs Menwynick, come in, come in, I was about to retire."

"I was just going to make sure the fire was damped down and safe for the night."

"Please, carry on, I'll just finish this glass."

Mrs Menwynick moved into the light, and dealt with the fire. She turned towards the door, but hesitated, and then spoke. "I do hope you don't mind me saying, sir, but we were all so sorry to hear about your parents."

"Why, thank you, thank you very much." He paused. "Would you sit with me, madam? I feel a little melancholic."

"I shouldn't, sir."

"Mrs Menwynick, it is still Christmas Day for a little longer, there are no distinctions, and I would be grateful for your company a while. Please, sit down."

She took a seat across the table from Michael. After a moment's silence she spoke. "I remember when I lost Mr Menwynick. That was in '93. He was killed when a hay wain tipped over. Dreadful it was, sir, but at least I had a body. My two boys, they were at Trafalgar, you know, sir. My youngest, thank God, was on the Prince, and came home safe. But my eldest was killed on the Victory, with Admiral Nelson, put over the side in a hammock, he was. It's hard to lose loved ones, particularly when you can't bury them. But you have to carry on, sir, the people you loved would want you to. I was fortunate, your grandfather needed a housekeeper, and here I came, and here I stay. That's all a widow can do. That, and curse that damned Corsican, begging your pardon, sir. 'Tis all his doing. 'Tis him as killed my boy, and 'tis him as drove your parents to sea in November. So I curses him, sir, I curses him. 'Tis all I can do." She paused for a moment, and calmed herself. "But you, sir, you're a young gentleman with your whole life ahead of you. You can do something. You can't bring your parents back, but you can do something." She stood. "And I've said too much, sir. 'Tis that wine of your grandfather's, I ain't used to it. So I'll beg you to forgive me, and bid you good night, Mr Michael." So saying, she left the room.

Michael hadn't moved while Mrs Menwynick had been speaking, now he sipped the last of his port and considered her words. She was right, she had simply put into words what he felt, the need to do something. He felt that there was a suggestion in her words, something that resonated with him, but his head was thick with drink, and he needed his bed, perhaps it would all be clearer in the morning. He took a candlestick and made his way to his room. Sleep came quickly.

Overnight a band of light rain passed over Cornwall, raising the temperature and softening the ground enough to make the going good across country. The day itself was another bright one, and as they rode they were joined by others going to the meet. By the time they reached the inn where the meet was, their party had grown to nearly twenty riders and almost thirty horses, as grooms led hunters and second horses. At the inn itself there was already a large gathering, perhaps a hundred riders in all, for the Four Burrow Hunt was popular and respected. The Reverend Isles was a well known figure, and Michael and Jocelyn were introduced to many there, others they knew a little, one or two were old friends from Falmouth. By ten o'clock the Reverend had got himself snuggly ensconced in a coach with two ladies whose husbands were hunting. There were warm rugs and provisions, and he happily waved Michael and Jocelyn goodbye when the Master, Sir John Rogers, and his huntsmen moved off with the pack of some fifteen and a half couple of hounds.

Michael had exchanged his hack for his hunter, a black gelding, just under sixteen hands, called Johnny. He was young, fit, fast and sharp, to say nothing of brave. Scobell stayed in attendance on the Reverend and the hacks, but Choak rode with Michael and Jocelyn, as happy as a sand boy as the Reverend had lent him his hunter for the day.

There followed almost two long, cold, fruitless hours, the horses getting restless, the cold seeping into boots and freezing toes. Flasks were gradually emptied. One or two riders slipped miserably away. Then the hounds were put into a small copse, and found almost immediately. The fox, a fine, large, dog fox, broke cover and the chase was on. Jocelyn was a steady rider, and Michael soon left him behind with the bulk of the field as he, and perhaps a dozen others, rode hard to keep up with the huntsmen. The hounds were in full cry and stone walls were taken at speed. Michael felt a wonderful thrill, the exhilaration of galloping, Johnny stretching out under him, going who knew where. At one wall a huntsman to his left crashed to the ground as his horse fell on landing. He pressed on without a backward glance. A brook was taken with barely a break in stride. Three, four miles flashed by. Most of the field was now far behind, but alongside Michael was a gentleman he didn't recognise. He was well built, in his early thirties, with large brown whiskers, and was mounted on a magnificent bay horse. They went neck and neck through an open gateway, and their stirrups touched for an instant. Michael glanced across, the man grinned at him, then urged his horse forward to greater effort, and he pulled slightly ahead. Johnny couldn't match the bay on the flat, but the fox ran into bad ground, strewn with rocks and gorse bushes, and there Johnny's agility told, and as they cleared another wall onto open ground they were a few lengths ahead.

Now Michael could see the hounds closing on the tiring fox. He was up alongside the Master, but taking care not to get in front. Ahead there were only the two remaining huntsmen. The fox, the hounds, and the huntsmen went up a steep bank and disappeared over a low wall at the top. Michael and the Master followed, and cleared the wall together. On the other side the ground dropped away quickly, and Johnny checked slightly and almost fell as they slid rather than rode down the slope. Michael needed all his skill to stay in the saddle. The Master was more fortunate and pulled ahead.

Then it was all over. The lead hound brought the fox down, and in a moment it was dead. One of the huntsmen dismounted and rescued the carcase from the hounds. Michael brought Johnny to a stand, flanks heaving, a yard or two from the Master who called out to the huntsmen,

"Well done, well done Teague, well done Harvey". He turned to Michael with a smile, "Well done, sir, well ridden," he brought his horse closer and offered Michael his hand, "John Rogers." Michael shook the hand, "Michael Roberts, Sir John."

"Ah, then you must be Isle's grandson, glad to know you sir, glad to know you. And, please, my condolences for your loss."

Before Michael could respond the rider on the bay came up to them. "Damn it, Sir John, that was a fine run, but I fear your huntsman has a broken arm for his troubles." He turned to Michael. "And you, sir, very well ridden, that's a good horse you have there."

Sir John spoke, "Colonel Vivian; May I introduce Mr Michael Roberts of Falmouth, his grandfather is the Reverend Isles."

"Pleased to make your acquaintance, Mr Roberts, excellent riding, better than some of the officers in my regiment."

"Colonel Vivian is with the 7th Light Dragoons," Sir John explained.

"Hussars now, Sir John, we have reequipped, and a damn complicated business it was too. Everything has changed."

Sir John laughed. "Good luck with that Colonel, now, if you will excuse me, I must see to the hounds." He rode off calling to huntsmen and hounds alike.

Now other riders were beginning to arrive, among them Choak, who was grinning like an idiot at the exhilaration of the ride. One of the riders waved at Vivian. "That's my cousin," explained the Colonel, returning the wave. "I am visiting family in Truro for Christmas." Just then a huntsman sounded his horn and the pack moved off in search of more quarry, and the two men found themselves following, side by side.

"Tell me, Mr Roberts, what are you engaged in, in Falmouth?"

The question, asked innocently enough, brought the conversation with Musgrave crashing back into Michael's mind, and once again, he felt honesty was his only option. "I am afraid that I am entirely unoccupied at present." He went on to tell Vivian about Lisbon and the loss of his parents.

"My condolences, Mr Roberts, and forgive me, I did not mean to pry."

"It's quite alright, Colonel. I need to find something to do with myself, but I know not what."

"There's a fine tradition of Cornish naval officers."

"Indeed, but that has little appeal, and I fear that I am now a little elderly for the gun room."

Vivian laughed. "Very true, Mr Roberts, very true."

They rode on together a little further before Vivian spoke again. "Have you considered the army? The cavalry, of course. A good horseman such as yourself could do well."

"No, sir, I haven't."

"Well, perhaps you should. I'd be glad to see you in my regiment, but we've no vacancies at present. It's being hussars, ye see, damned fashionable, and to tell the truth, damned expensive as well. Anyway, my cousin seems to be trying to attract my attention, I had better see what he wants."

"Of course, Colonel, glad to have met you."

"Likewise, Mr Roberts, likewise," and Vivian rode off.

The rest of the day offered nothing so good as that first run, and the party from the Vicarage set off for home at about two o'clock. The party was in good spirits, and

Choak took delight in giving the Reverend Isles his eyewitness account of Michael's part in the first, splendid run, not omitting his own enjoyment. Michael rode quietly, smiling at the stories, but also wrapped up in considering Colonel Vivian's words. It was thus a happy, but tired group that returned to the vicarage, tired save for the Reverend who admitted he had passed a perfectly pleasant and undemanding day.

Later, after another fine dinner provided by Mrs Menwynick, the three gentlemen were sitting comfortably in the parlour, replete and relaxed. Michael and Jocelyn were again going over the day's events, telling the Reverend again what had occurred, although he had seen some of it, as the carriages had tried to follow events from the roads and lanes. Other news had reached him from mounted followers calling it a day or looking for their second horse.

The Reverend asked Michael, "I understand that you made the acquaintance of Colonel Vivian?"

"Indeed, I did, grandfather," Michael hesitated for a moment, glancing nervously at his uncle before he continued, "and he put an idea into my head that I should like your opinion on."

Jocelyn and the Reverend exchanged a glance, "Oh? Go on," said the Reverend, "I will help, if I can."

"Well, it has occurred to me that I might take a commission in a cavalry regiment."

Somewhat startled by this suggestion out of the blue, Jocelyn replied first, while the Reverend studied Michael closely. "What! It's out of the question!" he blustered, furiously. "You have agreed to enter the legal profession! Did the Colonel make the suggestion? It's outrageous."

"Yes, uncle, he did. He was complimentary about my riding, and then said he would have me in his regiment, if they had any vacancies, which they don't."

"Michael, my boy," the Reverend's voice was quiet, but grave, "this is a very serious thing that you are suggesting. Leaving aside all the practical questions, might I enquire as to why you are considering this?"

"Yes, yes" added an angry Jocelyn, "why?"

"Because," replied Michael, "it seems to me that I must do something. I have no money of my own, no inclination to enter business, or a profession, no, not even the Law, uncle, forgive me. I do not wish to be dependent upon relatives for my subsistence, and, in any case, I have no wish to idle my life away, as I have so far. I am young, fit and healthy, and I am informed I ride as well as many an officer. What else can I do? And in the circumstances, with my parents driven from their home and lost because of French aggression, it seems a perfectly reasonable means of doing something."

"It's out of the question," Jocelyn stated bluntly. He turned to the Reverend. "Well, John, what say you to this? I admit to being taken aback."

The Reverend paused, thoughtfully, for a moment, as Michael waited, nervously, for some response. "You know, of course, Michael, that I was a chaplain to a cavalry regiment, that I have seen something of war?"

"Yes, I do, sir."

"Indeed I was with my regiment in Portugal in '62 and '63, and again when it went to the American colonies in '76. So, you will acknowledge that I have some understanding of what it is that you suggest?"

"Yes, sir."

"It is a hard life," continued the Reverend, "you would have to face death and injury every day." Michael started to object, but the Reverend held up his hand. "No, no, I do not mean your own, I have no doubt, Michael, of your personal courage. No, I mean that of your fellow officers, some of whom would become as brothers to you. And that of the men, men with whom you would share dangers and discomfort, who would be reliant upon you, and you upon them, for your very survival. There is no rhyme nor reason on the battlefield, only savagery and fortune, good and ill. You will lose friends and horses in brutal ways, and without warning." He paused again, and looked at Michael. "And when you are not on the battlefield, which is most of the time, there is an endless round of duty and frequent spells of interminable boredom, when the close company of others is inescapable and trying. But, if you can accept that, and face it cheerfully, there is nothing like the comradeship forged on campaign and in battle. If you can conduct yourself with dignity, but also laugh at yourself, if you behave with honour and courage, and respect those qualities in others, you will have riches beyond mere money, and, who knows, you may even reach great rank and gain tangible wealth."

Michael took a deep breath. "I think I can do that, sir."

"Ha!" Jocelyn exclaimed. "Have you thought about the expense?" he asked. "Commissions don't come free, ye know, and I'll not pay for one, and there's no officer but doesn't have a private income."

"No, uncle, I am afraid I hadn't, although Colonel Vivian said something about hussars being expensive."

The Reverend snorted, "Hussars, ha! Popinjays more like. Nothing wrong with an honest dragoon regiment. But, still, your uncle is correct, commissions don't come free you know."

"Yes," Jocelyn broke in, "your father sent money for me to look after you, not throw it away on some fanciful idea that might get you killed! No sir, you shall become a lawyer, and that's an end to it."

Michael felt disconsolate, and lost for words.

"However," continued the Reverend, "I think that this is something you and I should discuss tomorrow, Jocelyn. I think you plan to leave us at about midday?" Jocelyn nodded, "then I suggest that we send this young man out for a few hours after breakfast and let you and I discuss this idea of Michael's, if he hasn't changed his mind after a night in a warm bed!"

"If you insist, John, but I tell you now, I am against it."

The following morning, after breakfast, Michael took himself off for a walk around the village and surrounding countryside. Jocelyn and the Reverend retired to the latter's study and sat themselves in comfortable chairs on either side of a warming fire. "Tell me, Jocelyn," began the Reverend, "I realise that you are Michael's guardian, but are you really so set against his proposal?"

Two hours later Michael returned, and walked nervously into his grandfather's study. The Reverend was pouring a cup of tea, "Ah, Michael, will you join us? Mrs Menwynick saw you returning and has only this moment brought the tea in."

Michael took a cup and settled carefully into a chair. His uncle, to his surprise, looked a little smug, but sat in silence.

"Well, Michael, I have persuaded your uncle that if you do not have a chance to explore further your idea, you will always wonder about it, and, possibly, even come to resent us for having prevented you." Michael made to protest. "No, Michael, hear me out. As I said to you last night, what you propose to undertake is a serious matter. I assume that you have not had second thoughts?"

"No, grandfather, not at all, rather I have come to wish for it wholeheartedly."

"Very well, then. Now, your uncle has raised reasonable concerns about the expense, not least the cost of a commission. The price of a Cornet's commission in a dragoon regiment is, I believe, seven hundred and thirty five pounds. A considerable sum. We have agreed, however, that if I obtain such a commission for you, your uncle will pay for your outfitting. We have also agreed that, if you do obtain a commission, you will receive a small but adequate allowance from the monies received from your father, and the sale of the diamonds that I understand he sent. The alternative is that you accept your uncle's wishes, and enter into the legal profession."

Michael's heart sank. He knew his grandfather depended almost entirely on his stipend, and could not buy him a commission. It was a meaningless arrangement. His uncle now had a slight smile on his lips. His grandfather took a sip of his tea, and then continued.

"I can also tell you;" he looked at Jocelyn, "and forgive me if I did not mention this, Jocelyn, commissions are sometimes given without purchase." Michael saw the smile disappear from his uncle's face to be replaced with one of shock. "That being the case, I will write to my old friend William Harcourt about your desire. He is now a Lieutenant General, and Colonel of my old regiment, the 16th Light Dragoons, but he was just a young Captain when I first knew him. He will, no doubt, grant you an interview, and perhaps be willing to accept you into his regiment, without purchase." He paused to sip his tea again.

"You didn't tell me that!" exclaimed Jocelyn. "I will not allow it, no sir, I will not!"

"Really?" The Reverend Isles had a look on his face that Michael had not seen before. "And how will it look to the good people of Falmouth if you renege on your word? Answer me that!"

"You wouldn't…"

"Do you wish to find out, sir?"

Jocelyn slumped back in his chair, speechless. Michael was stunned. He had never seen his grandfather so angry, for that was what he plainly was, but he was also in complete control of himself. Michael had a fleeting recollection of an occasion, the only occasion so far as he knew, when his mother had got angry with his father. She had been the same. Another memory came to him, of a fight in Lisbon, he too knew that anger.

"My grandson wishes to enter into an honourable profession, to do his duty for his country and his King, and to do so with the money provided for him by his father. And, by God, he shall if I have anything to do with it! And, Michael, I make you no promise other than to try, so you must promise me that if I am not successful, you will become the best lawyer in Cornwall."

Chapter 3

Michael knocked nervously on the door, and, in response to a muffled "Enter," opened it and walked in. Captain Ashworth looked up from his desk as the young man closed the door, stepped to the front of the desk, and gave a passable salute.

"Cornet Roberts, sir. Lieutenant Barra said I should report to you, sir."

Ashworth looked him over. He was correctly dressed in the uniform of the 16th, Queen's, Light Dragoons, white leather breeches, black hessian boots, dark blue jacket with its rows of silver lace and ball buttons, red sash, and his Tarleton helmet tucked under his arm. From his waist hung a sabre and sabretache. Ashworth guessed that Barra, the regiment's adjutant, had inspected him before sending him to find the Captain. He looked fit and healthy, lean, light, and not tall, that was good in a light cavalry officer. Slightly dark complexion, brown hair and eyes. Ashworth hoped there would be no trouble with the ladies of Dover, whether real ladies or the other sort.

"Sit down, Roberts." He pointed at a chair near the desk, and picked up a sheet of paper with Michael's details on it. As he scanned it he asked, "I see your cornetcy is without purchase," he looked up at Michael, "how did that come about?"

"Through my grandfather, sir, the Reverend Isles. He was the regiment's chaplain, and knew General Harcourt. They were in Portugal and the Americas together. He left the regiment in '85, and now has a parish in Cornwall."

"Hmm, and I suppose you have a sufficient income? The General asked you about that?"

"Yes, sir, not a great deal, but enough."

"And Collyer has seen you fitted out with all you need?"

"Yes, sir." Collyer was the regiment's agent, and had guided Michael through the complex business of acquiring uniform and equipment.

"Good, and there's one other thing."

"Sir?"

"Yes, your hair. You are going to have to grow it long, until you can queue it. In the meantime we can get one of the barbers in the troop to attach a false one for you. We can get that taken care of tomorrow. Well, I think that covers everything for the moment, we had better get you started. Welcome to E Troop."

Somewhat taken aback with the news about his hair, Michael could only manage a "Thank you, Sir."

The next hour passed in a rush as Michael was introduced to Lieutenant George Thompson, a genial type in his late twenties and Ashworth's second in command, who undertook to show him around. Next he met Sergeant Flynn, the troop's senior sergeant, a tough looking Irishman in his early thirties, but with a ready enough smile and soft brogue that spoke of southern Ireland. Then an orderly showed him his room, in the same house as Ashworth and Thompson, and where all his kit had already been placed, sent in advance by a carrier, but not unpacked. Michael had been to the Regimental Headquarters in Hythe; it was there he had seen Barra and been sent on his way to Dover. Thompson explained that the individual troops were scattered around the villages near Hythe. E Troop, however, had been billeted in Dover, which was a mixed blessing, as the convenience of the town was counterbalanced by the number of ale houses and taverns that attracted the dragoons in the evening. He was then shown the stables for the officer's horses, where his horse, Johnny, had already been put up.

That evening, after trying to unpack and get his uniform and equipment into some semblance of order, Michael dined with Captain Ashworth and Lieutenant Thompson. When he made his appearance in the dining room Ashworth stressed that they did not talk Troop or Regimental business over dinner, but that he might tell them a bit about himself. Thus it was that Michael found himself telling them about growing up in Lisbon. That consequently he spoke Portuguese like a native, as well as very passable Spanish, which drew a comment from Ashworth.

"That will be rather useful, if we go out to Portugal!"

He explained about how his father had worked for Baron Quintela, and how he had come to England three years ago, in '05, when Spain declared war on England. The mood had turned sombre when he told them about his parents' flight from Portugal, and the disappearance of their ship. What Michael didn't tell them about was his uncle's opposition to Michael joining the army.

After dinner the three men retired to a small drawing room, and there, once settled with a bottle of port, the conversation turned more practical.

"Now," began Ashworth, "let me say that Thompson and I are very pleased to have you join us, at the moment there are only the two of us to run the Troop, and we need all the help we can get, even from a novice like yourself. We shall need to get you up to snuff as quickly as possible. That will fall mainly to Thompson and Sergeant Flynn. He's a good man, a fine horseman, and he rules the ranks like a martinet, which makes life easier for us. Not that he isn't a fair man, he is, very, and the men like him for it. He's been with the regiment a long time, he was at Beaumont in '94, along with the Colonel, General Harcourt. He has the rare distinction of having been taught to use his sabre by Le Marchant himself."

Michael was puzzled, "Le Marchant, sir?"

"Ah, yes, no reason why you should know. Our sabres, all the light cavalry's sabres, were designed by Colonel Le Marchant. He is now in charge of the Military Academy at Marlow, but when he was a major in the Sixteenth he designed the sabre and wrote the manual for its use, back in '95, and the manual and sword were officially issued in '96. General Harcourt is the governor of the academy, and they haven't always got along too well, so best not to mention Le Marchant in the General's company." Ashworth paused. "Well, we have to start your military education somewhere, so I think that tomorrow, you should join Thompson for stables at six o'clock, and after breakfast you can observe the watering parade, see what happens. Then I'll introduce you to our Quartermaster, Redmain. He's our senior NCO, but mostly concerns himself with the interior economy, the administration, of the Troop. After lunch, Sergeant Blood, our rough rider, can have a look at you and that horse of yours. D'ye have a copy of the Cavalry instructions?" Michael nodded. "Good, you better start getting familiar with that, one or other of us should be around to help, the technicalities are bit obscure until you get the hang of them. Anyway, it's all best learnt by doing, not from a book."

Thompson broke in, "There's another thing, sir; he will need a servant."

"Damn me, yes." Ashworth turned to Michael. "You've not brought your own servant have you?"

"Err, no, sir, should I have?"

"No, no, not at all, we will find you a dragoon to be your batman tomorrow. You'll need to pay him a couple of shillings a week, but no more. But tomorrow I'll get my man to call you at five, that should give you plenty of time before stables, eh, Thompson?"

Thompson, laughed. "Indeed, sir, and welcome to the army, Roberts."

As promised, Michael was roused from his sleep at five by Ashworth's dragoon servant, who brought him a very welcome cup of steaming hot coffee, and hot water for shaving. It was still dark and the single candle made shaving tricky. Just before six he was collected by Thompson and, with daylight slowly breaking, was taken around the various billets where the men were all busy caring for their horses. Every horse was fed and watered, thoroughly brushed and rubbed down, manes and tails combed and the stalls mucked out. On the tour he met the Troop's other sergeants, Blood, Taylor, and Mitchell.

"It's all a bit difficult in billets," explained Thompson, "the men are rather scattered around, their horses with them. It's much easier in barracks, or in camp, when everyone is together. It means we have to rely more on the NCOs. Fortunately ours are all very good, which reminds me, I've had an idea about your batman, but I need to speak to Ashworth and Sergeant Flynn about it."

Stables were finished by just after seven and Michael and Thompson made their way back to their billet for breakfast. Thompson explained to Michael that his horse was being taken care of by his batman, and would be by Michael's batman, once he had one. Because they also had to look after their own horse, and some officers had two horses, as well as taking care of their officers' needs, they were excused from all normal duties. Over breakfast Thompson broached his idea with Ashworth.

"Forgive me raising this just now, sir, but I have had an idea about a dragoon for Mr Roberts."

Ashworth looked up from his plate of bread rolls. "Really, who?"

"Lloyd."

"What! Lloyd? You can't inflict him on Roberts!"

Michael's bemused expression earned him an explanation from Ashworth. "Lloyd is an arrant knave. He's been broken from Corporal twice, far too fond of the bottle. He's lucky he hasn't been flogged into the bargain. Flynn despairs of him at times. If he wasn't such a good horseman, and the very devil with a sabre, probably the best in the regiment, he'd... oh! Oh, yes, I think I see what you are suggesting." He looked at Michael, and then turned to Thompson. "If it worked, but it seems a little unfair to burden Roberts with such an out and out reprobate."

"Yes, well, I'm not sure either," replied Thompson, "but perhaps we might put the idea to Flynn, see what he thinks?"

"Ha, probably just be glad to be rid of him." Ashworth paused and thought it over for a moment. "Very well." He called out for the orderly dragoon, "Richardson! Ask Sar'nt Flynn to join us."

Michael had been a complete bystander, but now he asked, "If this Lloyd is such a bad character, how did he become a corporal?"

"The thing about Lloyd," replied Ashworth, "is that when he's sober he's one of the best dragoons in the regiment. He knows horses very well. In fact the last time he got broken from corporal was for insubordination when under the influence. He was drunk and told the Veterinary Surgeon what he thought of his treatment for a horse." Ashworth smiled. "He would have been flogged as well if he hadn't been correct. Even Peers, the Veten'ry Surgeon, accepted that."

"I see," said Michael thoughtfully. "So you are thinking that if Lloyd was to stay sober, he would help me to learn all I need that much faster?"

"Something like that, yes," replied Thompson.

"And there's another thing," Ashworth chipped in, "everyone in the Regiment knows Lloyd and what he's like. If you can keep him on the straight and narrow, you will learn an awful lot in the process, and make a good impression into the bargain." He looked at Thompson, "I'm thinking of Major Stanhope."

"Ah," said Thompson.

"Yes, ah!" Echoed Ashworth. "That last time Lloyd was demoted, it was the Major who wanted to flog him into the bargain. If it hadn't been for the Veten'ry…"

At that moment, the door opened and Sergeant Flynn marched in, coming smartly to attention and saluting. "You sent for me, sir?"

"At ease, Flynn," Ashworth responded. "In fact, take your cap off, sit down, and have a cup of coffee."

"Sir?"

"Oh, come on Flynn, we want to ask your opinion about something, and I think we have known each other long enough to know when not to stand on ceremony."

Flynn smiled, and did as Ashworth had said. "Well, that's very true, sir, very true, and thank you. Now, what is that you are thinking about, Captain?"

"We were discussing a suitable dragoon servant as Mr Roberts' batman, and Mr Thompson had a rather interesting suggestion. We thought we would ask you what you think." Ashworth paused as Flynn waited, expectantly. "What do think of giving him Lloyd?"

"Lloyd!" Flynn almost shouted, "you cannot be serious! I beg your pardon, sir, but Lloyd?"

"Think about it, Sar'nt," responded Ashworth. "He is a superb horseman, and one of the best in the Regiment with the sabre. He's been good enough to make corporal twice, and could have been a sergeant by now if it wasn't for the drink. If Mr Roberts can keep him sober and out of trouble, then Mr Roberts stands to learn a great deal, very quickly, which will be good for us. We are rather stretched, are we not, Sar'nt?"

"Well, sir, since you put it like that, 'tis worth a try, if Mr Roberts is willing, sir."

The three men all turned to look at Michael, who realised there was only one answer. "Of course I am, sir."

"That's settled then," said Ashworth. "Flynn, can you tell Lloyd and send him over here? This afternoon Mr Roberts is going to take his horse and Sar'nt Blood is going to have a look at both of them. Lloyd can bring his horse and all his belongings here, and then see to Mr Roberts' horse when he has finished with Blood. And he can start to get Mr Roberts things into order. He can go in with our two men for quarters."

Flynn rose to his feet with a "Right you are sir, and thank you for the coffee." He saluted and marched out.

"Right," said Ashworth, "you had better get yourselves along to the watering parade, Mr Thompson is taking it this morning, and the sooner you can, the better for us, eh, Thompson? And, Thompson, see what you can do about a false queue for Mr Roberts, after the Watering Parade."

The dragoons of the troop were in their watering caps and jackets with off-white stable trousers, while the horses were in their bridoons only, with just a blanket held by a surcingle on their backs. Thompson explained to Michael, "Sometimes this is a parade to take the horses off and water them, but here there is water available in the stables, so it's more of an opportunity to see that all horses are present, fit and well. Follow me and you can see what I look at when I inspect the troop."

Michael followed, aware of the dragoons looking at him with a degree of curiosity. Accompanied by Flynn, every horse, over sixty of them, was carefully examined, its shoes checked, that the fitting of the bridle was correct, and that it had been thoroughly groomed.

After the parade had been dismissed Thompson took Michael in search of the troop barber, and half an hour later he had fixed a false queue into Michael's own hair. It felt most odd, but Thompson just laughed, and told him he would soon get used to it. Then Michael and Thompson headed back to their billet. As they walked Thompson explained to Michael more of the daily routine, of the stable calls three times a day, if not out or exercising, and Michael began to get some idea of the complexity of managing a troop of dragoons. He realised that getting to grips with his new profession was going to take application and concentration.

On their return to the billet Ashworth took over from Thompson and introduced Michael to Quartermaster Redmain, and the administration aspects of the troop, the pay rolls, the musters, the inventories of arms, equipment, accoutrements and uniform. It was all very confusing, and he hazarded saying so to Ashworth, who laughed. "Of course it is, it is a system that is designed to keep Clerks at Horse Guards happy. You'll soon get to be completely familiar with it."

After lunch Ashworth sent Michael off with Thompson again. "Thompson will show you the way to the exercise ground. Your horse should be ready for you, and Blood will be waiting. I shall see you for dinner."

Michael's horse, Johnny was indeed ready, but not in the tack he was used to seeing. He knew the saddle was a little different, it had been ordered from Gibson, the London saddler, along with everything else, and the breastplate was much as he used for hunting. The main difference was the pair of pistol holsters strapped to the front of the saddle and covered with a black sheepskin flounce. That and the crupper running from the cantle and around under the dock of Johnny's tail. From the way he was flicking his tail he wasn't happy about it.

"That's good," said Thompson, "he already has a nag tail." He referred to Johnny's tail which was trimmed to about a foot in length. "He'll soon get used to the crupper as well."

"I hope so," replied Michael, "and that's quite a bridle." A double bridle was nothing new to Michael or Johnny, but this one went on over a head collar that was trimmed with red leather, and had cross pieces from nose band to brow band, creating a large X on the horse's face. Johnny was tied by a leather lead rein that ran from the head collar.

"Just make sure you tie that lead rein securely to the front of your saddle," advised Thompson, "it's damned dangerous if it comes loose."

Michael untied Johnny, mounted and walked him along beside Thompson towards the Exercise Ground. Michael's sabre was banging against Johnny, and clattering on his spur. "He doesn't seem too bothered by your sword," observed Thompson, "that's always a good sign." They were approaching the Ground and could see a tall, straight figure standing, schooling whip under his arm, waiting in the middle. "That's Sar'nt Blood," Thompson told Michael, "he's a very good man, and a good horseman. If you've any bad habits prepare to lose them. Good luck. Oh, don't forget to return his salute."

Michael left Thompson at the entrance to the Ground and walked Johnny across to Blood, who snapped off a neat salute when Michael reined in. Michael did his best in return.

"Good afternoon, sir," Blood opened the proceedings, "it's Mr Roberts, isn't it?" Before Michael could respond Blood went on. "Now then, sir, perhaps you would be so good as to show me your horses paces, and what you and he can do?"

For the next hour Michael rode Johnny around the Ground, walk, trot, canter, walk to canter, leg yielding at walk, turns on the forehand, they ran through all the basic riding skills, and through it all Blood kept up a steady stream of encouragement and advice. Finally Blood called out, "That will do sir!" and Michael rode into the middle where Blood stood. Both Michael and Johnny were sweating profusely as they came to a halt. "Very good, sir, very good, indeed."

"Thank you, Sergeant."

"Yes, sir, you've a good, deep seat, soft hands, and your horse is sound and seems intelligent, and a quick learner. He soon forgot the sword, sir."

"Good Lord, so he did."

"Yes, sir, regular instruction for a few weeks and then regular practice, and you'll soon be the equal of most of our dragoons, sir. Now, sir, if I might, I suggest you walk him around for five minutes, and then take him back to the stables. I believe Lloyd will be waiting there for you, sir, and will take of your horse."

Michael wondered if he detected just a flicker of a smile as Blood mentioned Lloyd, but he simply thanked Blood, who threw him another perfect salute, and marched off as Michael tried to return the compliment.

Michael walked Johnny around, wondering, as he did, how best to tackle the imminent meeting with Lloyd. He was a little surprised, he had assumed there would be some sort of introduction by Ashworth or Thompson, or even Flynn, but it seemed he was being left to work things out for himself. As he approached the stables he decided that he would be formal, and try to use Johnny to break the ice. If the man was as good around horses as they said, he couldn't be a complete lost cause.

As Michael rode Johnny into the stable yard behind the billet, a dragoon who had been sitting on an upturned bucket jumped to his feet and saluted. Michael returned the salute and halted Johnny. The man was on the short side, slight, but wiry, not thin, with black hair, and a slightly suspicious look on his face. In time Michael would come to know that was his usual expression.

"Lloyd, is it?"

"Yes, sir," Lloyd replied, with a sing-song Welsh accent.

"I'm Cornet Roberts."

"Yes, sir."

Michael raised himself out of the saddle, swung down to the ground, and untied the lead rein. "And this is Johnny, six years old, not sure of his breeding, but he's sharp and fast."

"Yes, sir."

Michael took a deep breath, this wasn't going to be easy, to hell with keeping it formal; that clearly wasn't going to work. "You haven't been an officer's servant before, have you Lloyd?"

"No, sir."

"Well, that's alright, because I haven't been an officer before." Michael looked hard at Lloyd. "It seems to me that I have got a lot to learn, and Captain Ashworth thinks you might help me. Tells me you're one of the best in the

Regiment with a sabre?" Michael thought he saw a flicker of interest in Lloyd's face. "It seems to me that an officer who can't use a sabre well could get into serious difficulty with the French, and I don't want that. So, I would be grateful for your help. If it helps you, it's a chance to show Sergeant Flynn what you can do." Now Michael thought there had been just a hint of a smile. "Captain Ashworth also tells me that you are good with horses. Taught the Veterinary Surgeon a thing or two?" Almost a grin there, thought Michael. "And I need someone I can trust to look after Johnny here." Lloyd's eyes flickered over the horse.

"He looks very fine, sir, not fancy, but sound, reliable, well put together. I got a glimpse of you with Sar'nt Blood, sir."

Michael hid a sigh of relief. "I'm also told that there's an extra two shillings a week in it for you."

"Duw, that would be very acceptable, sir." Lloyd actually smiled for a moment.

"Very good, Lloyd," he offered the lead rein to Lloyd who took it, and Michael felt a bargain of some sort had been struck, what it was he would work out later. "I'm going to get some tea, and then start to sort my stuff into some order. When you've done with Johnny, come to my room, and you can tell me what it all is. And tomorrow you can show me all the horse accoutrements and how they go on."

Chapter 4

Over the next few days Michael began to get into the routine of the troop, five o'clock starts were the norm. The mornings were devoted to the activities of the troop, afternoons to Michael's military education. His introduction to the Sword Exercise came courtesy of Sergeant Flynn, and Lloyd. They met by a brick wall at the back of the billet by the stables, on which had been chalked a large face, with three lines on it, one running horizontally, the other two diagonally. Flynn and Lloyd came to attention and saluted when Michael appeared, and he returned their salutes.

"Good afternoon, sir," said Flynn. "As we have Lloyd here, I thought we might start with him running through all the Exercise, sir, to show you what we are working to achieve."

"That sounds very good, Sarn't," Michael was learning the language of the army and its colloquialisms.

Lloyd placed himself about six feet in front of the face, and Flynn called out, "Draw," Lloyd's right hand went to his sword hilt and through the sword knot, taking a turn around his wrist, "Swords!" The sabre slid out of its scabbard with a rasping sound, and Lloyd brought it to the vertical, forearm level at waist height and pointing forwards. What followed was, Michael realised, a virtuoso performance by Lloyd as he went through the six regulation cuts individually, his blade flashing along the lines on the face, and then one after the other in what Flynn said was called the Assault. Lloyd's sword arm was straight out in front of him and the blade was a blur.

"You see, sir," said Flynn, "with an enemy horseman the face is your target, because it isn't protected by anything, and by attacking with the assault as you approach your opponent, it puts them on the defensive, which means they aren't trying to kill you."

"I see," said Michael, impressed by the thinking behind it.

Flynn then got Lloyd to run through the cuts against infantry, the parries and defences, and finally the divisions, the set sequences that pulled all the elements together and represented various opponents in different circumstances. Michael was both impressed and daunted. Flynn caught the look on Michael's face.

"Don't you worry, now, sir. Given six weeks or so and you should make a passable go of it."

"Six weeks?"

"Yes, sir, with an hour or two every day."

"Very well, Sarn't, six weeks it is. What say you that you leave Lloyd to run through the beginnings with me?"

"Very good, sir." Flynn, shot Lloyd a glance that spoke a thousand words, saluted and marched away.

"Right, Lloyd, let's get started, and just for now, don't stand on any formality, I want to learn this, and learn it well. I have no intention of being skewered by some damn Frenchie."

At that moment there was the clatter of hooves and an officer rode into the yard. Lloyd suddenly snapped to attention, and hissed at Michael, "Major Stanhope, sir."

Michael turned to see an immaculately dressed officer just dismounting from a superb dark bay horse, with spotless saddlery and accoutrements. Michael followed Lloyd's lead, coming to attention and saluting. Stanhope returned a rather languid salute, looked Michael up and down, and glanced at Lloyd with his sword, and the drawing on the wall.

"Ah, you must be Roberts. I'm Major Stanhope. You've Lloyd teaching you the Sword Exercise, eh? Good luck with that." An orderly dragoon appeared and Stanhope gave him the reins of his horse. "Captain Ashworth at home, is he?" He addressed the orderly, who replied that the Captain was in his office. Stanhope looked across at Michael and Lloyd again. "Carry on," he said, and walked off with a chuckle.

The orderly also went off with Stanhope's horse. Michael looked at Lloyd, whose expression was completely blank. "I get the idea that you don't like Major Stanhope?"

"Sir," was all that Lloyd replied.

"Then we had better make sure I learn the Exercise well, eh, Lloyd?"

For once Lloyd smiled. "Yes, sir, I think we can do that."

Over the next few weeks Michael's military education continued. On visits to Hythe with Captain Ashworth he gradually got to meet the other officers of the regiment, in particular the other new Cornets, five in all. They all seemed to be going through much the same experience as Michael. On one visit, however, while waiting for Ashworth, who was in with Colonel Anson, Major Stanhope chanced to come into the same room. Michael saluted, and got Stanhope's usual wave in return. Stanhope looked at him.

"Getting on with your Sword Exercise, Roberts?"

"I like to think so, sir."

"Hmm, well, don't concern yourself too much, no one expects much from trade."

"I beg your pardon, sir?" Michael could barely believe he had heard correctly.

"Trade, Roberts, trade. That's where you're from, ain't it? Portuguese at that. Takes a real gentleman to make a good officer, ye know?"

Michael felt himself colour, and his anger rising, he was struggling to find a response, as Stanhope stood looking at him, a slight sneer on his face. At that moment, the door opened and Colonel Anson and Ashworth came in.

"Ah, there you are Stanhope," Anson cut through the tension in the room, "glad to find you, need to speak to you about a few matters. Come into my office, would you?"

With an "Of course, Colonel," Stanhope and Anson were gone.

Ashworth spoke, "What the hell was that about?"

Michael realised he was holding his breath and exhaled with a deep sigh. "Sir?"

"Oh, don't you come the old dragoon with me, Mr Roberts, you could cut the atmosphere with a knife when Anson and I came in, and don't think the Colonel missed it either." He paused. "I'm finished here, let's get our horses and go home, you can explain on the way."

As they rode back to Dover, Michael repeated what Stanhope had said to him. Ashworth rode on silently for a while, before speaking. "You have to remember two things about Major Stanhope, and the most important is that he is a very good soldier, very good indeed, and that you can rely on completely. But he sets high standards and has views on the sort of man who can reach the standards he thinks an officer should. And that brings me to the second thing, which is that he fancies himself above most of we mere mortals. His father is the Earl of Harrington, currently the Commander-in-Chief in Ireland. His mother is one of Queen Charlotte's Ladies of the Bedchamber. So he's rather well connected, and has plenty of money, but he's the second son, hence the army. Still, he sees himself as one of the Beau Monde. He joined the regiment in '98, and made Captain by '02, jumping over four Lieutenants senior to him to do it, which didn't help his popularity. He made Major last year, so he's junior to our other Major, Clement Archer. Now he's very different from Stanhope, got married last year, on leave in Wimbledon just now. Anyway, I suppose the thing about Stanhope is that he's driven, ambitious, very ambitious, and very jealous for the officer class."

The two men rode on in silence for a few minutes. "So, Mr Roberts, how and why did you decide to join? Obviously I know about your grandfather, and your parents, but I would like to hear how it all came about? If you don't mind?"

"No, sir, not all. I suppose it all came about at Christmas, just after we realised my parents were lost, as I told you, I was living with my uncle in Falmouth, and we went to visit my grandfather. On Boxing Day we went hunting, I was on Johnny here." And as they rode on, Michael told Ashworth the story. "We had a splendid, long run after a magnificent dog fox, it must have been upwards of five miles, over difficult country, all stone walls and gorse. At the kill there was only myself and one other gentleman from the field still up with the hounds, and the Master introduced me. It was Colonel Vivian of the Seventh."

"Was it, by God, that was well met!"

"Yes, sir, and he asked me what I was doing in Falmouth. I explained about my parents, and then said I wasn't engaged in anything, but I also said that I was looking for something to do with myself, and he suggested a commission in the cavalry. The rest you know, sir."

"Indeed, and thank you. Now, we are almost home, and an hour to dinner, time for a bit of reading, eh, Mr Roberts?"

Before dinner Michael did read, but not any of the cavalry manuals. There was a letter waiting from his uncle. It was not welcome. His uncle had enclosed a cutting form the latest edition of Lloyd's Register, for April 23rd, 1808. In a few words it listed as lost the Venus, the ship his parents had sailed on from Lisbon. The finality of the simple statement left Michael suddenly drained, and his loss washed over him like a breaking wave. Memories of his parents flashed through his mind. Silent tears ran down his cheeks as he recalled happy times in Lisbon. Then the clatter of passing horses brought him back the present, and he took up the letter and read it.

Jocelyn informed him that he was going to apply to the Prerogative Court of Canterbury to grant probate, this being necessary in the case of those lost at sea. He went on to add that while this would make no material difference to Michael's legal situation, it could be important should they ever discover the identity of the mysterious Augusto and recover any property still in Portugal. In his letter Jocelyn continued, he had discovered that Quintela had gone to the Brazils, and that he would write to him by the next Packet, enquiring about the identity of Augusto, however no reply could be expected until late August at the earliest.

The real sting came at the end of the letter. Jocelyn wrote that once he had probate, and Michael's parents were formally declared dead, he had decided he would act with his full authority as Michael's guardian and insist that he give up the ridiculous idea of an army career. If Michael did not comply with this instruction, he would cut off Michael's allowance. Jocelyn went on to state that although the allowance, and the cost of Michael's fitting out as an officer, had come from the proceeds of selling the diamonds sent by Michael's father, the letter and packet had been addressed to him, not Michael, and there had been no instructions as to what use they should be put. Accordingly, Jocelyn considered the money to be his, but he was prepared to be generous and to spend it on Michael's legal training.

Stunned by the cold formality of the letter and its implications, Michael sat, staring hopelessly into space. Clearly his uncle had decided that his position was strong enough to face down his grandfather. He supposed that, as a lawyer, he was correct in his claim about the diamonds and the proceeds from their sale. Even if that was not the case, Michael did not see how he could challenge the claim. In any case, he was still a minor, and his uncle was his legal guardian, and controlled his money. Eventually, Michael roused himself and went for dinner.

The following morning Michael had little time to dwell on his problems. A little after nine o'clock, a rather harassed looking Lieutenant Barra, the adjutant, rode in looking for Michael, and found him in the drawing room, reading the Cavalry Instructions, which were slowly becoming clearer.

"Ah, Mr Roberts, there you are, excellent. Urgent orders for you, you are to leave immediately for London, General Harcourt has sent for you, and you are to be at Harcourt House by four o'clock tomorrow. It seems he is having a ball and there are some Portuguese attending, he wants you on hand in case of any language difficulties. Oh, and don't go in uniform. You will be able to leave your horse in the General's stable, he always has a few spaces."

Ashworth had walked in as Barra was speaking. "Barra? What the devil is going on?"

"Beg your pardon, Captain Ashworth, but that's all I know. An urgent message arrived from the General this morning for the Colonel. The next thing is he's shouting for me to find young Roberts here, and get him on his way to London. Damn it all, I've not even had me breakfast!"

Ashworth turned to Michael. "You heard Mr Barra, get on with you now, get changed, get packed, and get on your way." He stuck his head out of the door and bellowed for the orderly. "Richardson; find Lloyd, tell him to get Mr Roberts horse ready now, his civilian saddle and bridle, and tell him he's got ten minutes."

Michael rushed off to his room, and Ashworth turned to Barra. "Well, Mr Barra, what can you tell me?"

"Nothing, sir. I have no idea what's going on, but Colonel Anson was rather terse about it. I don't think he knows either. And Major Stanhope looked put out that a new Cornet was summoned to Harcourt House." He smiled.

"I expect he was," replied Anson, also smiling, "now, let's see if we can find you some breakfast."

It was going to take Michael the best part of two days to ride to Harcourt House, with an overnight stop in a coaching inn at Sittingbourne that Ashworth had suggested. There was a hint of spring in the air, tomorrow was May Day. Once he and Johnny had climbed up, out of Dover, they began to make good time towards Canterbury, and his spirits rose a little. The long ride gave him plenty of time to think about his situation. He had no idea how long he had before his uncle got his parents formally declared dead and got probate for his father's will. He determined to make the best of it. As soon as he could, he would write to his grandfather. He might be able to intercede on his behalf again. Perhaps he could speak to General Harcourt? He wondered if the summons from the General boded ill for him. He had only met the General once before, when he had travelled to London to be interviewed by him, and Colonel Anson, for admission to the Regiment. What he did know was that he had found something he enjoyed and he thought worthwhile, and he wasn't going to relinquish it easily. He wanted to be a good soldier, and a good officer. And he would be, and to hell with his uncle, and Major Stanhope. He wondered if it was possible to live on just his pay, he suspected not.

It was a little after three o'clock when Michael rode through the gates of General Harcourt's house in Cavendish Square. He was expected and met by a groom in the forecourt. In a short time Johnny was in the stables, unsaddled and being washed down to remove the sweat from his coat. Once he was satisfied that the horse was in good hands, and carrying his valise, Michael made his way to the house entrance. There, a footman informed him that the General was currently out, but that a room had been prepared for him. That, thought Michael, was a relief, he had wondered what he might do for a billet, nothing had been said before he was rushed out of Dover. The footman led him through the pillared entrance hall and up the grand staircase to the third floor. His room, overlooking the back of the house, was simply furnished, but pleasant enough. He unpacked his valise and changed from top boots and pantaloons into breeches, stockings, and shoes to be ready for the ball. Then he went in search of refreshment.

He wandered back the way he had come to the top of the main stairs. He walked slowly down the broad stairs with their deep, carpeted treads, the walls painted a fashionable light green and hung with paintings. Perhaps not surprisingly, there were many portraits of horses and dogs, but only a few people. Michael passed the first floor and the drawing room where he had first met General Harcourt some three months ago. It was there that the General had interviewed him for entry to the Sixteenth. As he continued down he felt a little like an intruder in this grand London house. It was a far cry from his uncle's house, if anything it reminded him a little of the Palacio Quintela in

Lisbon, which he had visited as a boy, but not quite as lofty and airy.

The same footman who had shown him to his room was in the hall, he led Michael into a reception room and, in answer to Michael's request, brought him a pot of tea. It struck Michael that the house was very quiet, and showed little sign of preparations for a ball. Half an hour later he heard voices, among them that of the General. As he glanced towards the half open door he caught a glimpse of General Harcourt passing by, and then another man, who looked vaguely familiar. The voices receded in the distance, and then Michael remembered. Musgrave! That was the man's name, in Wynn's Hotel. He recalled clearly their meeting; it had been so odd. What the devil was he doing here at General Harcourt's?

Chapter 5

As Michael puzzled over what Musgrave could be doing with the General, the footman reappeared and took him to the General, in the same drawing room where he had first met him. Musgrave was standing with his back to the room, looking out of a window.

"Ah, Mr Roberts, excellent" said the General, "this is Mr Musgrave."

Musgrave turned and addressed him in Portuguese. "Mr Roberts, it is a pleasure to meet you again, and once again to have an opportunity to practice my Portuguese."

"Indeed, Mr Musgrave?" Michael replied stiffly. "Although, once again, you have me at a disadvantage."

Musgrave smiled, "Yes, I'm afraid I do. You see, I do like to keep track of those who might be useful. I saw your commission gazetted, my congratulations," Michael nodded in acknowledgement, "and finding that I have need of someone with your skills, your presence here was easily arranged."

Michael wondered how ordering up an officer from Dover might be considered 'easy'. "Forgive me," he said, "but I fail to see how I can be of help to the Post Office."

Musgrave smiled at that. "Ah, yes, the Post Office. I must confess that is something of a misleading suggestion, although suitably uninteresting to enquirers. But, now, I must be brief before the General loses patience. When I had the good fortune to meet you in Falmouth, and I assure you that it was entirely fortuitous, I already knew your father, he occasionally corresponded with me."

"Indeed, sir?" Michael was more than a little surprised.

"Yes, and I am aware of your misfortune, your loss, please accept my sincere condolences?" Michael nodded in acknowledgement. "I met your father, and your mother, just once, at an embassy reception in Lisbon. We talked a little, and subsequently he wrote to me with snippets of news about the situation in Lisbon, and Portugal generally. Working for Baron Quintela meant that he was well placed to hear interesting news. And that is how I knew him, and of you. But tell me, do you know Baron Quintela yourself?"

"No, I was only sixteen when I left Lisbon in '05, I knew him by sight, of course, and he me, but I cannot claim any real acquaintance."

"And now you are a young man, with whiskers, and I doubt that any passing acquaintance with a sixteen year old boy would know you now?"

"I would very much doubt it, sir."

"Excellent." Musgrave turned to the General who had been standing by, an impatient spectator, as Michael and Musgrave had conversed in Portuguese. "Forgive me, General, but this young man will suit my purpose entirely."

The General looked pleased. "Then I shall leave him in your care, Musgrave." He turned to Michael. "Mr Musgrave has a task for you. You have been shown your room?"

Michael nodded, "Yes, sir."

"Good. There is always a footman in the hall, whatever the hour. You will return to the regiment when all is done, whenever that is. In the meantime, the room is yours, and you are Mr Musgrave's, consider yourself under his orders." The General paused. "I think that is all, Musgrave,

I shall bid you good day." With that the General left the room.

"I fear the General is a little out of sorts with me," said Musgrave, switching back to Portuguese, "and you, no doubt, are still a little puzzled? Let me explain your task, and why I have need of you. There is, indeed, a ball tonight, but not here, it is at Carlton House. And, yes," Musgrave anticipated Michael's question, "the Prince of Wales will be there. However, what concerns us are a number of Portuguese gentlemen who will also be there. They have somehow got to London by way of Spain and Gibraltar. They say they are from Lisbon, and that they represent the opposition to the French, but we don't know them, and with the entirety of the Portuguese court and government in the Brazils, and our diplomats expelled, we have no way to check on them. We, by the way, is the government, not the Post Office, but specifically the Office for Aliens. I am its Superintendent, and that, however, is a piece of confidential information, and I'll ask you to keep it so. The General knows, of course, and so, unfortunately, do the Portuguese. That is why I need your help. You are completely unknown to anyone. All that I need you to do is stay close to them and listen to what you can. My hope is that if they see that I am not within earshot they will speak freely to each other. If they are not what they claim, it might be that they will give themselves away. Of course, it is imperative that they don't discover that you speak Portuguese, or Spanish for that matter. D'you understand what I want?"

"Yes, sir." Michael had done nothing but nod throughout Musgrave's explanation.

"Excellent. Consider it an opportunity to help Portugal." He smiled. "And now, there's a coach waiting for us, I want to be at Carlton House ahead of everyone. I see you are already dressed, so there's nothing to delay us."

Musgrave led the way out of the house and to the waiting coach. The drive took a quarter of an hour, and during it Musgrave talked to Michael about Lisbon, asking him about his life there, and since. It was only when he called to the driver to stop that Michael realised that they were still conversing in Portuguese. Musgrave led the way to a side entrance to Carlton House, where a rather large man with a definite military bearing admitted them in response to Musgrave's knock. They followed the man in silence through a maze of corridors, stairs, and rooms, emerging at last into a large reception room.

With a start Michael realised that the man standing in the middle of the room, apparently giving instructions to a crowd of people, was none other than the Prince of Wales, the Prince Regent. Musgrave led the way forward until they were a mere few yards from the Prince. He waved a dismissive hand at the crowd, which broke and scattered, then he turned and saw them.

"Ah, Musgrave!" Musgrave and Michael bowed to the Prince who walked towards them. "So, this is Harcourt's young Portuguese speaker, eh?"

"Your Royal Highness, may I present Cornet Roberts of the Sixteenth Light Dragoons."

The Prince looked at Michael. "Musgrave's explained everything, I suppose?"

"Yes, Your Royal Highness."

"Good, good." The Prince pulled out his watch. "Well, there's an hour before anyone will arrive. You'll find refreshments in the room beyond the throne room." He looked again at Michael. "Stay close to them, Mr Roberts, close." He turned and walked away, as Michael and Musgrave bowed to his retreating back.

"Come along, Roberts, it's likely to be a long night, we must prepare, refreshments and a thorough reconnaissance, you also need to know who else I have here, and they must know you."

Musgrave and Michael strolled through the various rooms that were to be in use for the evening's affair. There was an entrance lobby, and then a sequence of rooms leading to the throne room, which for tonight would serve as the ballroom. Off the ballroom was the circular dining room, where refreshments were available. Beyond that another sequence of rooms led back to the entrance. The scale and decoration was almost overwhelming, with gold leaf and crimson velvet everywhere. Huge chandeliers hung in every room, and the walls were covered with portraits and mirrors. In every room were at least half a dozen footmen, and at least two in every room were Musgrave's men.

Returning to the refreshment room the two men took a moment to rest themselves and take a glass of punch and some food. "As I said," Musgrave was again speaking Portuguese, "we know very little about these men, beyond what they claim. They are certainly gentlemen, and have money. They could well be what they claim, but we must be sure, they could equally be agents of Buonaparte, and that could be extremely dangerous for many reasons. Not least if they get near the Prince."

Musgrave's words brought home to Michael the seriousness of the situation, and its potential dangers.

Distant voices reached them, and Musgrave gave Michael his final instructions. "Now, if you place yourself near the entrance you will hear them announced, there are only those three Portuguese here tonight, so I don't think you will have any trouble identifying them, but just in case, I have a man at the entrance who will rather ostentatiously blow his nose when they enter. His idea, not mine, still, he's a good man in case of trouble. And remember, you don't know me. Keep well clear of me, keep close to them." With that Musgrave rose and walked off.

Michael took a glass of punch, and made his way towards the entrance hall. There he waited patiently, half hidden behind a tall pillar, while outside carriages arrived and disgorged their finely dressed occupants. He watched them arriving, heard the names, Lords with the insignia of different chivalric orders, and their Ladies in satins and silks, working their fans in the warmth of the spring evening. Barons and Baronets, and Generals in scarlet coats with their decorations. There were a couple of Admirals and a few Post Captains in dark blue and gold lace with brilliant white waistcoats. Amongst the guests was General Harcourt, who ignored Michael completely. Meanwhile, he could hear the distant sound of dance music, and an increasing volume of chatter from the inner rooms. Michael would have been the first to admit that it was a long way from the regular assemblies at Wynn's Hotel in Falmouth.

There was a stir at the entrance, and in came a guest who had not been mentioned, the Duke of York, the Prince Regent's younger brother and Commander in Chief of the Army. He was dressed in uniform, on his left breast the star of the Order of the Garter, and accompanied by a single Aide de Camp. He quickly passed from view, and Michael returned to his watch on the entrance.

Almost at once the three Portuguese were announced. Michael would have known them as such without the names, or the ostentatious nose blowing by a rather portly looking gentleman who had completely avoided Michael's notice. Nose blown, he threw a glance at Michael, and then he was gone.

Michael moved slowly after the three men as they walked towards the first of the reception rooms. As the crowd of guests got thicker, he tried to get closer. For a while they seemed content to stand and watch the dancing, Michael could hear nothing of their conversation over the music and chatter of guests. Then they took the opportunity of a break between dances to skirt the ballroom and enter the refreshment room. As they stood at the table Michael was able to get right alongside them. He took his time refilling his glass. One of the men was speaking in a low voice, with an air of authority. All he caught was a reference to a Duke. Then, to his horror, they divided, one walked off through the room in the direction that Michael knew led to the entrance, and the other two, including the one who had spoken, turned back towards the ballroom.

Michael hesitated for a moment, left his glass, and then he too turned towards the ballroom. The man who had spoken had taken up a station in the ballroom, just to the right of the door, but his companion had walked on, also towards the entrance. Michael turned away to the left, and then he too stood by the wall, ostensibly watching the dancing. As he surreptitiously glanced to his right he caught a glimpse through the crowd of a woman standing on the far side of the room. His glance was held. He had never seen a woman like her. She looked to be about thirty, certainly older than he was. She had a face that, while not pretty, was strong and handsome, but what had caught Michael's eye was her hair. It framed her face with ringlets and was coiled artfully on her head, it was the most vivid, stunning, copper colour. Michael was entranced.

To his surprise he realised that she was watching the same man that he was. Then her look caught his. Her head tipped a little to one side. Their eyes held each other. Michael was suddenly overcome with a passion unlike any he had felt before, and as she held his gaze he knew that the feeling was mutual. A slightly surprised smile flickered across her face. In the ballroom the guests were congregating, numbers swelling. The music stopped, and the noise of chatter rose. The Prince Regent had just entered, the crowd thickening as everyone pressed toward him, to get a glimpse, perhaps even a word. The crowd between Michael and the woman thinned, and he could see her more clearly. She was tall, perhaps unfashionably so, but stood straight, and without her moving he knew that she was graceful and that her well formed frame was strong.

Then her eyes flickered away from his and she gave a slight nod in the direction of the Portuguese. With a start Michael looked to the Portuguese, he was turning and walking away, back into the refreshment room. Michael moved quickly after him as the man passed through the doors. Musgrave's footmen were at the doors, peering in the direction of the Prince and watching the surrounding crowd, they took no notice of either the Portuguese or Michael as they passed between them.

As Michael walked in he realised the refreshment room was empty of guests, except for the Portuguese and the Duke of York. The Duke was taking advantage of the attention on the Prince to get a glass of punch. The Portuguese man was only a few paces behind him when Michael saw him shake his left arm and a long, slim shape dropped out of his sleeve into his hand. His right hand came across to take the handle of the dagger. As he drew the dagger out and raised his arm Michael shouted, "Look out, sir!"

The Duke spun around and seeing the danger swung at his attacker with the punch ladle. The man avoided the blow, but it slowed the attack long enough for Michael to hurl himself forward, crashing into the man, grabbing at the arm with the knife. The man twisted and they fell across the table, food, plates, glasses flying everywhere. Michael felt a stinging, burning pain across his left cheek as the man slashed at him. Then Michael had the man's knife-hand grasped in his as they rolled onto the floor. He pulled the knife towards him, and then he bit, very hard on the man's wrist. He screamed and in reflex dropped the knife.

Help arrived in the form of Musgrave's two footmen from the door, they seized the man's arms and pinned him to the floor. Outside, in the ballroom there were screams and shouts. Over it all Musgrave was shouting, "Find those men, close the doors, secure the building, no one goes in or out." Then Musgrave appeared in the room with a handful of his men. "Close the doors, don't let anyone in." Michael rolled away on his back, and lay on the floor panting. He put his hand to his cheek, and the pain made him pull it away quickly. It was covered in blood. He closed his eyes.

"Lie still." It was a woman's voice. Then a napkin was placed gently on his cheek, making him wince. He opened his eyes; it was the red headed woman. She looked away from him and spoke to someone, "He's alright, but he needs a surgeon."

Michael put his hand on the napkin, on the woman's hand, "Thank you, madam, but it's nothing, a small cut." Their eyes met again, and they held each other's gaze. Looking at her from so near, Michael could see bright green eyes, and unfashionable freckles. For a moment her hand stayed where it was, then she gently pulled it away. He rolled over and pushed himself upright and on to his feet. A hand gripped his arm and steadied him; he was surprised to see that it was the Duke of York.

"I am indebted to you, sir, indebted." The Duke released his arm. "Musgrave, would appear to be busy, so, tell me, who are you, sir?"

"Cornet Michael Roberts, sir, Sixteenth Light Dragoons."

"And tonight here with Musgrave?"

"Yes, sir."

The Duke turned and addressed the red headed woman. "And Lady Travers, I suppose you are also here with Musgrave?" Lady Travers smiled and dropped a small curtsey by way of reply. "Then, please, be so good as to take care of this young man, get his wound attended to." He turned back to Michael as Lady Travers dropped another curtsey, looked at Michael for a moment, and then he turned and walked away.

At that moment Musgrave reappeared. "Got them all." He sounded relieved. "And thank God you were here, Roberts. Good Lord, man, have you seen yourself?"

Michael turned towards one of the mirrors in the room. His face was covered in blood, a red mass of napkin clutched to his cheek, the cuff of shirt and coat stained and ruined. Musgrave took his arm, and found him a chair to sit on. Lady Travers spoke, "The Duke has instructed to me to look after him, I don't think there is any immediate danger, but we must get him attended to soon."

"Perhaps I can be of assistance?" The speaker was a slightly built man, with an open expression.

"Doctor Vaughan, I do believe you can." Lady Travers looked at Michael, "Mr Roberts, this is Henry Vaughan, the King's physician."

"Excellent," said Musgrave, "I shall leave him in your care, Lady Travers, Doctor Vaughan," he bowed at both, "I have rather a lot to attend to. Mr Roberts, I shall see you again, soon." With that he strode off.

Vaughan issued his instructions, sending a footman for his bag, and then Michael was led off to a room where hot water and clean linen were quickly brought. Vaughan gently washed the blood from Michael's face, and then closed the gash in his face with sutures. A footman came in with a bottle of brandy, and glasses, and left again.

Vaughan spoke, "I think we could all do with a little of that, eh, Lady Travers?"

Lady Travers poured three generous measures into the glasses and passed one each to Michael and the Doctor. Michael drank his swiftly, and felt the brandy burn its way down his throat. His cheek burned like fury, but he was still being carried along by the excitement of the moment.

Vaughan drank half his glass and then peered closely at Michael's cheek. "The bleeding has stopped, it looks clean, should leave you with quite a striking scar." He chuckled, "Something to attract the ladies, eh? Keep it clean, give it a week, and then come and see me and I will remove the sutures. Lady Travers, I shall leave him in your care." He bowed to her, Michael stood to shake the Doctor's hand, he took one last look at Michael's cheek, and was gone.

Michael suddenly realised that he was alone with Lady Travers. He looked at her, uncertain what to do, and she looked back at him with her head again tipped a little to one side, and the same slight smile, almost mocking, but also quizzical. In her eyes he saw the same look that he had seen in the ballroom. He gathered his courage, and took a step towards her, "Lady Travers," he began.

A soft finger on his lips stilled his words. "Be quiet, Mr Roberts," she spoke softly, still smiling, "you might open your wound." Then she leant forward, and her lips replaced her finger. The kiss was long, and deep. His hands went to her waist, her hands rested on his arms. There was a knock at the door.

They both dropped their hands, "That looks much better now," said Lady Travers, directing her gaze to the sutures as the door opened. It was the portly nose blower. "Ah, Mason, look here, Vaughan has done a splendid job on our young hero." Michael's blush deepened, but now there was a legitimate reason for it.

"Indeed, Lady Travers. Mr Musgrave sent me to see how Mr Roberts is. He suggested that we might see to it that he gets home. He is staying at General Harcourt's house."

"Thank you, Mason, perhaps you could arrange a carriage and I shall see him safely delivered?"

"Mr Musgrave has made his available, my Lady, I shall call for it now."

It was a short drive from Carlton House, and little was said in the dark, cramped interior of the carriage. They sat side by side, arms touching, Michael all too aware of a warmth and a delicate perfume. He wanted to kiss her again, but dared not, for fear of refusal. He sat unmoving, at a complete loss for what to do, or say. His cheek stung like the very devil, distracting, stopping him thinking clearly. He was all too aware of the rapidly passing journey, and felt that something was slipping away from him. But as the carriage entered Cavendish Square, Lady Travers turned towards him and took his hand in hers. "Now, Michael," her voice was quiet, the tone firm, "you must promise me to rest, and be careful, and say nothing of this to anyone, anyone at all, please?"

"Of course, I promise, but when shall I see you again?"

"Soon, Michael, soon. Now, quickly, a kiss."

The carriage clattered through the entrance and drew to a halt in the courtyard of Harcourt's house. Michael composed himself, and climbed down, not trusting himself to speak until he was standing firmly on the cobbles. "Good night, Lady Travers, and thank you for your help." He closed the door and watched as the carriage drove away.

Inside the house General Harcourt had just returned himself from Carlton House, it was still before midnight, and he was more than a little surprised at the sight of Michael. "Good God, what happened?" He knew nothing of the events of the evening, beyond that there had been some sort of disturbance, and he demanded a full account from Michael. It was another hour, and a couple of strong brandies before Michael got to bed.

He lay in bed, his mind racing. Was it really only two days since he had received the letter from his uncle? The letter that seemed to herald and end to his ambitions. It seemed an age ago. Since then he had been introduced to the secret side of government, probably saved the life of the Duke of York, been scarred for life, and met the most amazing woman. Then exhaustion took him, and within moments he was asleep.

Chapter 6

Michael was woken by a knock on his bedroom door, and one of the General's footmen entered carrying a tray. "Tea, sir, and the General's compliments, could you join him as soon as possible in the dining room?" He put the tray on a small table.

"What time is it?" Michael asked, feeling slightly groggy.

"A little after eight o'clock, sir," replied the footman and left, quietly.

Michael groaned; his cheek throbbed like blazes. His room faced West, but the summer morning's light was enough to make him screw up his eyes until he got used to the brightness. He swung his legs out of bed and sat up. He touched his wound carefully, it had oozed a little in the night, and there was blood on the sheets and pillow. He reached for the teapot, and found his hand was trembling slightly. Carefully he poured himself a cup of tea, and added a little milk. His hand steadied as he raised the cup to his lips. The hot liquid seemed to scour away the bad taste in his mouth. Thirstily, he swigged down the tea, and poured himself another. The second cup he sipped at, and took a look around. There was a washstand and mirror, but looking at himself Michael decided that today he would not shave, there was no hot water anyway.

He looked for his clothes. His blood-soaked shirt and neckcloth had both disappeared during the night, to be replaced with pristine ones. His coat, the left cuff stained with blood, and his blood speckled waistcoat, breeches and stockings were still there. Fortunately, he had the pantaloons and boots he had worn to ride up to town. Ten minutes later he was finding his way downstairs. On the ground floor he heard voices, and the clatter of dishes and cutlery. Guessing that such sounds could only come from the dining room he made his way towards the sounds, and was proved correct.

"Come in, Roberts, come in, you must be starved." The General waved him in from the head of a long dining table set for breakfast. "Help yourself from the sideboard, and come and join us." Also in the room was Musgrave, sitting near the General and looking rather tired. As Michael got himself some breakfast the General went on. "Musgrave, here, has been up all night, dropped in for something to eat and a word with you." Michael took a chair opposite Musgrave, the General waved at his butler, "Markham, pour Mr Roberts some tea, and then leave us, we are not to be disturbed until I ring."

Once Michael had his tea and the men were alone, the door firmly closed, the General continued. "Quite a stir last night, you did well, Roberts, very well, but, now, here's the thing, it never happened."

Michael frowned quizzically at that, and Musgrave interrupted. "Perhaps, General, I might explain?"

"What? Oh, yes, carry on, please."

Musgrave addressed Michael. "The fact of the matter is that last night's incident could have serious repercussions. Of course, not as many as if you hadn't saved the Duke's life, for which a lot of people, not least the Duke, are very grateful to you. But I don't have to tell you about the situation in Portugal. If it were to be known that there had been an attempt on the life of the Duke of York by a Portuguese assassin, then I fear all support for any possible expedition to Portugal would be lost, and all the Iberian Peninsular would be at the mercy of Buonaparte."

He paused to take a sip of tea. "Consequently, it has been decided that there was no attempt on the Duke's life. There were no Portuguese assassins. An unfortunate Portuguese gentleman suffered a fit, and, in falling, crashed into a table in the refreshment room. You went to his assistance, and, unfortunately, suffered a nasty cut from a broken glass. Regrettably your help was in vain, the gentleman died." Musgrave looked hard at Michael. "Oh, yes, the gentleman died, of that you may be sure. Once we finish questioning him. In fact, this week isn't a good time to be a Portuguese in London. Another was killed in a robbery next Saturday, and a third fell from London Bridge and drowned, next Monday."

For a moment Michael wasn't sure if had heard Musgrave correctly. "I beg your pardon, sir, I don't follow."

"Yes, you do," Musgrave replied curtly. "I tell you this so that you realise the seriousness of the whole business. This is about more than the attempted murder of the Duke of York. It is part of the war with France, and it goes on all day, every day, everywhere. Make no mistake about that Mr Roberts, all day, every day, everywhere. Thinking otherwise has cost men, and women, their lives, I would hate you to be one of them. You were extremely useful last night, and I might want to call on your services again. That being so, the fewer who know about you the better. Anonymity is a life saver in this business. Clearly, those of my department who were there last night know you, and may be relied on not to give you away. Similarly, the General, the Prince Regent and the Duke of York. However, there must not be a word of this when you return to your regiment, Mr Roberts, not a word. The General will help with that." Musgrave looked at General Harcourt.

"Yes, of course. I thought I might travel down to see them next week. We can wait until your sutures are out, and then you can go down with me, Roberts. That should make everything well, I'll tell 'em all what happened, officially, and distract attention from you."

Michael listened to all this with a sense of bemusement. He had thought he had merely done his duty and that was that, but it now appeared he had become involved in something that he did not understand, not at all.

"That sounds an excellent idea, General, and in the meantime, Roberts can get some new clothes, we can't have him wearing blood stained clothes. I'll send some funds over to you, ready money, can't have any paperwork like tailors bills to explain. I am afraid that there will not be the rewards that might be expected for saving the life of a Royal Prince." Michael started to speak, but Musgrave cut in. "No, Mr Roberts, you deserve a reward, but there will be nothing tangible. Just the gratitude of some quite influential people. Which is probably worth a damn sight more than money."

"No, sir, I expect no reward," Michael bristled, he might be confused, but he would not be insulted, and his tone was accordingly hard. "I was not going to speak of such a thing, sir."

Musgrave looked at Michael, "Then I beg your pardon, Mr Roberts, forgive me, I am rather tired." He smiled, "And perhaps I have spent too much time in the company of those whose motives are purely mercenary."

Michael nodded his acceptance of Musgrave's words. "No, sir, I was about to say that I am happy to serve my country in any way possible, but, to tell truth, sir, I find this intrigue all rather strange and confusing."

"Indeed, it is. And it may be that you will have no further involvement with the Aliens Office, but it will do you no harm to have a little awareness, and to take a little care, Mr Roberts. That is all. And I ask for your discretion not just for your own safety, but also that of those who work with me."

Lady Travers came suddenly into Michael's thoughts. "Then, Mr Musgrave, you may be assured of my discretion."

The next two days passed slowly for Michael, with nothing achieved save his new coat, waistcoat and breeches, which were better than his old ones, and had been produced at lightning speed, Harcourt's name had worked wonders with his tailor. Apart from that, he was reluctant to go out more than was necessary, his wound was startling in appearance. The General was hospitable, but left Michael to his own devices, much to his relief. He was still somewhat daunting for Michael to feel able to relax in his company. However, Michael learnt much about the regiment's activities in America, including the capture by the General of the American General Lee.

On the third day Michael's spirits positively soared. There was a note for him. It gave an address, a time, one o'clock, the words 'today, Tuesday', and was signed 'Travers'. He looked at his watch, it was still only half past nine, plenty of time. He called for hot water, and shaved, very carefully, around his wound. It took him a while, but when he had finished, he felt fit to meet a Lady. He dressed with care, a new shirt, a freshly starched neckcloth, his new waistcoat and coat. His pantaloons were thoroughly brushed to get the dust of the road out of them, his top boots were polished to a high finish. White kid gloves, a top hat, also carefully brushed, and he was ready. He checked his watch, another hour before he need leave.

Five minutes later Michael left the house in Cavendish Square and set off towards Hyde Park. Reaching the park, he turned south, strolling along the edge of the park, down an avenue of trees. The day was turning warm and the shade was welcome. Reaching Piccadilly, he turned eastwards. Anyone observing him would have seen a handsome young man, a young gentleman, well dressed, who gave the appearance of not having a care in the world beyond enjoying the fine spring day. Some stared at Michael's wound, he didn't notice, he barely noticed the fine quality of the day. His mind was a seething turmoil of hope and despair, passion burned hot, alternating with a cold reality that mocked him. He had no idea what to expect from the summons, surely he had no right to any expectations. The evening at the ball had been one of heightened emotions, and tackling the assassin had raised his blood. Had he imagined that Lady Travers, a Lady for goodness sake, had shared his passions? Had she allowed him unforgivable liberties because of his actions, his wound, his confusion? Was he about to be put firmly in his place for his imagined fancies? Did Musgrave know? Would he tell the General? Would his career be over before it had started? He was a bundle of nervous anxiety.

He arrived at the address in Covent Garden, a small, double fronted house in a terrace near the opera house. He knocked on the door. He was punctual to the second. A few anxious moments passed, and the door was opened, by Lady Travers herself! "Mr Roberts, what a pleasure it is to see you again, please, do come in." She stepped back, allowing Michael to pass into the hallway. The door closed behind him, he turned, they were face to face, a mere yard apart. The hall was dark after the brightness of the street, but a fanlight above the door gave enough light for him to see her face. Michael removed his hat and gloves, and put them on a small console. She smiled, and her head took on that slight tilt, she gestured to a door, "I have just made tea, would you care for a cup?"

In the small drawing room Michael took the chair indicated to him. He was wondering what to do, what to say. She poured tea for Michael, and walked to him with it. "I hope it is alright, I live here very simply, just a cook, a manservant, who is the cook's husband, and a maid, and they are all out today." She avoided his eyes as she spoke. As he took the cup and saucer from her, she bent down close to him, looking at his wound. She reached out to touch his cheek gently. "Is it very painful?" She looked into his eyes. Michael put the cup down on a side table and stood up. Mere inches separated them, but Michael feared to say or do anything.

For a moment, neither spoke. Then Lady Travers broke the silence. "Michael?"

"Yes?"

"Will you promise me something? Well three things, actually." She smiled, and her head tipped.

"Yes, anything."

"First, anything between us must remain a secret, an absolute secret."

"Of course."

"And when we are alone you must call me Elaine, I think Lady Travers a little too formal."

"Yes, of course. Elaine."

"And finally," she took his hands in hers, and looked into his eyes with an intensity that was full of passion, but also fearful, "you must never, never fall in love with me."

"Elaine?"

"Promise me, Michael, promise me that, or there can be nothing between us."

"Of course, I promise, but…"

Once more she stopped him with a finger on his lips. "No, no buts, no arguments, you have promised."

Holding him by one hand she led Michael out of the drawing room, up the stairs, and into her bedroom. As she pulled him in, she turned to him and they embraced and kissed. She leaned away from him, supported by his arms around her waist. "Now, my maid is out, you will have to help me." And she turned her back to him.

Later they lay in bed together, Elaine's hand gently resting on Michael's chest. "Tell me, how is it that you speak such fluent Portuguese?"

Bit by bit, Michael told her his whole story. About growing up in Lisbon, about his Portuguese boyhood friends, the scrapes and fights, learning to look after himself in a fight where knives were common. At that, Elaine smiled, and asked Michael if that was where he had learnt to bite? He laughed, and said "and more". Then he told her about fleeing Portugal, about his parents, about losing them, about his difficulties with his uncle Jocelyn, about the diamonds, about Christmas at his grandfather's. He told her of the mystery of Augusto. He held nothing back, except his uncle's recent demands.

When he had told all, they lay quietly in silence. Michael felt completely at peace with the world. Content, happy, slightly wondering at his good fortune. He turned his head to look at Elaine. "And you? What is your story?"

She paused, thoughtfully for a full minute. "A brief marriage, my husband was a diplomat, in Switzerland. More than ten years ago, now. He went on a trip to meet a French agent. He didn't come home. His body was found at the bottom of a ravine near the French border. The French agent disappeared. That was how it happened that I knew William Wickham. He was the ambassador, and then he recruited me for the Aliens Office. And now I work for Musgrave, which, Mr Roberts", she tapped him on the chest with her forefinger, "is a State secret. Men don't always take much notice of a woman. I hear things no man would. I can pass unnoticed while I watch. I help with the fight against Buonaparte, it's a small form of revenge."

Somewhere in the house a door banged. Michael started with surprise. Elaine laughed. "It's alright, Michael, that will be Marianne, my maid. Now, don't look at me like that. If you hadn't thought the house empty… Anyway, I trust her completely, and so can you." She ran her hand down his chest, and onwards. "And now that you know, let us see how quiet you can be."

Elaine lay propped up on one elbow, watching Michael dress. At least he had accepted the necessity of discretion, she thought with relief. She had never experienced such an intense and immediate attraction to a man, and giving in to that attraction had been a huge risk. Secrecy was something that underpinned her entire existence. It kept her alive. She hadn't told Michael half of it, but she had no regrets. She had asked him for the note she had sent, with her address on, and he had seemed unsurprised when she burnt it. She liked him, liked him a lot. She would not like him too much, that way lay vulnerability. She would not love him, the only man she had loved was in a grave in Switzerland. No, she would not fall in love with him. She would not leave herself open to so much hurt again.

As Michael walked away from Elaine's house his mind was spinning. He barely believed what had just happened, it seemed unreal, fantastic. If he had been distracted on his way to Elaine's he was now in a trance. He felt, rather than understood, that he had touched the edge of a world he had not known existed. More than that, much more, he had met a woman, a wonderful woman, someone he could never even have dreamt of. Mysterious, capable, and, ultimately, he knew, unobtainable on terms other than hers. He was elated and excited, saddened and dismayed, all at the same time.

A week after the ball, Michael paid an early morning call on Doctor Vaughan. The doctor was happy with the healing of the wound, and removed the sutures. He commented that it would probably leave a scar some two inches long, but that in time it might fade. To protect the wound he covered it with a plaster, told Michael that it would fall off on its own in a few days, but the regimental surgeon would be able to replace it, and not to worry, the bill was taken care of. It was a much-relieved Michael who left the doctor's, partly because he caught sight of himself in a hall mirror, and decided he no longer looked quite so startling.

He was expected at Elaine's for lunch, and this time Elaine's manservant answered the door, and Marianne was in attendance on her mistress when he was shown into the small drawing room. "Michael, this is Marianne, Marianne, this is Mr Roberts. And that was Mr Johnson who admitted you, and Mrs Johnson is preparing a light luncheon for us. Thank you, Marianne, that will be all."

The luncheon was served in Elaine's dining room, Michael spoke about the Regiment, but still made no mention of his uncle's demands. He spoke of how he hoped to become a good officer, a good leader and to win the respect of the men, to have that easy relationship with them in the way that the likes of the Regiment's Captains and Field Officers did. Not overly familiar, but comfortable, with mutual respect. Elaine suggested to him that he needed to get to know them, to talk to them when he didn't have to, to be around when he wasn't on duty, to care for them, take an interest in them, to be firm, but fair. The conversation flowed easily, with no awkwardness between them, and when she looked at him, when they held each other's gaze, she felt her feelings growing.

After lunch they retired to Elaine's bedroom.

In the afternoon they walked together to St James' Park. Elaine felt that she was losing control of the situation, of her feelings, of her emotions. Everything was happening too quickly, far, far too quickly, she couldn't let it happen. It was ridiculous, it was impossible, it was outright foolishness. But being with Michael just felt so right, so comfortable, so easy, so good, so loving. A long suppressed emotion rose and overwhelmed her. No, she scolded herself, no, she should not, must not let that happen.

At breakfast the following day, Michael found the General there ahead of him. "Ah, Roberts, there you are. How's the face? Looking better. I have decided that we shall take ourselves down to Hythe on Friday, Get there for dinner on Saturday. They're not expecting me, so the surprise and confusion will help to cover your return." The General chuckled at the prospect. "Surprise 'em. Like I did Lee at White Plains." He laughed again. "That gives us a couple of days to finish up any business in London, and it's time we got you back to Regimental duties."

Michael had little to do, he called in on Collyer, the regiment's agent, more for form than any need. He wrote to Elaine, a brief note, explaining his imminent departure. In return he received a note that simply said, "Wednesday, 11 o'clock." There was no signature.

Wednesday was a fine warm day, and they walked across London to the Tower. It was a pretty walk, and took them past the majestic mass of St Pauls, towering above all around it. At the Tower they saw the menagerie, laughed at the monkeys, but thought the lions rather poor and flea bitten. Michael found the various Armouries of interest, Elaine not so much, except for the Line of Kings, who all looked very proud and noble in their fine armours. They paid their shilling each and visited the Crown Jewels, and stood in awe of them.

They were easy and comfortable in each other's company, and time passed easily. They returned to Covent Garden and dined at Elaine's home. Mrs Johnson's dinner was quite excellent. A chicken soup was followed by roast beef, and the meal was rounded off with an apple tart, all accompanied by some very fine claret. During the meal their conversation had been general, Michael telling her more about life with the Regiment, and Elaine listening attentively, and laughing when he told her all about Lloyd. On her part, Elaine spoke a little of balls and parties that she had attended, many, she implied, at the behest of Mr Musgrave.

"Is there not some danger attached to this work?" Michael asked her.

"Some, I suppose, Michael, but not much, and I am never alone on such occasions. There are always other agents present. And if I venture out anywhere, then I always take Johnson with me. I can assure you that he a most capable man in case of any trouble. Which reminds me, Michael, I have a small present for you." She rose from the table and retrieved a long, slim package from the corner of the room.

Michael quickly removed the paper covering to reveal a fine, silver topped cane. There was a small cartouche on the side of the silver top, which was engraved. He held it to the light of a candle and saw 'MR from ET'. He looked across at Elaine. "Elaine, it is far too kind of you."

"Not at all," she replied, "and do not think it is a sentimental gesture, Michael, see, there is a small catch there."

Michael pressed the small stud set near the top of the cane. The top came lose, and from the shaft of the cane he drew a fine, wicked looking blade, that glinted in the candlelight. "Good Lord, that's wonderful! Thank you Elaine." He slid the blade back into the stick, rose from his chair and walked around to where Elaine stood, smiling at his obvious pleasure, her head with its characteristic little tip to the side. Taking her in his arms he looked into her eyes, "Elaine, you are a truly wonderful woman." It was as far as he dared to go, it wasn't the whole truth, but he had made a promise. He shackled the emotion that he really wanted to give way to, swallowed the words he wanted to say.

She kissed him lightly. "And I am rather fond of you, Michael Roberts, and I would not like to see you come to any harm, wandering around the streets of London." She grinned, mischievously, "I do believe I would miss you, a little. Now, shall we leave the dining room so that the table can be cleared?" She took the stick from him, led him out into the hall, and propped it against the console with his hat and gloves. "There, it will be quite safe until you leave." With that, she turned and led him up the stairs.

The single candle flickered slightly, and Michael thought it made Elaine's hair glisten like gold. He put his hand out and ran his fingers through it. Elaine stretched towards him and kissed him, long and slow, pulling him to her. He ran his hand down, through her hair, over her shoulder, and down until rested on her hip. He was overcome with contentment.

"You're not falling asleep on me, are you?" Elaine teased him with her hand, scratching gently.

"No, not all."

"Good, now listen carefully, I have something to tell you, it's to do with Musgrave and the Alien's Office."

Michael groaned. "Elaine, please, not now."

"Yes, now. It's important. Those three Portuguese, do you remember?"

"How could I forget?" Michael lowered his head to kiss her.

"Michael, listen, there weren't three of them, there were four."

"What?" Michael was suddenly very attentive.

"Yes, there was a fourth who was watching the three to see what happened. They didn't even know about him. We only found out two days ago; an intercepted letter alerted us."

"Us? Do you mean Musgrave and his office?"

"I do indeed."

"But what has that to do with me?"

"It seems the fourth man is still in London, and apparently asking questions about what happened that night. Musgrave is concerned that he might find out about you, and seek revenge for foiling the assassination attempt."

"Ah, now that would be a problem."

"Yes, and we can't deal it with it until we find him, and until we deal with him, we can't be sure what he might do. That sword stick really isn't a sentimental gesture."

"Not even the inscription?"

"Well, perhaps that, a little." Elaine smiled.

A thought struck Michael. "And what about you? Are you in any danger? If this fellow is after revenge might he seek it by attacking you?" For a moment Michael forgot himself. "Elaine, I don't know what I would do if anything happened to you."

"Now, Michael, there is no reason to suppose that this man knows anything about me. But, you are not the only one to have that thought. I am being well protected, I can assure you, but it does mean that Musgrave now knows about us." She stilled Michael's response with a finger to his lips. "It is of no matter, Musgrave will not be concerned, nor will he share that particular piece of intelligence. He needs me too much. He has no one else who can move freely in society as I can, and gain confidences, and listen in corners. And seduce handsome young cavalry officers." Elaine kissed him. "Now, show me how much you like the inscription."

When Michael woke it was getting light. He slowly turned his head. A tumbled mass of red hair covered the pillow next to him. Slowly a hand appeared, parted the hair, and a green eye peered out at him. Michael laughed and kissed the hand. "Good morning, My Lady."

Another hand stretched out, followed by a naked arm, the hand reached the back of his head, and pulled him close. "Mmm, good morning, Lieutenant."

An hour later an arm reached out again, this time for a bell pull, and tugged on it. Then Elaine tossed and turned, threw back the bedclothes, and stood naked, her back to Michael. Slowly she turned to face him, raised her hands to her head and ran her fingers through her hair, she smiled a wicked smile and tilted her head. A knock at the door and she skipped behind a folding screen in the corner of the room. "Come in," she called out and Michael burrowed down under the bedclothes. The door opened and Marianne came in with a tray bearing tea.

"Marianne, bring some hot water for the Lieutenant, he will need to shave."

"Yes, My Lady." She gave Michael a smile, and left the room, closing the door behind her.

Elaine emerged from behind the screen, pulling on a long shift. "Why, Mr Roberts, I do believe you are blushing."

"Ha!"

"Now, now, but I do think you should at least put your shirt on before the hot water arrives."

"But my razor is at General Harcourt's."

"You will find all that you need in the drawer of the washstand. I find that one has to be prepared for all eventualities."

Shaved and breakfasted, Michael prepared to walk back to Cavendish Square. Johnson was handing him his hat, gloves and cane, when he said, quietly, "You will have company on your walk, sir, Mr Musgrave has set a couple of his men to watch your back while you are in London."

Elaine merely smiled at this, and tipped her head to the side as if to see him the better. Johnson vanished, and Michael kissed Elaine, hugging her tight. "Shall I see you tonight? I must return to Dover tomorrow."

"No, Michael, I am already engaged." She kissed him tenderly. "Soon, Michael, soon, now go, and take care." She watched him walk away, and felt something she hadn't felt for a long time, hadn't felt since the happy days in Switzerland.

Chapter 7

General Harcourt's unexpected arrival in Hythe caused quite a stir. Poor Joseph Barra found himself running around looking for suitable quarters for the General, his coachman, valet and footman. Colonel Anson was informed that the General wished to visit all the quarters over the next two days, starting at Dover, and to meet all the officers together for dinner on the second day. Then, if he was happy that all was well, he would return to London. It was a simple matter for Anson to dispatch Michael to Dover, with no questions, but a hard look at the plaster on his face. As he trotted away on Johnny he caught a glimpse of Major Stanhope, who also gave him a look, with a deep frown.

At Dover it wasn't so easy to avoid questions. Ashworth and Thompson were just sitting down to dinner when Michael joined them. "Good God, Roberts," exclaimed Ashworth, "where the devil have you been? What's happened to your face? Richardson?! Another place for Mr Roberts."

The rule against talking business was forgotten as Michael explained his prolonged absence, with Musgrave's cover story. Then he added that he had returned to Hythe with General Harcourt, in his coach, with Johnny trotting along behind. Finally he added that the General would be inspecting all the Regiment's quarters over the next two days, and then dining with all the officers in Hythe.

At this news Ashworth bellowed "Richardson!" again, and sent him to fetch Quartermaster Redmain and Sergeant Flynn at once. In the following confusion there were no penetrating questions about Michael's absence. Indeed there were no questions at all, and Michael's absence and wound were hardly remarked on. The occasional comment was easily deflected. The dragoons in his troop seemed to have got hold of the idea that a woman was involved somewhere. That gave Michael a few nasty moments until he recalled that they thought a woman was always involved somewhere. He found the best course of action was to ignore the odd remark that he was meant to overhear, and just smile. And it was easy to smile at the thought of Elaine.

The following morning General Harcourt arrived just after ten o'clock, accompanied by Colonel Anson and Lieutenant Barra, and riding a horse he had apparently borrowed from Major Stanhope. He was in jovial spirits. "Morning Ashworth," he called out as he dismounted, and then to the orderly dragoon that took his horse, "See you take great care of this horse, I'd hate to see Major Stanhope looking any more miserable." Then he saw Sergeant Flynn, "Flynn, good man! How the devil are you?"

Flynn snapped off a salute and replied, "Very well indeed, thank you, sir."

"Excellent, excellent. Now, let you and Captain Ashworth conduct me around the billets, and then we shall have coffee and I'll tell you what I think." And with that the inspection began.

Michael, Thompson, and Redmain followed at a discreet distance, and, so far as they could tell, all seemed to go well. And to Michael's relief, Thompson asked no questions about London. A little over two hours later, and they were all taking coffee in the small drawing room. Redmain and Flynn were there, at the General's insistence.

"Very well, Gentlemen." The General began. "I am very satisfied with what I have seen this morning, and I am sure there will be further improvements as Mr Roberts is able to take on more duties. I will save his blushes, but suffice it to say that he was of great assistance in London, it was just unfortunate that he received such a nasty injury. Still, Captain Ashworth, work him hard, see what you can make of him. And now, Colonel Anson, we should get on or we will not around five troops today and the other five before dinner tomorrow!"

After the General had had gone there was a sense of the calm that follows a great storm, and the troop heaved a collective sigh of relief. Michael's only moment of concern came when, after dinner, Ashworth said, "Thank the Lord that's over, we could do without unannounced visits like that. Mr Roberts, you were in London, any idea why the General suddenly felt the need to travel down here?"

"Err, no, sir, none at all." And Ashworth merely shrugged.

The dinner passed off almost uneventfully. By the time Michael, Ashworth and Thompson arrived the story of how Michael got his injury seemed to have become common knowledge, and there were no questions. The only cloud was as the gathering was breaking up. Michael was with a few of the other new officers, when Stanhope joined them and spoke to Michael, "So, Carlton House, eh? I suppose the General would need someone to fetch and carry his refreshments for him. I do hope it wasn't all too exciting for you?"

At that last remark Michael almost burst out laughing. In sheer devilry he replied, "No, sir, not at all. It quite reminded me of the Palacio Quintela in Lisbon, but not so airy." Poor Penrice almost choked, and Stanhope stalked off looking cross.

Following the General's visit, routine was quickly re-established. Michael found himself riding in a squad with seventeen dragoons, as the quickest way to learn the drill. With two ranks of nine there was nothing that couldn't be taught and practiced under the watchful tuition of Sergeant Flynn. He learnt the difference between 'shoulders forward' and wheeling. He grappled with the difficulties of wheeling by threes, where each group of three had to turn their horses in the space they occupied. Going backwards on a tight curve through ninety degrees was challenging. But, gradually, he and Johnny learnt what was required and began to acquire some proficiency. As the make-up of the squad was varied every day, he soon got to know all the dragoons in the troop by name.

Work on the Sword Exercise also continued, and both Flynn and Lloyd worked him hard, insisting on a ramrod straight arm, directed at his opponents face, with all the action of the blade coming from the wrist alone. They also made him understand the necessity of some of the requirements. Such as when cutting against infantry. Michael was standing in front of the chalked face. "But, Sar'nt, when you cut against infantry, why do you have to turn your body to the side you are cutting on? Surely it can't make any difference to the power of the cut?"

"None at all, sir, but just you make the cuts standing square to the wall."

Michael did as he was bid. The blade came down from his left shoulder to behind him on his right, he then turned the sabre and made the reverse cut, back up.

"Right, sir, you see where the blade passed?"

"Yes."

"Diagonally across your front, sir?"

"Yes."

"Now, where would your horse's head be, sir?"

"Oh! I see. Thank you, Sarn't."

"That's alright, sir. See, if you turn your body, the blade passes alongside your horse, sir."

Michael turned, cut, and understood.

Michael's education went on through the rest of June, and he steadily gained the knowledge and experience to make a contribution to the running of the troop. Under the tutelage of Quartermaster Redmain he began to understand all the administrative details. His riding also improved, and Johnny proved such a quick learner that Blood began to push the boundaries of what was normally expected. As he put it to Michael, "You see, sir, the charge is the thing, but after it, when everything is confusion, that is when it is most dangerous, and that is when you want your horse to be quick and agile, sir. You can't do any of this fancy footwork like Mr Angelo teaches, you can only move as well as you can get your horse to move."

At the end of June Michael got the chance to put Sword Exercise and horsemanship together, as he made his first runs against targets, turnips set on poles at the height of an enemy horseman's head. "Now, sir," advised Lloyd, "don't pass too close to the target, keep your arm straight, and remember, you only want to strike with the last four to six inches. That way your sword won't get stuck in the enemy, sir. And it's the part of the blade that is moving the fastest, so it will slice his face open nicely, sir."

Michael touched his spurs to Johnny, and within a few strides the horse was at a flat gallop. He straightened his arm, pointed it at the target as he flew towards it, then he brought the point of the sabre over his left shoulder, and with a flick of his wrist made cut one. He missed. "Never mind, sir," shouted Lloyd, "it will soon come."

Watching from a little way off, Ashworth smiled to himself. Young Roberts was certainly coming on apace, he showed plenty of promise with the sabre, and Blood was enjoying teaching him and his horse. And more than that, he could see a change in Lloyd, who was becoming quite attentive to his officer. The gamble appeared to be paying off.

Late in June came the news that a British expedition was preparing to sail to Portugal. Two days later Michael was summoned to the regiment's headquarters in Hythe by Colonel Anson. Ashworth shrugged; he had no idea what it was about.

At Hythe, Michael was escorted by an orderly to the Colonel's office. In answer to his query the orderly informed him that Major Stanhope was away on a few days leave, at which Michael relaxed a little. Anson was at his desk. "Ah, Mr Roberts, come in, come in, sit you down." Anson paused, looking at a letter. "I have the damnedest request, no, order, here, from General Harcourt. It seems you are required elsewhere." He shifted his gaze from the letter to Michael. "Do you have any thoughts as to why the General wants you in Ramsgate as soon as possible?"

"No, Colonel, none at all."

"Part of the expedition to Portugal is assembling there. The town and barracks will be packed. However, there is a room waiting for you at the Albion Hotel. Good Lord, Roberts, that's probably the best in the town! Your orders are to go there, in uniform it says, although why you wouldn't go in uniform. I don't know, and there you are to wait. What for it doesn't say." Anson put the letter down and stared at Roberts. "Is this some business like the ball at Carlton House?"

"Sir?"

"When the General wanted you to interpret for some Portuguese coves?"

"Oh, that." Michael had wondered for a moment what Anson knew. "I suppose it could be, sir, perhaps it's something to do with the expedition to Portugal."

"Yes, I expect that's it, although you can't be the only Portuguese speaker in the army. Well, you had better get on. And try not to get injured." Anson nodded at the scar on Michael's cheek, now healed, but still red.

"Yes, sir, thank you, sir." Michael spoke as he rose and got out of the office as quickly as he dare. The comment about his uniform had him wondering if this was anything to do with Musgrave again.

It was a good thirty miles or so to Ramsgate, and Michael had to call in at Dover, collect some baggage, and tell Captain Ashworth that he was off, he knew not for what or how long. Ashworth asked if the orders had come from the General, and then just looked resigned.

By the time Michael rode Johnny into the stable yard of the Albion it was late afternoon. An ostler took care of Johnny, and promised to take great care of Michael's saddlery and accoutrements. Michael found his way into the hotel where he was relieved to find that there was a room for him. He was delighted to be handed a note with the name of a suite of rooms on it. It was simply signed E. He hurried to his room, dropped his baggage, and went in search of the suite. A porter directed him, and he was soon tapping on the door, wondering what to expect.

He wasn't entirely surprised when Johnson opened the door, and he glimpsed Marianne. He was only a little more surprised to find Musgrave sitting comfortably, a glass of wine in hand, and amiably chatting to a woman in a simple, plain dark blue dress, with dark, brunette hair. It took Michael a moment. "Elai…, Lady Travers?"

Elaine laughed and Musgrave smiled and urged him into the room. "Mr Roberts, come in, very timely, will you take a glass of wine? You must be tired and hungry after your ride? Eh?" He poured Michael a glass of claret, and Elaine took the opportunity to explain.

"Oh. Michael. The look in your face! And I think you may call me Elaine while we are amongst friends. I fear that I am just too easily known by my hair, and if we are to be successful tonight, I must not be recognised."

Musgrave handed Michael his glass. "I trust your room is acceptable. As the town is full of army officers, I am afraid we had to turn someone out from it for you. If you see a rather cross looking Major, I wouldn't say anything to him." Majors, thought Michael, what is it about majors? Musgrave continued. "We have a little problem, well two, in fact. It's two Portuguese gentlemen, they do keep popping up all over the place, don't they? But I suppose that one cannot blame them for fleeing before the French?"

"No, Mr Musgrave, not at all, many did."

"Oh, my, please forgive me. Mr Roberts, I meant no insensitivity. Your parents were a sad loss. Very sad indeed." Michael nodded his acceptance of Musgrave's apology. "And now, we must seek your assistance again. My, your scar looks a little livid, is all well?"

"Yes, sir, it is, the redness is diminishing. The cut itself is quite healed."

"Excellent, excellent. Now, where was I? Ah, yes. As I am sure you know part of the expeditionary force for Portugal has gathered here, and should sail in a week or so. Two Portuguese gentlemen have turned up, offering to go with the expedition to help free Portugal from the French. Say they are from Lisbon, know people, have good contacts there, and so on. Could be useful. If they are what they say they are. I have interviewed them extensively, and they seem to be genuine, but I am not entirely convinced. If they are, in fact, French agents, sympathisers, afrancesados, they could cause all sorts of problems."

"And do you want me to speak to them?" asked Michael.

"Oh. Lord, no, not yet at least, I might ask you to ask them some questions about Lisbon, see if they really are from there. For the moment, I have only just left them, and they are about to have dinner in the hotel dining room. It's Carlton House again, I fear, but, hopefully, without assassins. They will be shown to a particular table, you and Lady Travers will be shown to the adjacent table." Michael glanced at Elaine who simply smiled at him. "They don't know either of you, you, sir, are simply a young officer, dining with his companion. They will have no reason to suspect that you speak Portuguese, and that you know Lisbon well. And you must not let them know that. Your skills and their ignorance are all we have on our side."

Michael had left his sword in his room, and he and Elaine were able to make their way directly to the dining room. The dining room was very busy, crowded, but a waiter showed them to a table, and they made themselves comfortable only feet away from the two Portuguese. The two men had been engaged in conversation, but stopped to look at the couple sitting so close.

Elaine leant across the table, "So, Michael, how many days leave do you have, before I must return to my lonely house in London."

Michael played the game. "Only three nights, Elaine. I hope it will be enough?"

The two men returned to their conversation while Michael and Elaine continued to flirt outrageously, both rather enjoying it. Then the waiter brought menus and silence fell while they decided what to eat. Michael was listening to the men, but they were talking about the hotel and the food, and how bad the wine was.

Michael and Elaine continued to alternately chat away, and try to eavesdrop. Elaine kept the conversation going while Michael, not really listening to her, concentrated on the two men and their conversation. The wine flowed, or appeared to. When their wine came Michael took one sip and looked very askance at Elaine, who whispered to him, "It's well watered down," and smiled mischievously. "Unlike theirs."

As the evening wore on the two did seem to be getting a little louder, making Michael's job easier, but giving him no clues, except he thought he detected a slight northern accent. Then one of the men said, "But what shall we do when we get to Lisbon?"

His companion replied, "We shall just have to be careful, try not to give ourselves away, but once we know the English plans we can head north to Oporto." He laughed. "Perhaps we can hire a Lisbon servant or two who know their way around."

At that moment Michael heard a voice he knew only too well. "Roberts! What the devil are you doing here?" It carried clear across the room, the interruption silencing the diners. It was Major Stanhope. Michael started to rise, to forestall him, he saw the two men staring. Stanhope went on, every word clear in the silence. "Not more of this Portuguese speaking nonsense I hope?"

The two Portuguese started to rise, Michael turned towards them, away from Stanhope, who said loudly, "Don't be insubordinate, Roberts!"

Out of the corner of his eye Michael saw Johnson, Mason, and, behind them, Musgrave, coming into the room. The man facing him, who had been sitting with his back to the wall, produced a small, but mean looking pistol, his companion also reached into his coat. As the first man cocked his pistol, Michael threw himself at the other. There was a loud report as a pistol went off, and then Michael was on the floor, grappling with the other man. In seconds Johnson was there, and subdued the man with a sharp blow to the head from a short club. Michael climbed to his feet; Mason looked up from the other man. "He's dead."

Michael turned at Elaine's voice. "I fear I shall need a new reticule; this one has a hole in it!"

There was complete confusion in the dining room, over which Stanhope could be heard. "Roberts, what the bloody hell is going on?" Michael wasn't present at the subsequent interview between Musgrave and Stanhope. He was helping Mason question the surviving Portuguese.

Michael and Mason discovered that the pair were indeed afrancesados, anti-monarchist, republican supporters of Napoleon. They had been recruited by the French in northern Portugal and neither had ever been to Lisbon. They had no particular objective, other than to get back to Portugal with the British expedition, discover its plans by offering local knowledge, and then make their way to the French army. The man was taken away by two of Musgrove's men, accompanied by Mason, who parted from Michael with "I'll take care of this. You'll probably find Musgrave with Lady Travers; you can find out what's happened with that loud-mouthed major. He nearly ruined everything."

Musgrave was indeed with Elaine. They were sitting, drinking coffee with Johnson and Marianne in attendance. "Coffee, Mr Roberts?" Musgrave waved at a chair, "And sit down, it's been quite a night."

Elaine had removed her wig, and let her hair hang loosely over her shoulders. It caught the candlelight and shone like gold. Michael smiled at her, and thought she was the most wonderful woman he had ever known. If only he might love her, and she him, he thought ruefully.

"You will be pleased to know," said Musgrave, "that I have spoken to your Major Stanhope. An interesting man. An excellent officer, I believe, very well connected, as Lady Travers informs me, and yet he seems to have a fear that capable men might emerge from classes below him and usurp the natural order of things." He shook his head. "One begins to understand the causes of the Revolution. Egalite, Fraternite, Liberte, and all that. But just look where that has got the French. Hmm, perhaps he has a point? No, we also had our Republic, and then saw sense, but then we are very different from our French neighbours."

Elaine coughed, "Perhaps you could tell Michael what passed between you and Stanhope?"

"What? Oh, yes, of course. I have made it clear to him that Mr Roberts was here on the most delicate business, that might have been handled delicately, save for his unfortunate intervention. I stressed that Mr Roberts' actions were authorised at the highest level, the very highest, let him make of that what he will. I may have hinted that any indiscretion on his part about this evening could very well have a detrimental effect on his career. I may have mentioned the Duke of York." He shrugged. "Anyway, Mr Roberts, you may return to your regiment assured that no word of tonight will escape the Major's lips. I also took the liberty of telling him you would be needed here for another day or so." He paused. "However, I think it only fair to warn you that he does not approve of this sort of thing, as he put it. I also think he doesn't quite approve of you either, Mr Roberts, so I would advise caution where the good Major Stanhope is concerned. I understand that he can be vindictive. And now I must leave you. I must check on our Portuguese survivor with Mason, and then try to get a little sleep." He stood and made for the door. "I shall bid you goodnight, do not expect to see me tomorrow, I shall probably leave for London at dawn with our man." With that he was gone, Johnson closing the door behind him.

Elaine smiled at Michael, then addressed Johnson and Marianne. "I think that you can both retire. Marianne, a late start tomorrow, I think. We will return to London the day after tomorrow."

Once they had gone, Michael moved to sit next to Elaine, taking her hand in his, and giving her the kiss that he had longed to give since he arrived. She smiled and tipped her head a little, and Michael fell further into love. "Now," she said, "tell me how you have been? How are things with the regiment? And tell me about Stanhope. You must be careful of him. I know him a little, thank goodness he didn't recognise me."

"You know him?"

"Oh, yes, very much one of the Beau Monde, a society that I do move in, occasionally. The Honourable Lincoln Stanhope. You know about his mother and father, I suppose?" Michael nodded. "Well, take heed of Musgrave's warning. But, now, tell me, how are things with you."

The question brought all of Michael's problems back to him, and he slumped slightly. "Stanhope thinks I am not good enough to be an officer, not the right sort, not a gentleman, trade, as he put it." Elaine squeezed his hand. "And my uncle doesn't want me to be in the army either. He wants me to resign and become a damned lawyer." He explained to her Jocelyn's demands, his threat, and his seizing the money from the diamonds for himself. "I am still waiting to hear from my uncle, but I expect to find any day now that he has cut off my allowance, and then what shall I do? Just when I feel that I have some purpose." Michael's anger and frustration with his uncle were clear. They sat in silence for a moment, then Michael roused himself. "Still, the earliest I can hear from him is when I get back to Dover, and until then I am here with you." He grinned at her. "What more could I ask for?"

Later, Elaine lay watching a sleeping Michael by the light of a candle. His scar caught the light, and looked red and sore, although he had assured her it no longer caused him any discomfort. She thought about his problems, what he meant to her, she had become very fond of him, very fond indeed. And, no, she would not fall in love with him. But she would do what she could to help him.

Chapter 8

Two days later Michael was back in Dover, and once again threw himself into the routine of the Troop and his military education. Flynn, Lloyd and Blood were now all working him hard with the Sword Exercise on Johnny. Improving his technique with the sabre, and as a rider. It was a good time. Every day saw improvements, and the smiles from his instructors were all the reward and encouragement he needed. Of Major Stanhope there was no word, but Michael kept in mind the warnings of Musgrave and Elaine.

In mid-July Colonel Anson was called to London, leaving Stanhope in command of the regiment for a few days. Anson was no sooner gone, than orders arrived from Stanhope. Ashworth called Michael into his office.

"Roberts, Major Stanhope wants to see all the new Cornets in Hythe tomorrow. Says he has concerns about the standards of horsemanship and wants to see how you all are with a sabre. Damn peculiar if you ask me, never heard the like. And just when Anson is away." He looked hard at Michael. "Is there anything I should know?"

"No, sir, nothing I can think of."

"Well, I think I shall ride over with you, just for my own peace of mind, and we'll take Flynn and Lloyd along as well. One word of advice, you have been doing very well, I have seen some of the things Blood has been teaching you and that horse of yours, far beyond the requirements of the drill book. And I know Flynn and Lloyd have been working you hard with the Sword Exercise. But I would suggest that you don't show off too much tomorrow. I know how good you are, and so does the whole troop, and that's what matters. So don't be the best, and don't be the worst, eh?"

There were six new Cornets, all told, leaving aside Barra, who had been commissioned from the ranks to take on the job of adjutant. When they all met at the drill ground just outside Hythe it was quite a convivial gathering. Ashworth was not the only Captain who had come to see how his Cornet compared with the others. There was a fair crowd of off duty dragoons hanging around to watch as well. Then Stanhope arrived, accompanied by Barra, Regimental Sergeant Major Williams, and a large, rough looking sergeant on a big horse that Michael didn't know. Lloyd did, and he spoke quietly to Michael. "There's a nasty piece of work, look you, begging your pardon, sir."

"That sergeant?" asked Michael.

"Yes, sir, Butler, seen him break a man's jaw with a wooden practice sabre." Lloyd was referring to the wooden sabres used when beginners were practicing against each other.

When Stanhope arrived all conviviality evaporated. He informed the waiting Cornets that it was all very well going through the drills as laid out in the various Divisions. He wanted to see how they performed putting all the Sword Exercise into practice. So, he would see them all run at the same series of targets, of his own devising, that represented a mix of both cavalry and infantry targets. No one was keen to go first, then Stanhope shouted, "Alphabetical order, gentlemen, off you go, Mr Bence."

Michael thought quickly, Bence, Osten, Penrice, Roberts, Sawyer, Tomkinson. That made him fourth, not a bad place to be. There were six targets, in a line down the drill ground, three were infantry height, three cavalry, of which one was a ring, not a turnip, requiring a thrust, rather than a cut. Bence missed one infantryman and the ring, probably the hardest target. Osten went next. He was actually a German, Wilhelm, Baron von Osten, who had transferred from the King's German Legion. He had grown up riding and learning to use a sabre, so there was no surprise when he hit all the targets and lifted the ring. Penrice got the ring, but missed a couple of his cuts. Then it was Michael's turn.

He took his time. He steadied Johnny at the start of the run, then drew his sabre. A moment's pause, a squeeze of his legs, and Johnny was off into a nice, collected canter. He cut the first turnip neatly, then used his left leg and shifted his weight to push Johnny sideways a touch, to put the next turnip of the harder near side, and quite deliberately missed, hoping it would look like a riding error. The three infantry targets were next, near side, off side and near side again, and he took them all easily. That left the ring. He managed to miss it by an inch. Not bad, he thought as he trotted Johnny back, should look about average. Stanhope's face was expressionless, and he just called out for Sawyer.

Michael reined in next to Captain Ashworth, who said quietly, "Nicely done Mr Roberts." Sawyer missed three targets, and Tomkinson got everything except the ring. Then Stanhope pushed his horse forward and addressed the gathering.

"Not too shabby, gentlemen." He paused. "I was disappointed by Mr Robert's riding." He looked at Michael. "Perhaps it would motivate you to greater efforts and application if you have a little demonstration of why we need to practice all of this, and become expert?" Stanhope turned to Barra. "Please be so good as to find two practice swords."

As Barra looked round, Sergeant Butler rode forward. "I've two 'ere, sir."

"Ah, Butler, good man. Give one to Mr Roberts. And you shall have the honour of giving Mr Roberts a lesson in the realities of battle."

Ashworth swore, "Damned man's never been on a battlefield, either of them."

Butler handed the wooden sabre to Michael with an evil grin, "Ere you are," there was moments pause, "sir." Then Butler turned his horse and cantered gently down to the far end of the ground.

"I shall take post in the middle, and signal when to begin," shouted Stanhope, and he rode off.

"Be careful, Roberts," said Ashworth, "I want you in one piece."

Michael nodded, and walked Johnny forward. His mind was in turmoil. Stanhope was obviously setting him up to fail, demonstrating the inadequacy of 'trade' in front of a suitable audience. He hefted the practice sabre in his hand. The weight was the same as the real thing, but it was a thick piece of timber, and could easily inflict injury if wielded with any great force.

Stanhope called out "Begin." Immediately Butler pushed his horse into a canter towards Michael, who followed suit a moment later. Rapidly they closed the ground between them. This was much quicker than a stationary target, but Michael had practiced against Sergeant Flynn, and wasn't too concerned. Then Butler came at him with a fast assault, all six cuts delivered in a single sequence. Michael caught one on his sword as he parried, and he was shocked at the sheer power of the impact. Butler had made no attempt to pull his cuts. Then they were past each other, and turning at the end of the ground.

Michael turned Johnny and set off back, turning a little faster than Butler, and getting a slight start. This time

Butler dropped his sabre slightly, aiming a vicious cut at Michael's ribs. Michael just managed to parry it, but the force of the blow knocked his wooden sabre back towards his shoulder. Michael reached the end of the ground where the watching officers were gathered. As he pulled up to turn Johnny, Ashworth called out to Stanhope, "A moment, Major, if you please?"

Stanhope had no option but to call out "Stop!" and then, "What the devil is it Ashworth?"

"I thought I saw something come loose on Mr Roberts' accoutrements, sir." As he shouted Lloyd rode forward, and placed himself between Michael and Stanhope. He bent as if adjusting something at the front of Michael's saddle.

"Sir, Sar'nt Flynn says to tell you that Butler's been promised five guineas if he breaks a bone of yours. And he says he's bet the Regimental Sar'nt Major a guinea that you will see off Butler, sir, and that you'd better use some of that fancy riding Sar'nt Blood's been teaching you." He grinned. "And I've two shillings on you as well, sir. Good luck, sir." He turned away, and called out towards Stanhope. "Beg your pardon, sir, everything is fine." Stanhope glared at Lloyd as he rode back to the watching crowd.

Michael recalled the insolence of Butler, and what Lloyd had said about the big sergeant. It was clear that Stanhope had arranged all this. He felt anger rising in him. An anger that burned hot, but left his thoughts ice cold. An anger he hadn't felt since Lisbon, since he was a boy, and the fight when knives had been pulled. He thought quickly, he had to beat Butler, for himself, and for Flynn and Lloyd, who had put their faith in him.

Stanhope called out, "Begin!"

As Butler approached him, he gave Johnny a touch of off side leg and shifted his weight to his left, Johnny veered, and the two riders passed each other harmlessly. At the end of the ground Michael turned Johnny quickly, and saw he was quicker and sharper than Butler's big horse. He knew what to do.

Again the two riders set off towards each other, and again Michael swerved away at the last moment. Stanhope bawled out, "Come on, Roberts!" But as they passed each other, Michael was pulling Johnny up, spinning him right around on his haunches, and clapping his legs on, pushing Johnny into a flat out gallop. Butler was a few yards away, slowing his horse for the turn. He didn't hear Johnny coming until it was too late, as he pulled up and started to turn, Michael drove the point of his sabre into Butler's left shoulder, with the combined weight of man and horse at speed. Butler flew forwards, over his horse's shoulder, and lay in a heap on the ground, screaming in pain. Michael pulled Johnny up at the end of the Ground, and then trotted gently back, past Butler who was being attended to by a surgeon's mate, and stopped just in front of a stunned audience, his face a cold, expressionless mask, hiding the fury. Ashworth nodded, Flynn smiled, and Lloyd grinned.

Stanhope rode away without a word to anyone.

As they rode home to Dover, Michael spoke to Lloyd. "Did you collect your winnings?"

"Yes, sir, thank you."

"And, of course, you wouldn't be going to drink them away, would you? I don't want a drunk looking after Johnny. The horse that won you the wager."

"No, sir, I wouldn't do that."

"Good," was all that Michael said. And Lloyd had a few celebratory beers, and whilst not sober, didn't get drunk.

Michael was concerned about repercussions over the injuries to Butler. At Ashworth's suggestion he went to see Butler, who was nursing a broken collar bone, and a very nasty bruise to his shoulder. Butler was surprised to see him, and was initially hostile, thinking Michael meant to make trouble for him. For his part, Michael was more magnanimous than he felt, he remembered the sergeant's grin and insolence all too well. However, he made it clear that he knew where the responsibility for the incident lay, and pressed home the point by giving Butler five guineas. The story of the contest had flown round the Regiment, thanks to the many witnesses, and Michael's generosity also became widely known, and approved of.

Anson returned a few days later, with news that the regiment was going to Wimbledon Common at the beginning of August, where the whole Regiment could camp and exercise together. He was not pleased when Barra told him what had passed. There followed interviews with the Regimental Sergeant Major, Captain Ashworth, and, lastly, Major Stanhope. And then, nothing more was said, officially. It was left to Ashworth to speak to Michael, one evening after dinner, when Thompson was away on some duty or other. They were in the drawing room, having a glass of port.

"Anson was rather vexed when he heard about the injury to Butler." He paused to sip his port, and Michael waited without speaking. "Yes, quite vexed. However, between Mr Barra, the RSM, and myself, I think he got a fair understanding of what had gone on. He also seems to have some knowledge of why Stanhope has taken against you so." He waited for Michael to comment.

Michael limited himself to "Really?"

"Yes. Anyway, I think you can consider the matter closed, officially, that is. What Stanhope thinks and might do is another matter. Hopefully he will also treat the matter as closed, the whole regiment knows what happened, and the sooner it is forgotten the better. All said and done, he knows his business, and if we go to Portugal we will need that. Just be a little careful where the Major is concerned, Mr Roberts."

"Yes, sir, of course." Michael wished he could share Ashworth's optimism, but what he knew of Stanhope told him that he and Stanhope might be comrades, but they would never be friends.

The Regiment's mind was soon distracted by a General Order that arrived a few days later. It was for the removal of all queues. Michael was mightily pleased, he was still trying to grow his hair long enough to queue it, and thought all the Regiment would be equally pleased. To his surprise there were many who didn't like the idea, having spent months, years growing and tending to their queues. The opposition was considerable, and all the officers had theirs removed first to set an example. Soon the whole Regiment was getting used to the strange sensation, but also realising the benefit of not having to spend hours preparing and maintaining it. It was thus a short haired Regiment that made its way to Wimbledon Common.

Wimbledon Common in the first week of August was hot. Men sweated, horses sweated, the flies were inescapable, horses stamped and swished their short tails, getting fractious, men swore when the flies bit them. Sleep was difficult, even in tents. Drills were carried out at the crack of dawn, and late afternoon as the sun sank and the temperature moderated a little. In the heat of the afternoon little moved, save men with buckets of water, and the tails of the horses.

Major Archer rejoined the regiment, and Michael found him to be a very different character from Stanhope, who used Archer's presence to take every opportunity to slip away to London. Archer was older than Stanhope, and the senior Major. He had joined the Regiment in '84, knew everyone, he was somehow related to Captain Swetenham, knew everything, and knew how to make the Regiment run smoothly. He was living on the edge of the Common with his new wife and their baby daughter. His wife became a familiar figure around the camp, and was very popular with all, taking an interest in the men's wives, and inviting officers to tea. With the whole regiment together, and all the officers gathered into a single mess, Michael quickly got to know all the other officers well, when, in Dover, they had been for the most part, just names.

The Regiment hadn't been in camp for long, when Michael was sitting a little way off from the horse lines, in the shade of a magnificent horse chestnut. It was mid-afternoon. He leaned back against the tree and closed his eyes. In his hand was a letter from his uncle, Jocelyn, and it was every bit as bad as he had feared. Jocelyn informed him that his parents had now been officially declared dead, lost at sea, and that consequently he had obtained probate on Edward Robert's will. All his property was left to Michael, but the will named Jocelyn as Michael's guardian. As Michael would not come of age for more than a year, Jocelyn intended to exercise his full authority over Michael and his inheritance as his guardian. Consequently, he was giving Michael a month to resign from the army, return to Falmouth, and take up the study of the law. If he failed to comply with these instructions, Jocelyn would immediately cut off his allowance, and write to General Harcourt, requesting Michael's release from the army. Michael didn't know what the legal position was regarding the threat to write an appeal to the General, it would certainly cause him no little embarrassment, but cutting off his allowance would be sufficient to drive him out of the army, out of the regiment, and back to Falmouth. The only bright spot was the month's grace. That and the knowledge that in a few days he had a little leave, and would spend a couple of days with Elaine.

There was a standing arrangement that, with the Regiment so close to London, any officer could stable his horse at the General's, which put any officer under an obligation to call on Harcourt, and so he was able to keep his finger on the pulse of the Regiment. When Michael called he was soon shown into the General's presence, in the usual drawing room.

"Mr Roberts, come in, come in, Markham, coffee, if you will. Now, Roberts, sit yourself down, and tell me, how are things at Wimbledon?"

Michael told Harcourt what he could, and answered his questions while the coffee was produced and served. An hour later Michael was able to make his escape, mightily relieved that the subject of Major Stanhope and Michael's fight with Butler had not been mentioned. That was not the case at Elaine's. He was admitted by Johnson and was soon in Elaine's drawing room, drinking more coffee. She got quickly to the point.

"What is this I hear about you and Major Stanhope and a fight with a sergeant at Hythe?"

He told her the whole story. Then he told her about his uncle's letter.

"Musgrave was right to warn you about Stanhope, but you seem to have managed the matter quite well." She smiled and her head gave its characteristic tip. "Now, come and sit next to me, and give me a kiss. As for your uncle, we shall have some luncheon, and then go out, we have an appointment."

Michael did as he was bid, before asking, "What appointment?"

"A rather timely one, given your uncle's letter. We are going to see Mr Rutherford, my solicitor. We are going to see what he might be able to advise, or do, where your uncle is concerned."

Mr Rutherford was, to Michael's surprise, a huge bear of a man, with a jovial air, receding hair, and a pair of spectacles perched on his nose. He welcomed them both into his office, a dark room, with one grimy window, and walls lined with dark panelling and huge bookcases. Once they were settled, Rutherford addressed Michael. "Now, Mr Roberts, Lady Travers has told me something of your troubles, but I would like to hear your story from your own lips, and then we can see what we can do to help you." He smiled encouragingly, and settled back in his chair.

There was something about Rutherford that encouraged frankness, and Michael told him everything. He told him about his parents, Lisbon, Quintela, going to Falmouth, living with his uncle, the loss of his parents, his father's letter, the diamonds, the strong box key, his grandfather's intervention on his behalf with General Harcourt, his uncle's threats, his latest demands. It took a while, and Rutherford listened without interruption, eyes half closed, nodding occasionally. When Michael had finished, silence descended. He glanced at Elaine, who smiled, and nodded reassuringly.

Eventually, Rutherford broke the silence. "Tell me, Mr Roberts, did your father send regular sums of money to your uncle?"

"So my uncle told me, and I have letters from my father telling me so."

"And you understood these monies to be for your support, your subsistence?"

"Indeed, sir, that was my understanding."

This seemed to please Rutherford.

"And your uncle has been making you an allowance?"

"Yes, a hundred and fifty pounds a year, paid monthly from Praed's to Mr Collyer, the Regimental agent. Collyer also receives my pay, and arranges to make it available wherever the Regiment is."

"And who paid for your commission and outfitting?"

"The commission was without purchase, my uncle agreed to pay for the outfitting from the sale of the diamonds."

"Hmm. Let us see now. Your outfitting would be, what, some four or five hundred pounds?"

"Yes, Sir."

"And the diamonds sold for about five thousand pounds, which would leave, at 4%, an annual income a little in excess of the hundred and fifty he allows you. Excellent. It's not conclusive proof, of course, but compelling, which is all you need in the civil courts. It suggests that it would have been reasonable to assume that the diamonds were intended for your assistance, rather than an unexpected gift to him, leaving you penniless. I think I might be able to help." He glanced and Elaine who gave him an almost imperceptible nod. "Our first aim must be to enable you to continue in the army. That means securing your allowance. Secondly, your uncle must be deterred from writing to any authority seeking your discharge. Both, I think, can be achieved by a simple letter suggesting that he is at risk of being litigated against for the misappropriation of funds belonging to you whilst acting as your guardian." He smiled. "Believe me, Mr Roberts, such an action, even if unsuccessful, would be the end of him as a lawyer. I very much doubt actual litigation would be necessary. I think that such a letter might also contain a suggestion that any attempt to secure your discharge would also result in litigation." He chuckled. "Oh, yes, I think that will be sufficient unto our purpose."

"And you would write such a letter Mr Rutherford?" Michael asked.

"Oh, yes, certainly. It will be a pleasure to help any friend of Lady Travers." He bowed his head to her. "As to your greater inheritance, the money or other property left in Portugal, I would simply suggest that you do not find it until you are of age. With regard to your father's house in Lisbon, your uncle can do nothing without the deeds. I say that as a simple fact, not a suggestion that you conceal anything from your guardian." Rutherford and Michael smiled at each other, and Michael decided that he rather liked him.

That evening they dined at Elaine's.

The weather continued fine and hot, and in the morning Elaine insisted they take a walk to Bond Street. There she led the way into a small booksellers. "Now, Michael, we need to choose a book, a novel of some description." Michael was rather bemused by that. "Now, go on, just do as I say, I will explain later."

Michael browsed the shelves, looking at the occasional book, but entirely uncertain about what he was doing. Then Elaine appeared at his side with two books. "Here," she said, with a mischievous glint in her eye, "this will do perfectly." Before Michael could even see the title, the books were being wrapped and added to Elaine's account at the shop. "And now, back to Covent Garden! We are having an early dinner, and then, I have a surprise for you."

That night Michael achieved his ambition to visit Vauxhall Gardens, and not just on any night, it was the Prince of Wales' birthday gala, and Elaine had secured tickets. They dined early because, as Elaine advised Michael, "We will

have supper there, but the food is not of the best quality."
The day was still very hot when they set off, accompanied
by Johnson and Marianne, 'for security and propriety' as
Elaine put it, and walked down to the river where they
took a wherry for Vauxhall. Elaine had changed after
dinner, and wore the plain, dark blue dress she had worn in
Ramsgate, and a straw bonnet with a matching ribbon and
a heavy veil. The veil would protect her from the sun and
insects, as well as prying eyes. Marianne carried a spencer
and a shawl for Elaine in case it got cool later.

Vauxhall was everything Michael had imagined. It was a
garden of delights, and on that day only the best of London
society were there. Elaine had secured for them one of the
booths in the arcades around the central area, where a tall,
octagonal band stand lifted the orchestra well above their
audience. Leaving Marianne at the booth to secure their
occupancy, they strolled down the wide walks and through
the gardens, followed at a discreet distance by Johnson. As
the dusk grew deeper they returned, and witnessed the
almost simultaneous lighting of thousands of coloured
lanterns that transformed the gardens into something
magical.

For a while they stood and listened to the music, watching
people mill around and promenade. Once it was quite dark
they returned to their booth and ordered supper from a
waiter hovering in attendance. The booth was dimly lit,
and Elaine removed her veil to eat and drink. Once their
supper had been served, Elaine sent Johnson and Marianne
off to find themselves something to eat, and Michael felt
both completely alone with Elaine, but at the same time in
the midst of a great crowd of London society. As they ate
and drank, and talked about the wonders of Vauxhall,
Michael thought that he had never seen Elaine looking so
beautiful, and he knew beyond any doubt that he loved
her. The magic of the evening weaved its spell on him, and
he reached across the table and took her hand in his. Elaine

stopped whatever it was that she was saying, and the two of them simply looked at each other. "Elaine," Michael began.

"Lady Travers! Still looking after our young hero, I see." The voice from the front of the booth caused Michael and Elaine to look, and then rise quickly, bowing and curtseying.

"Your Royal Highness, what a pleasure to see you." Elaine recovered quickly from the surprise.

The Duke of York beamed at them. "Tish, tish. I see your wound has healed well, Mr Roberts."

"Yes, Your Royal Highness," Michael stammered. "It has, thank you."

"Ha, surprised I remembered you, eh? Well, Mr Roberts, I have, and I shall, I shall." The Duke gave a small bow in the direction of Elaine, and was gone, followed by a small crowd of courtiers and hangers on.

Michael and Elaine sat back down; Michael amazed to have been addressed by the Duke in such a casual manner. Elaine took a sip of her wine. "Well, that was quite exciting," she said. "You were about to say something, Michael, what was it?"

But Michael had come to his senses. He dare not tell Elaine what he thought, what he felt. He would risk losing her if she knew he had broken his promise, that he had fallen deeply in love with her. "Err, I was just going to thank you for this evening, for bringing me here. I can't recall a better evening."

Elaine smiled, graciously, and wondered if that was what he had been going to say. She feared it wasn't and feared that she knew what he had intended to say, but she was determined to give him no encouragement, she would hold him to his word. She would not leave herself open to so much hurt again.

Later that night, in bed, and by the light of a single candle, she gave him one of the two books she had bought, The Libertine by Charlotte Dacre. She explained. "If we are to correspond at all, and you may have some matter of intelligence to send to me, for Mr Musgrave, you cannot just write me a letter. You must use a code, and this is the simplest, yet one of the most effective. You find the word that you want in the book, write down the page number, and then the number of the line, and, finally the number of the word in the line. It only works if those communicating have the same book, hence the two copies." Elaine laughed, "I thought this might be a title that would appeal to a young cavalry officer." Michael's response was in keeping with the title.

She knew what she had told herself, that she would not leave herself open to so much hurt again. She knew, but as she watched him walk away the next morning she knew that she loved Michael Roberts as much as she had ever loved anyone.

Chapter 9

When Michael arrived back at Harcourt House to collect Johnny, the General's head groom, Jackson, and another groom were saddling up both Johnny and two other horses. "Ah, there you are, sir, the General's been looking out for you this last hour, you best call in quick, sir."

The General's footman took Michael upstairs to the now familiar drawing room. "Come in Mr Roberts, come in. Glad to see you, was wondering where you were. I trust you had a good few days. Eh?" He continued without waiting for a reply. "Good, good. Did you see Jackson? Are the horses ready? I am riding down to Wimbledon with you. Need to see the Regiment, a ride is always the better with company. Jackson will ride along as well."

Michael and General Harcourt were soon on their way to Wimbledon. The hot weather was holding, and it was a pleasure to cross Putney Bridge and reach the freshness of the countryside. An easy two hours riding found them at the camp of the Sixteenth. The General's unexpected arrival caused some consternation, but he instructed Major Archer that there was to be no ceremony, told him that he wanted to see all the regiment's officers in half an hour, and to find Colonel Anson immediately. In all the hustle and bustle Michael was able to slip away, hand over Johnny to the care of Lloyd and get changed into uniform.

Within the half hour some three dozen officers assembled in the mess tent. When the General walked in, accompanied by Major Archer and Colonel Anson, the buzz of conversation fell away as all the officers came to attention. "Thank you, gentlemen, please, take a seat if you can find one, although I shall not keep you long." General Harcourt paused while those who could sat themselves down. "I am pleased to tell you that on Tuesday next the Duke of York will do us the great honour of reviewing the Regiment. On the following Friday the Regiment will march to Woodbridge Barracks for the winter. Colonel Anson and Major Archer have the details, I am returning to London, and I will accompany the Duke on Tuesday. I am sure that you will all realise how important this review is." The General looked around the tent at the Regiment's officers. "If all goes well, we will be declared fit for service and in due course the Regiment will go to Portugal. If it does not go well, we shall be the laughing stock of the army. Thank you, gentlemen, that is all." He turned to speak to Anson and Archer while a babble of conversation broke out at the news.

The next few days passed in a bustle of preparation for the review. In the mornings the dragoons, wearing their stable dress, with sabres and carbine belts, went through the choreography of the review, each officer with his allotted place in the ranks of the regiment. The squadron commanders fretted over the correct distances being kept as the regiment formed from line to column of squadrons and back, and then column of half squadrons and back, and then did it all over again. In the afternoons, and late into the summer's evening, the dragoons worked at their uniforms and equipment, everything had to look its very best for the Duke. Lloyd had the added responsibility of preparing Michael's uniform and equipment as well as his own. A bottle or two of beer from Michael soon cheered him up. Michael was involved in innumerable briefings. With early mornings, hours in the saddle, and late nights Michael hardly had time to think about his London adventures, or Elaine, but he did.

On the day of the review, the whole regiment was up and about before first light, and by ten o'clock all was deemed ready. The ten troops, each of about seventy men, were drawn up, two deep, in five squadrons. The Captain commanding each squadron was a horse's length in front of his squadron, his second in command on the outer flank of his own troop. As a junior officer, Michael's post was behind the squadron, in the middle of his troop, and two horse's lengths back. He had little to do in the review, just remember where he was supposed to be and when. Despite that he felt nervous, glancing right and left to ensure he was aligned with the other officers behind the other squadrons. He licked his lips, and gently eased himself in the saddle. One of Johnny's ears twitched, and Michael muttered "steady lad," in his calmest tone.

Colonel Anson took his position at the head of the Regiment and there was a long pause. Then the orders started to come and the need for concentration drove any nervousness out of his head. The squadrons divided in the middle and wheeled to the right, and then they were off, marching to the review ground, a column of ten half squadrons, one behind the other, over seven hundred horses and men moving in unison and according to the orders of a single man, Colonel Anson.

At the reviewing ground, on Wimbledon Common, the Regiment formed its squadrons back into line, and waited. The early September day got hotter. Tails flicked as flies buzzed around. A horse stamped on the ground. There was little sound save for the occasional muttered word at horse or dragoon, horses chewing at their bits, scabbards gently scraping on spurs. Michael could feel sweat trickling down his face, his head itched under his Tarleton. He could sense Johnny getting restless, standing still had never been his strong point. Before very long there was a stir and straightening up in the ranks as small party of military men on horseback appeared, the Duke of York and General Harcourt leading. Colonel Anson's timing had been spot on, keeping to a minimum the time they had to stand waiting. Through the ranks in front of him, Michael caught glimpses of the reviewing party as it took up position. Then the orders started again and the review began.

Several hours later it was all over. It was a very tired and drained group of officers that gathered in their mess tent for food and drinks, no one had fallen off, no horses had spooked and bolted. On the whole the feeling was the review had passed off reasonably well. Then there was a flurry of movement at the entrance, and officers were leaping to their feet. The General entered the tent, with the Duke of York and his entourage. Smiling, the Duke waved them all back down, and was led by the General to the middle of the tent. A gesture from the General, and a mess orderly appeared with a tray of drinks.

After a moment, and a good draught of his wine, the Duke looked around at the officers waiting expectantly. "Well, gentlemen, that was very well done, my congratulations. I can report, without fear of contradiction, that the Sixteenth is fit for service." He paused and looked around again, his glance settled on Michael for a moment, "Yes, I can say I am very pleased," and he looked across to the officers on the other side of the tent. "Furthermore, I am delighted to be able to give you news that reached me only late last night. Sir Arthur Wellesley has beaten the French army under Junot!"

Immediately cheering broke out, which soon spread through the tent lines as word spread. The Duke looked around, smiling, then raised his hand for silence. "I can also tell you that you will soon be receiving orders for Portugal." A buzz of conversation broke out.

Anson barked brusquely, "Silence, gentlemen, if you please."

The chatter stopped abruptly, and the Duke continued, "You will be going to Portugal, but not immediately. I believe that General Harcourt has told you that the

Regiment marches next week to Woodbridge?" The General nodded. "There you will have a little more time to ready yourselves for campaigning, make the most of it."

The Sixteenth marched into Woodbridge Barracks on the day before Michael's twentieth birthday. After four days march in a warm, early September there was much to do caring for the horses. Farriers were kept hard at work, shoeing and then producing a spare set of shoes for each horse. Tack was repaired, overalls and other items of uniform were stitched back together. And then the training started, and Michael began to realise that there was a lot more to being a light cavalry officer than horsemanship, skill with a sabre and keeping the correct distances.

His troop was now combined with that of Captain Swetenham to form a squadron, and he was expected to act as the flank officer for a half squadron, which entailed ensuring that he kept exactly the right distance from the half squadron in front, otherwise, when they wheeled into line there would either be a gap in the middle of the squadron, or, worse, the lines of wheeling dragoons would collide. Ashworth and Swetenham took it in turns commanding the Squadron while the other rode in the rear, shouting instructions, advice, and curses when things went wrong.

After a week, the Squadron was able to carry out an advance over distances of up to a mile, holding the line straight as they went from walk to trot, trot to canter, or gallop as the army called it, and, finally, from the gallop to the charge. Once the two Captains were satisfied, each subaltern officer was given the chance to lead the Squadron in an advance.

When it was his turn, Michael took his place, a mere horse's length in front of the middle of the Squadron. The Squadron was some one hundred and forty men, formed two deep, and with only six inches between the knees of the dragoons. It stretched for thirty-five or forty yards to either side of Michael's position. He took a deep breath, hoped Johnny wouldn't spook, and shouted his first order. In the silence his voice carried clearly to all the dragoons, "Squadron," pause, "Draw," a pause to let everyone slip their right hand through the sword knot and take a grip on their sword, "Swords!" There was a loud rasping sound as all swords were drawn. "Squadron," another pause, "March!" As the Squadron moved forward at the walk, Michael, looking ahead, picked out a far distant tree directly in front of him that would keep him straight, and avoid the disruption that any deviation could cause in the ranks.

He kept the pace at the walk for a hundred yards then, "Squadron," pause, "Trot." The whole line moved forward into the trot, and now the noise level rose, hooves thumping, scabbards clanging on spurs, officers and NCOs calling out, keeping the ranks straight and together. The Squadron covered a good quarter of a mile before Michael increased the pace. Raising his voice as loud as he could he called out, "Squadron," pause, "Gallop," and heard it repeated. A gentle squeeze on Johnny's sides and he broke into a beautiful, smooth and collected canter. Behind, the Squadron followed suit.

It dawned on Michael that now was the time to hope that Johnny stayed as sure footed as ever. A stumble, or a fall could be fatal.

The advance had now covered upwards of half a mile, the time had come. "Squadron!," he was unsure who could hear him, he could only hear, and feel, the Squadron thundering forwards a few yards behind him. He thought he heard someone call out "Squadron." He took a deep breath, "Charge!" He touched his spurs to Johnny and felt the horse accelerate into a flat out gallop. He could feel the ground shaking, hear the hooves pounding, the shouts, the clattering of scabbards. Fifty yards on, his heart was thumping in his chest, it was terrifying, it was exhilarating, he felt invincible. He could feel the weight, the terrible power of the squadron behind him. A hundred yards, and then he heard the bugle call ringing out above all the noise, giving the command to halt. Michael threw his sword arm up and screamed a long drawn out "Halt!" He threw his weight back in the saddle and pulled on the curb rein, firmly, but not harshly, Johnny was nothing if not responsive. A few more yards and the whole Squadron came to confused halt. Officers and NCOs shouted to dress the line, to get the men back into straight ranks. Michael sat motionless, giving the direction that the Squadron was to face, waiting for the shouting to end.

As he sat, panting, his heart still racing, Captain Ashworth rode up with the Troop Trumpeter. He had been behind the Squadron and had ordered the trumpeter to sound the Halt. Michael saluted him with his sabre. Ashworth could see the excitement in the young man's face and grinned at the sight. Behind him the Trumpeter was also grinning. "Well done, Roberts, well done. Quite something, ain't it?"

"Yes, sir, thank you, sir!" Michael could not help grinning wildly himself.

"Very well, I think that is enough for today. And since you are so clearly enjoying yourself, be so good as to march the Squadron back to barracks. At the walk, if you please!"

Later in September came news that gave an extra edge to their training. One evening all the officers of the Sixteenth were gathered around the dining table in the mess. Colonel Anson was at the head of the table, Michael, as a mere Cornet, was near the bottom of the table with his fellow Cornets. Sawyer was telling a mildly amusing story about one of the dragoons in his troop when an orderly handed a letter to Anson. This unusual occurrence put an end to Sawyer's tale as Anson opened and read the letter.

"Gentlemen," Anson looked around the table at them, "this is from Major General Cotton. I congratulate you. Here is the order to prepare for foreign service!" There was an immediate buzz of excited conversation. "We are to prepare to go to Portugal in January."

Captain Cocks leapt to his feet and onto the table, glass in hand, and called out, "Gentlemen, three cheers for the Sixteenth, hip, hip…" The room resounded to three loud cheers and glasses were emptied and more bottles called for.

The Sixteenth was brigaded with the Fourteenth Light Dragoons and a troop of Horse Artillery, the brigade commanded by Major General Cotton. Cotton, then a Captain, had charged with the Sixteenth at the battle of Beaumont in 1794, when the Duke of York had won a stunning victory over the French. He was determined that the sixteenth would again excel itself in Portugal. Consequently he worked both regiments hard. And not just at drill and charging around. He knew very well that in Portugal the light cavalry would be the eyes and ears of the army. They would be expected to organise and maintain lines of outposts, pickets and vedettes to protect the army from surprise, and to send out patrols to ascertain where the enemy was and what they were doing. He intended to do his utmost to prepare his brigade for such work.

So it was, with the days growing quickly shorter, the weather turning wet, windy and cold, that Michael found himself wandering around the Suffolk countryside with a sergeant and half a dozen miserable dragoons trying to locate the Fourteenth. On another occasion Michael was posted with a line of vedettes along the River Deben, their orders being to prevent the Fourteenth patrolling across it. It was a long cold night when nothing happened, beyond keeping contact with the lines of the vedettes along the river to either side of his position. When dawn broke it was discovered that the vedettes to his right were from the Fourteenth, and had been posted to stop patrols by the Sixteenth.

During the day they practiced skirmishing with the Paget Carbine that every Dragoon carried. For several weeks now every feed given to the horses had been accompanied by the firing of pistols and carbines until the horses took no notice at all. First they went through the drill with blanks. The Adjutant, who was supervising this, lost count of the times he called to one dragoon or another that he had just fired at a comrade. Then came firing with ball, at first on foot at targets, then on horseback. Michael was relieved that there were no accidents.

Into October, and things were improving, a night out on picket was no longer a strange experience. The horses were also now used to the noise of artillery, who missed no opportunity to gallop into action and fire off blanks at all and sundry. Michael was enjoying it all. He felt he had a grasp of his duties and felt comfortable giving orders to the dragoons, even veterans like Sergeant Blood, who had been at Beaumont with General Cotton. He got on well with Captain Ashworth and his fellow officers, and, perhaps more importantly, the NCOs and dragoons of his Troop. Truth be told, he missed Falmouth not a jot.

Quiet moments were few and far between, one came when he was wrapped up in his cloak, sitting under a tree in the dark, Johnny's reins in his hands, waiting for something to happen. He was, to all intents and purposes, alone, the nearest dragoon was ten yards away. He let his mind wander over the last year and how much, how dramatically things had changed for him. He believed, he hoped, he had found his calling, but he knew that he was yet to be truly tested. He just hoped that he would not let anyone down. He did not believe he was a coward, nothing in his life suggested that he might be, and thousands of men of all nationalities managed perfectly well to be soldiers. He was, however, all too aware that until he heard shots fired in anger, until he charged across a field with French cavalry on the other side of it, until he crossed sabres with a Frenchman, until then he would not know that he could do it.

He also wondered how the latest news from Portugal would affect matters. No sooner had he beaten the French than Sir Arthur Wellesley had been succeeded by two officers who were both senior to him. They had concluded what many were calling a shameful agreement with the French, by which they would be evacuated from Portugal on British ships! Such was the reaction against this that all three had been called home for an enquiry, with command in Portugal passing to Sir John Moore.

He wondered if he would get to Lisbon and solve the mystery of Augusto.

And always not far from his thoughts was Elaine. He wondered when he might see her again, and if he would be able to keep his promise.

"Sir?" the softly spoken word from the dragoon brought him back to the present. "There's movement across the bridge, sir." Something was happening, probably a patrol from the 14th trying to find and cross the bridge.

The days shortened through October, and the training went on. One result of the intensity of the training was that Michael got to know the men in his troop better. Lloyd was a fairly constant companion, and the Welshman proved to have his strengths, and weaknesses. He was indeed a fine horseman and looked after both his own troop horse and Johnny with devotion and expertise, even if he was sometimes at odds, politely, with the Regiment's Veterinary Surgeon. When it came to looking after Michael's uniform and accoutrements he was not so efficient, and Michael found that minor repairs were best tackled by Mrs Taylor, wife of one of the troop's sergeants. The exception to that was the edge Lloyd put on Michael's sabre. As a swordsman, Lloyd was a demon, and Michael was glad to know that he would usually be near him in a fight. As for his drinking, Michael had not yet caught him drunk on duty, but he knew that he still liked a few drinks.

With the regiment preparing for active service there was a need to double up the number of lieutenants so that each troop had two. Consequently, being deemed fit for promotion, Michael received his lieutenancy, along with six other cornets. At the same time four new cornets arrived, with another three due by Christmas. Being an internal promotion there was no cost of purchase, which was a great relief, given the situation with his uncle. Under other circumstances that step would have cost him nearly three hundred pounds. The promotion appeared in the Gazette, and shortly afterwards Michael received a congratulatory note, in code, with an instruction to write if he was going to be in London at all, and simply signed E. London, thought Michael, that would be rather good, but not likely as the regiment worked at its field skills.

Michael also received a letter from Rutherford. He had heard from Michael's uncle Jocelyn, whose intransigence had collapsed under Rutherford's attack. He had assured Mr Rutherford that there must be some misunderstanding. He only meant that he would support Michael in a legal career, should he choose the leave the army. He had no intention of cutting off Michael's allowance, which came from the money received for the diamonds, sent by Michael's father for his subsistence. Enclosed in the letter was the strong box key, which Jocelyn had sent to Rutherford at the latter's request. It was a complete volte face. Mr Rutherford concluded that Michael should have no further concerns about his uncle, and that he would be honoured to give him any further assistance, should it be required.

Michael was mightily relieved. He opened his copy of The Libertine, and composed a letter to Elaine.

A few days into November, and Michael was relaxing in his room after breakfast, he had no duty or exercises that day. It was a rare day of rest. There was a knock on the door, Michael groaned, and for a moment wondered about pretending not to be in, then the door opened and Lloyd stuck his head in. "Begging your pardon, sir, Mr Barra wants to see you in his office, please, sir."

Michael levered himself to his feet. "Alright, Lloyd, help me with my sword belt and I'll go directly."

Lieutenant Barra was at his desk, as the Adjutant he was probably the busiest officer in the Regiment. "Ah, Roberts, thank you for coming so promptly." Barra smiled at Michael in appreciation. "Colonel Anson has asked me to have a word with all the new lieutenants who need second horses as they are likely to be going to Portugal. General Harcourt has written that Harris, the dealer, has some that might make suitable chargers. You are to ride to London the day after tomorrow, and see what you think. Penrice and Tomkinson are there now, due back tomorrow. Sawyer, Osten and Bence have already managed to get one, so it's just you. You had best take that scoundrel Lloyd with you, the man does know his horses. You are to put up at Harcourt House, Lloyd can bed down with the grooms. And try not to let him get drunk, there's a good fellow." Barra smiled wanly. "Try not to be more than a week, please?"

Michael laughed, "Of course I will be, Barra, and I shall do my best with Lloyd."

Michael returned to the officer's quarters, but Lloyd was nowhere to be seen. He was pretty sure he wouldn't be in his barrack room, too much chance of being told to clean his kit. Michael thought he would take a stroll down to the stables, it was a good bet that he would be there, but first, there was a note he had to write and get in the post.

Lloyd was grooming Johnny, giving him a rub down with a twist of straw, all the time talking to him in gentle, singsong Welsh. Michael watched for a moment, then Johnny saw him and gave a little snicker, drawing Lloyd's attention to his arrival. "How is he, Lloyd?"

"As fit as a flea, sir, all this work and fine feed is doing him a power of good."

Michael unbuckled his sword belt and propped his sword in a corner. As he started to remove his jacket he said "I'll carry on with that Lloyd, you look to your own Edward. We are off to London on Tuesday."

"Is that right, sir? And may I ask what for?"

"We are going to see General Harcourt, there are some horses to look at, for a second horse for me. We will be staying at Harcourt House; you'll be in with the grooms. We will be coming back for next Monday."

"Now that sounds very fine to me, sir. Staying at the General's? Duw, and Sergeant Taylor will be green with envy." He gave Michael a broad grin as he started to work on his own horse.

"That's as may be, Lloyd, but I am counting on you for two things, to help me pick out a good horse, and to stay sober, or at least not get drunk. Do you think you might manage that for me?"

"Well, sir, I think I can manage about a horse, sir, but the drink? That's a harder thing for me, as you know, sir."

"I do indeed, Lloyd, and I also know that the regiment is watching to see what I can make of you, damn you. So you stay sober, or I'll have your damned hide off your back, and send you back to general duties."

"Ah, now sir, do you not think Johnny would miss me something terrible? Probably go right off his feed, sir." Lloyd had his back to Michael, and a huge grin on his face.

"You are a miserable wretch, Lloyd," Michael laughed, "just don't let me down." The two men worked on their horses in companionable silence.

The ninety or so miles to Cavendish Square were covered by Michael and Lloyd in two days, and it was not long after darkness had fallen that they rode into the forecourt of Harcourt House. They were expected, and Michael just took his valise off Johnny and left Lloyd to look after the two horses. He told Lloyd to be ready by eight o'clock the following morning, and, aware of the General's groom nearby, simply added "and take care now, Lloyd, we are guests of the General," trying at the same time to give him a meaningful look. Lloyd's salute and "Yes, sir," were not entirely comforting.

In the house Michael was relieved of his valise, Tarleton helmet, and sabre by a footman, the butler informed him that he had been given the same room as before and that the General had given instructions that he was to see him as soon as he arrived. The butler took Michael up to the drawing room, announced him, and went on his way.

"Roberts, come in now, come in. You are just in time for dinner, will you take a glass of sherry? We have a few minutes."

"Thank you, General, a glass of sherry would be most welcome, and dinner will be as well, thank you, sir." Michael was a little taken aback by the General's rather effusive welcome.

"Very well, make yourself comfortable. Now, how's your face? Healed well?"

Michael's hand went to his left cheek and the long, thin scar, still red, that ran from his cheekbone to his jawbone. "Yes, sir, thank you, no problems at all."

"Good, good, I expect the ladies like it, eh?" The General laughed. "Now, I want to hear all about how the Regiment is getting on in Woodbridge?"

Harcourt seemed pleased with what he heard from Michael, it tallied with what he had heard a few days before from Tomkinson and Penrice. After dinner the General insisted they have a few glasses of port, and the conversation turned to more general matters.

"Tell me, how is your Grandfather, is he keeping well?"

"Very well, indeed, sir, and still gets out with the hunt on good days."

And so the conversation turned to hunting, horses and hounds. Eventually the General announced that he was retiring, and that he would see Michael at breakfast, at about eight o'clock, and then they would go and see Michael's new horse. It was only after he was in bed himself that it struck Michael as rather odd, the reference to Michael's 'new horse'. Harris would undoubtedly have a few to show to him, but even then he might not find one he liked enough to buy.

Promptly at eight o'clock Michael walked into the dining room, the General was already there. Markham, the General's butler was in attendance, as he had been at dinner the night before. Michael helped himself to some bread rolls while Markham poured him a cup of tea, with a quiet "good morning, sir." Conversation was desultory, although the General seemed quite pleased about something.

At last the General pushed his chair back and said "Well, shall we go and see this horse then?"

"Yes, sir, of course, are we to ride there?"

"Ride? Ride?" laughed the General, "why sir, I don't think we need to ride across the courtyard! The animal is in my stables?"

Michael was now thoroughly confused. "I beg your pardon, sir, but I don't quite follow. I thought I was to look at some horses that Harris has?"

"That, my boy, is up to you, but first you must come and look at the horse in the stables. Now, come along, sir, quick, quick!"

So saying, the General strode purposefully out of the dining room, pursued by a confused Michael. Was the General going to offer to sell him one of his own horses? Oh, Lord, what if it was no good? How could he refuse? Across the courtyard they strode and into the door of the stables. Lloyd was already there, looking at a horse in a loose box, the General's groom next to him.

At the sight of the General bearing down on him, Lloyd came smartly to attention and saluted, while the groom simply touched his cap.

The General looked the dragoon up and down. "Ah, you must be the infamous Lloyd? Well, man, you've seen the animal, what do you think, they tell me you know a thing or two about horses." Lloyd looked completely taken aback. "Come on man, d'ye think I don't know what goes on in my own Regiment?"

By now Michael could see the horse in question. It was a simply magnificent looking dark-bay gelding. The General turned to Michael, a large smile on his face. "Now then, Mr Roberts, what do you think of that, eh? Better than anything Harris has in his stables, I'll wager." He turned back. "Eh, Lloyd, so what do you think, is this a fit animal for Lieutenant Roberts to be seen on?"

Lloyd gave Michael a quick glance. "Well, General, sir, it certainly looks fine enough, and Mr Jackson here," he indicated the groom, "tells me he is sound and in good condition, sir. But there's many a trick to make a horse look fine, begging your pardon, sir, and yours, Mr Jackson. The real question is how does he go under a rider?"

The General laughed. "Very well, Lloyd, shall we take a ride over to Hyde Park? See what Mr Roberts makes of him?"

"Yes, sir, I think that is a very good idea of yours, sir."

"Ha, you do, do you, then best get him and yours saddled up. Jackson, saddle up a couple for us, we will go along for the entertainment. Right, we will mount in half an hour."

An hour and a half later the little cavalcade rode back into the courtyard at Cavendish House. Michael had put the horse through its paces and was impressed by the way it had dealt with the busy London streets, the noise and clatter leaving him unmoved. He was unbothered by Michael's sabre banging about at his side. His trot was comfortable, and his canter smooth and ate up the ground. He responded promptly to hand and leg, and was light in the mouth. In the courtyard they all dismounted, the General shouting at a servant for tankards of mulled ale. Michael handed the reins to Lloyd, raising his eyebrows, questioningly.

"That's not a days' hunting or a day's field exercise, sir, but, chwarae teg, he looks well enough. I doubt if Harris has anything better." Lloyd muttered quietly as he took the horse from Michael. "But he'll be worth a pretty penny, sir, and you can't be haggling with the General."

With a thoughtful nod, Michael hurried after the General, who was striding across the courtyard to the house. In the drawing room the butler soon appeared with the mulled ale, which both men were grateful for. Once they were alone the General smiled at Michael and asked, "What do you think then?"

"Oh, he's a splendid animal, sir, well-schooled, light in the hand, good paces. Of course, that wasn't the same as a field day, sir, but he looks strong enough."

"You like him then?"

"Yes, sir, I do, but…" Michael was about to question if he could afford to buy such a fine horse, but the General cut him short.

"Good, just as well, he's yours."

"What? I beg your pardon, sir, but I couldn't possibly accept…"

The General laughed, "Good Lord, man, I'm not giving him to you. He is a gift, but not from me, oh, no, no! He's a gift from the Duke of York! So it's just as well you like him, you can hardly send him back!" The General laughed at Michael's obvious confusion. "It's about all the Duke can do to thank you for saving his life without causing some sort of political scandal with the Portuguese. As Musgrave said, that never happened, so as far as the rest of the world is concerned, I have sold you a fine horse at a very good price out of my fondness for your grandfather. Now, not a word to anyone, particularly that rogue Lloyd. I suggest we agree on fifty guineas as a very, very generous price, what do you say?" The General was clearly highly amused by the whole business and beamed at Michael, his eyes twinkling with good humour.

Michael smiled back at General Harcourt. "Yes, sir, yes, a very generous price indeed."

"Excellent, now I have some damned meeting at Horse Guards and then dinner with the Earl of Pembroke, he wants to know my opinion of this business of the Convention that Dalrymple made with the French. If he asks me, I shall say I think Dalrymple is a fool, not that your heard me say that." The General wagged his finger at Michael.

"No, sir, of course not."

"Good, now, I suppose you can amuse yourself for the rest of the day?" Michael nodded. "Take your new horse out again, or something. Best eat out this evening, if that suits?"

Michael nodded again, aware that in his pocket was a note delivered to him while the horses were being got ready. He was very happy to be freed by the General that evening, it saved him making his excuses. He had a rendezvous in Covent Garden.

"Right, I shall be off, good day to you, Lieutenant." And with another chuckle the General was gone.

Michael sat quietly and supped his ale. He heard the General's coach clatter off, and strolled down to the stables. Lloyd was rubbing down the new horse, and looked up expectantly.

"Yes, Lloyd, I bought him."

"Did you get a fair price, sir, begging your pardon for asking?"

"Oh, yes, Lloyd, I did, very fair indeed."

"That's good, sir. And what's his name sir?"

Michael realised that he had no idea what the horse was called, it had never been mentioned, probably so it couldn't be connected to the Duke. He laughed as an idea struck him. "Duke, Lloyd, we will call him Duke."

Chapter 10

Michael had brought a change of clothes with him, civilian clothes, visits to London seemed to require them. As soon as he was changed he crossed over the courtyard to the stables. He found Lloyd and Jackson deep in conversation in a small room full of tack and saddles, but with a very nice little fire burning in the grate. When Michael appeared both men shot to their feet, Lloyd giving a passable salute.

"This is a snug little billet, Jackson. I hope Lloyd isn't being a nuisance?"

"No, sir, not at all."

Michael wondered for a moment if he should warn Jackson about Lloyd's predilection for the bottle, but decided against it. Lloyd had done well so far; he deserved a chance for that. "I will be out for the rest of the day, Lloyd, if you can give Johnny a stretch that would be good, your own nag too. Jackson, keep him busy."

"Oh, I can do that, sir," replied Jackson with a smile.

Leaving Cavendish Square Michael walked down to the Regiment's tailor on Conduit Street and ordered a new pair of Pantaloons and some shirts. From there he made his way to St James' to pay his respects to Nathaniel Collyer. With his promotion his pay had increased, and as a result there was a little business to conduct with the Agent.

Heading south down St James' Street, Michael passed by the Palace and emerged onto the Mall. He turned east, crossed Horse Guards, and turned north. He called into a coffee house and spent an hour reading the latest newspapers. By now it was getting dark. After checking his fob-watch, he left the coffee house and at three thirty precisely knocked on the door of Lady Travers little house.

Johnson answered the door and let him in. Taking Michael's hat, gloves, cane and topcoat he said, "Her Ladyship is her sitting room, sir."

Michael opened the door and let himself in, and closed it behind him. Elaine rose from her chair by the fire, and in seconds was in his arms. He kissed her, urgently, with all the longing of their separation, his arms around her, hands caressing. "Enough, now, Michael," she laughed and wriggled out of his arms. "Mrs Johnson has prepared a fine dinner for us, and she will be vexed if it spoils." She glanced at a clock on the mantelpiece. "But we have ten minutes, enough time for a sherry, I think?"

Over dinner Michael told her about Duke, and how things were in the Regiment. Elaine congratulated him on his promotion, and drank a glass to his health. She thanked him for the letter about Rutherford's success in dealing with his uncle. Their conversation flowed easily, and there was no awkwardness when it failed occasionally, just companionable silence. After dinner they went to the theatre, and saw Congreve's play, the Mourning Bride. Returning to Elaine's house they found a light supper waiting, it did not long detain them.

As he walked across London the following morning, Michael's thoughts were all of Elaine, of the tenderness of her touch, the softness of her skin, her scent, the little mewling sounds she made. He could not even begin to guess where her friendship might lead. He knew it would only be friendship, he might not have known her long, but he knew her well enough to know that she meant what she said, and expected him to keep his word, no matter the cost. And cost him it already had; he had quite lost his heart to her. He knew, beyond all doubt, that he loved her. The world she lived in was a mystery to him. The double world. High class London society on one hand, and the world of spies, assassins and intelligence services on the other. He shook his head in wonder. What a truly remarkable woman, he was glad she was his friend, he regretted that she would not be more. He consoled himself with her parting promise that she would see him again, soon,

Lost in his thoughts, Michael was soon back at Harcourt House. As he walked across the courtyard he heard laughter coming from the stables. He looked in and saw Lloyd and Jackson, obviously sharing some joke. Well, everything seemed to alright there. Lloyd was behaving himself, the more he had to do with horses, the better he seemed to be.

Inside the house John, the footman, took his hat gloves and cane, and helped him off with his top coat. "The General has been asking for you, sir, he's in the drawing room."

Michael ran up the stairs and made his way to the drawing room,'

"Ah, Roberts, there you, I was beginning to think we had lost you. Out all night, eh? Well, no harm in that, at least, I hope not?"

"No, sir, none at all."

"Excellent. Now I want your help today, and that rapscallion Lloyd. Harris has some possible remounts in, and I want the pick of them before anyone else gets to them. Steuart from the Twelfth has already been sniffing around. We'll take Jackson as well, see what we can get."

It was a long day, but satisfying. They managed to get to Harris before Steuart, and picked out a dozen good horses from the fifty or so in Harris' yard. Once again Michael witnessed the effect of the companionship of horsemanship. By the end of the day the four men were at ease with each other, pointing out defects or strengths of horses with very little ceremony beyond the occasional 'sir'.

By the time they returned to Harcourt House it was almost dark. Michael and the General got down from the coach, Jackson had driven, with Lloyd siting on the box with him. The General was clearly pleased with the day's proceedings. "Well, Lloyd, I have to admit you're not a bad judge of horse flesh, well done, man. And you as well, Jackson, a most satisfactory day, and we stole a march on Steuart, eh?" The General smiled and chuckled at the thought. "Take care of the horses and I'll send you a couple of bottles of claret. Right, Roberts, I think we deserve a drink ourselves before dinner."

As they settled themselves into chairs in the General's drawing room Michael felt obliged to speak. "I beg your pardon, sir, but is it such a good idea to give Lloyd a bottle?"

"No, I'm not at all sure about it, but he has been worth his pay these last few days, particularly today. Working with Jackson seems to have had an effect. We will give him a chance and see if he holds up, or lets us down."

Dinner over, Michael and the General were just taking a glass of port when there came the sound of a carriage in the courtyard, followed by raised voices and a disturbance at the front door. Michael and the General started to rise from their chairs as the door opened and John just had time to say "There's a man asking for the Lieutenant, sir, he seems…" when he was thrust aside to reveal Johnson.

"Sir, will you come at once, it's Lady Travers, she's been shot!"

"What? Yes, of course," Michael started for the door, followed by the General, "what has happened?"

"I'm not sure, sir, Mr Musgrave brought her to the house in his carriage, and she asked for you, sir."

Michael seized his cane and coat as he made for the door. They reached the courtyard where a carriage stood, the horses sweating. A light shone from the stables. "Lloyd!" roared the General. Lloyd appeared a moment later in his stable trousers and jacket. "Lloyd, get your sabre and go with Mr Roberts." Jackson also appeared. "Jackson, get Lloyd a coat to cover his uniform, sharp now!"

Michael and Johnson were already climbing into the carriage. "Hold a moment," said the General, "take Lloyd, you might need him."

Lloyd came running across the yard, carrying coat and sabre to where the General was holding the door for him. "In you go, Lloyd, look after the Lieutenant now."

The driver cracked his whip and the carriage flew forward and out of the archway of Harcourt House. Inside, Michael and Lloyd struggled into their coats and onto seats. "For God's sake, Johnson, what has happened?" Michael demanded.

"I don't know sir. My Lady went out early, she said she didn't need me to go, it was just a small gathering she said, nothing to worry about, and Mr Musgrave was sending a couple of men along. Then the next thing is Mr Musgrave is hammering on the door saying her Ladyship was shot. We got her into the drawing room, Mr Musgrave has sent a man for Dr Vaughan. She asked me to get you, sir, Mr Musgrave said to take his carriage, and that's all I know, sir."

It seemed to Michael like an eternity until the carriage was pulling up outside Elaine's house. He leapt down, followed by Lloyd and Johnson. A man stood in front of the door, one of Musgrave's, and recognising Michael he stood aside for him. "He's with me," Michael called over his shoulder, indicating Lloyd. In the hall Musgrave was speaking to two men who looked like porters. Seeing Michael he just gestured at the drawing room.

In the room Elaine was lying on the chaise longue where she and Michael had often sat together. Her eyes were closed, her face was white and a red stain had soaked into cloths covering her left shoulder and breast. Marianne was standing by, almost as pale. Dr Vaughan rose from Elaine's side as Michael came in. He looked him in the eye, and gave a tiny shake of his head. Michael dropped to his knees beside Elaine and took her hand. Her eyes opened and she saw him.

"Elaine, Elaine." He felt overwhelmed by a complete sense of helplessness.

"Michael, hush now." She drew a deep, ragged breath, frowning at the effort. "I am glad that you are here, see, I said it would be soon." She smiled, and her head tilted towards him a little. "Michael?"

"Yes?"

"Do you remember that promise you made me?"

"Yes. Of course I do."

"Do you think that you might have broken it?"

"Elaine, I already have. Forgive me?"

"I forgive you, Michael, and I am glad you have, because I have too. You have made me so happy, as I never thought I would be again. Kiss me, Michael."

Michael bent his head to hers and kissed her gently, he felt her hand squeeze his. He raised his head, she smiled at him, a beautiful, radiant, happy smile, and then she slipped quietly away.

The doctor stepped up to them and felt for a pulse. "I am sorry, Mr Roberts, so very, very sorry." He walked out into the hall and shook his head at Musgrave. "Best give him a few moments. It was serious, wasn't it?" With that he took his leave.

Back in the drawing room Michael still held Elaine's hand, and knelt by her as his heart broke into a million pieces.

Nearby stood Marianne, sobbing into her handkerchief. Eventually Michael forced himself to let go of Elaine's hand. He brushed a strand of that copper coloured hair from her forehead, and bent to kiss her one last time. He rose slowly to his feet. "Marianne?"

"Yes, sir?"

"Take good care of her," his voice started to crack as he felt anger welling up in his chest. "The very best of care, do you hear?"

"Of course I will, sir."

He turned towards her and spoke, his voice more gentle. "Yes, Marianne, I am sure that you will. Forgive me."

He saw Musgrave standing in the doorway, and something snapped. He hurled himself across the room and seized Musgrave by his waistcoat, pushing him into the hallway and against the wall. "What happened, damn you, you were supposed to be protecting her, what the hell happened, who did this?"

Musgrave's two men started forward, and Lloyd started forward as well, his hand going to the hilt of his sabre. Musgrave raised a hand to halt his men, and everything froze. Musgrave looked Michael in the eye. "I don't know, I just don't know."

Michael looked hard at him for a moment and slowly released his grip. "Then you had better tell me what you do know. In here." He pushed Musgrave into the dining room and closed the door, leaning on it, shutting everyone else out. "Now, tell me everything."

Musgrave sat down on one of the chairs at the table. He indicated another chair, "Please, Mr Roberts, please, sit down, and I will tell you everything, although it isn't much."

Reluctantly Michael took the chair indicated, and waited.

"All I know is that Lady Travers went to a small soiree this evening. It was a gathering of French Royalist emigres, a regular meeting, we monitor it, keep an eye, but everyone who goes has been checked, and checked again, and they are all genuine. The risk was considered to be negligible, but I still sent a couple of men along to keep an eye on things. It is held at a hotel on The Strand. I was surprised to receive a note from Lady Travers, by hand, brought by a page at the hotel, asking me to come at once. Of course, I did, she is not," he hesitated for a moment, "was not a woman to take alarm easily. I arrived at the hotel, and I was just speaking to one of my men, at the hotel entrance, the other was patrolling around, when I heard a shot. I ran in and up to where the soiree was being held. Lady Travers was on the floor, a French physician was attending to her. I sent for Dr Vaughan and brought her here in my carriage. And that is all I know." He paused for a moment, and took a deep, calming breath before he continued.

"I have men questioning all the guests at the soiree, some left immediately, but we will speak to everyone. It is a small group, who all know each other. Once we find who fired the shot we will hunt them down, and see them swing from the gallows for this, that I promise you."

Michael had been sitting, head down, listening. Now he looked at Musgrave. "I shall hold you to that promise,

Musgrave. And you had better keep it. Unless I get to them first."

Musgrave had absolutely no doubt of Michael's sincerity.

As the following days passed, a little more was discovered. Musgrave came to see Michael at Harcourt House. "I have some information, but very little. It appears there was a new face at the soiree, we don't yet know how he got in, but he spoke of being a refugee from Lisbon."

Michael looked up at the mention of Lisbon. "Oh, he was French," continued Musgrave, "but claimed to be a Royalist supporter from the south of France who had fled south and ended up hiding out in Lisbon. Yes, well, not very convincing, but not impossible. But then it seems someone thought they recognised him, and Lady Travers sent me that note. He smelt a rat, started leave, and she challenged him. He drew a pistol and shot her. Disappeared in the smoke and confusion." He paused. "I believe Lady Travers told you that we thought there was a fourth Portuguese?" Michael nodded. "Well, now we think it was this Frenchman, with enough Portuguese to pass as such in London. What he was doing at the soiree, I don't know." Musgrave looked at Michael, "Look, I give you my word that I will keep you informed of our search for this, this bastard! You must understand, it will take time, but I want him as much as you do."

"Oh, I doubt that, I doubt that very much," replied Michael.

The following day General Harcourt wrote to Colonel Anson, informing him that he was attempting to buy more remounts, and that as Michael and Lloyd had proven so helpful, he intended to keep them in London a little longer. As for Lloyd, he had learnt a lot that awful night, from the Johnsons and a grief stricken Marianne. He felt for Michael, his Lieutenant as he now thought of him. A few days later he was alone in the stables when Michael wandered in to see Johnny and Duke. After Michael had fussed the two horses for a while, Lloyd nervously cleared his throat.

"Begging your pardon, Mr Roberts, sir, and I hope you don't mind, but I should like to offer my condolences, sir." Michael stood stock still, his back to Lloyd. "Mr Johnson put me in the picture that night, sir. And I would like you to know that there won't be any loose talk around the horse lines from me, sir. On that you have my word."

After a moments pause, still without turning, Michael spoke. "What's your Christian name Lloyd? I should know it, I'm sorry, but I don't."

"Emyr, sir."

"Well, Emyr Lloyd, I thank you for your words, I thank you very much indeed." He turned and walked out of the stables, not daring to look Lloyd in the face.

Lady Elaine Travers was laid to rest in the churchyard of St Pauls in Covent Garden. The funeral was attended by many of London society who had known her, and many French exiles who had seen her as something of a guardian. Musgrave was there, and there was a sprinkling of his men around the church and in the curious crowd of onlookers. Mr and Mrs Johnson and Marianne were there. Some were surprised to see Lieutenant General Harcourt in attendance, but none took any notice of the lieutenant acting as his orderly.

The day after the funeral Elaine's will was read. Michael was surprised to have been asked to attend. He found that there were only four other people at the reading, Elaine's lawyer, Mr Rutherford, Mr and Mrs Johnson and Marianne. Rutherford explained that he had seen Lady Travers only a few weeks previously, and that she had had a new will drawn up. First there were bequests for the

Johnsons and Marianne, and not small ones either, enough to give them independence and security, Michael had not realised just how wealthy Elaine had been. The ladies sobbed and Johnson looked rather close to tears himself. The house in Covent Garden was rented, but a quarter's rent had been paid at Michaelmas. They would have time to arrange their new lives.

Finally the lawyer read, "To my very good friend, Michael Roberts, I leave the residue of my estate, to be held in trust until he is of age, and the contents of the package addressed to him and held by my lawyer." The lawyer looked over his glasses at Michael. "There are still a few matters to be settled before we can be entirely sure of the value of Lady Travers' estate, but I would estimate the residue to be in the region of ten thousand pounds." He picked up a small package from his desk. "And here, sir, is your package."

Stunned, Michael took the package. "Thank you, sir."

"Her Ladyship asked me to act as trustee for your inheritance, Mr Roberts." He smiled ruefully. "I am sure you understand why?"

Michael nodded his agreement; he was too overwhelmed to speak.

"And, if you are content, when all is settled, I shall invest it Government Bonds, and pay you the interest through your regiment's agent, Mr Collyer, I believe?"

"Yes, Mr Rutherford, that will be most acceptable."

"Now, unless there are any questions? No? Then I shall be in touch very soon about the arrangements for payment of the bequests. Please accept my condolences, Lady Travers was a very fine lady, and it was always a pleasure dealing with her." The lawyer sniffed, took out a large spotted handkerchief, and removed his glasses to dab at his eyes and blow his nose. "Forgive me, as I said, a very fine Lady. And now if you will excuse me, I shall leave you alone for a few minutes, my clerk will show you out."

After the lawyer had left, the four of them sat silently for a while. "I must say," said Michael, "that I had no expectation of anything. Frankly, I am rather taken aback, and embarrassed. You are far more deserving of her kindness than I am."

"No, sir." It was Marianne who replied. She looked at Mr and Mrs Johnson, and then back to Michael. "She was a great lady, sir, and it us who owe her much for her kindness. I was with her in Switzerland when her husband was killed. She never got over it, sir. That is, not until she met you. I know it might seem odd, you had such a short time together, but she was happy again, sir, really happy. And for that, I thank you."

Back at Harcourt House Michael opened the package. Inside was a folding picture frame. On one side was a miniature of Elaine, on the other, a lock of her bright copper coloured hair. With it was a letter.

'My dearest Michael,

If you are reading this it means that I am dead, how, I cannot guess. I hope that this gift will keep my memory fresh in your mind for many, many years to come. I hope that I have had the time, and the courage to tell you what you have so very, very quickly come to mean to me. I never thought that I would love again, you proved me wrong, something I don't usually take kindly to, but in this instance I am only too, too happy to be wrong. My darling Michael, I love you.

I hope that you have loved me, I hope I know that you do before I die. If not, I hope you will remember me as a dear, dear friend. If you do love me, do not, my love, do not make my mistake of thinking love comes only once. I hereby, most sincerely, release you of any ties, real or imagined.

Remember me, your ever loving Elaine.'

No, he would never, could never forget.

The next day Michael and Lloyd set off to return to the Regiment at Woodbridge. Leaving Harcourt House had been a subdued affair, little was said, or needed to be said. Two days later they rode into Woodbridge Barracks, Michael on Duke, Lloyd leading Johnny. A slightly awkward interview with Colonel Anson followed, but Michael avoided too close a questioning by speaking highly of Lloyd's behaviour, and usefulness. He also knew that Harcourt had written to Anson.

Over the next few days, however, the Regiment became aware that a changed Lieutenant Roberts had returned from his long sojourn in London. Duke was much admired, and Michael was considered to be a lucky dog that his Grandfather had served with General Harcourt. But Michael himself seemed no longer to be quite the light hearted subaltern he had been. Moreover Lloyd had become sober and very protective of 'my Lieutenant'. Michael threw himself into preparing himself for war. He practiced the Sword Exercise relentlessly. He became a reasonable shot with his pistols. The men in his troop noticed that he had become much more attentive to them, talking to them in the stables, asking the married men how their wives were.

Captain Ashworth was both delighted and concerned. Michael's conscientious approach to all professional matters made his life a lot easier, but at the same time he became aware that Michael had acquired an edge, a seriousness, a focus that was, frankly, a little disconcerting. The consensus, out of the hearing of Michael or Lloyd, was that something serious had happened in London, but none of the other officers felt able to make enquiries, and as Sergeant Flynn observed to the Captain, "Lloyd is not saying a word to anyone about London, sir, and he's leaving the bottle alone." Ashworth raised his eyebrows questioningly. "Yes, sir, it's true."

Chapter 11

As it turned out, the Regiment had little time to wonder about the change in Michael. With the likelihood of orders to march for Portugal expected at any time, Colonel Anson embarked on a reorganisation of the regiment. Of the ten troops, eight would be going, while two stayed behind to form a depot for recruiting and training, both men and horses. Personnel had to be allocated so the troops that went were the strongest, brought up to eighty men each, but while also allowing the two remaining troops to function effectively. There were also the new Cornets to deal with. They had arrived through November and December, and were still novices in many aspects of their rank. E Troop got George Keating, a quiet young man of seventeen, who promised to be quietly efficient. Sergeant Blood was moved, to Michael's dismay, into Captain Cock's Troop, in exchange for Sergeant Evans, newly promoted from corporal. Major Stanhope would be going, while Major Archer remained to command the depot.

By late December they were on the march, ordered to Falmouth, there to board transports for Portugal to join Sir John Moore's army. On the way they heard the outcome of the Court of Inquiry into events in Portugal that autumn. Generals Dalrymple, Burrard and Wellesley had been exonerated. At Exeter their march was halted, and Michael was rather relieved, he had not been looking forward to seeing his uncle again. But it seemed their transports were now required for another purpose and they went into quarters in and around Exeter.

Towards the end of January came the news of the disastrous retreat of Moore's army and its evacuation from Corunna. Transports arrived at every port from Falmouth to Portsmouth. Such was the state of the returning troops that the Sixteenth was moved to Dorchester to make room.

All through this Michael continued to work hard and push himself hard. Captain Ashworth was forced to order him to do less. Michael just took to riding out all day, on Johnny or Duke, when he had no duty. Sometimes alone, sometimes with Lloyd.

The delay in going was too much for Captain Cocks, who managed to arrange to go out to Portugal anyway. General Cotton had also gone ahead.

Gradually, almost imperceptibly, the pain of Michael's loss began to ease. He got a week's leave, and realising he couldn't avoid it for ever, he rode to see his uncle. He found his uncle on the verge of writing to him; he had received another letter from Baron Quintela. Following the expulsion of the French from Portugal and the occupation of Lisbon by the British, the Baron had written to Lisbon, instructing his chief clerk, Rodrigues, to give Michael, should he manage to get to Lisbon, whatever help he could in identifying the mysterious Augusto. Their meeting was awkward, Michael kept it as brief as he could, saying that he was also going to see his grandfather.

Leaving Falmouth behind, a four hour ride took him to his grandfather's house. He told him about everything, about Elaine, and about his uncle. His Grandfather listened without interrupting while Michael unburdened himself. When he had finished the Reverend sat silent for a while.

"The situation with your uncle is a very difficult thing. He came to see me a little while ago. He wanted my advice on how he might dissuade you from pursuing your way in the army. I told him that he should not. That when one has found one's calling, one must follow that, and I pointed out that I am well placed to know about that." He gave a chuckle. "He didn't like that very much. I asked him why he thought the army was not suitable. He said it was no profession for a gentleman." At the irony of that Michael pulled a fleeting wry smile. The Reverend continued. "I fear that like so many he cannot conceive of what it means to belong to a regiment, nor, I suspect, to have a true vocation. However, I will not speculate further on his motives. He asked me, I told him."

"As for Lady Travers, Michael, what you have told me is a terrible thing, but it is also a very beautiful thing. She sounds like a truly remarkable woman. I should have liked to meet her. You did, Michael, and more than that you loved her, and she loved you in return. That is something wonderful and precious, and little though it might seem, it is more than many have, and you should treasure it and give thanks for it."

Michael took more than a little comfort from his Grandfather's words.

On his way back to the Regiment Michael could feel a hint of the coming spring. In sheltered corners the occasional brave daffodil was showing itself. The very air smelled different. He began to think of Elaine without always seeing her lying in her drawing room, life slowly leaving her. Instead he was able to recall the good times, their conversations, her advice, her life, not her death.

In Dorchester her life came back to see him. Musgrave was there. He arranged to meet Michael privately, in one of the town's hotels. They sat in a small parlour, a fire burned merrily in the hearth, but the atmosphere was frosty. Michael pointedly concentrated his gaze on a tankard of mulled ale.

"How are you?" Musgrave asked, solicitously. "I have heard that you have been pushing yourself too hard."

"Have you? After what happened, what did you expect?" Michael's response was rather sharp.

Musgrave paused; this was not how he wanted things to be. "I don't know, I really don't know, but I find that I need to know that all is well with you? Or as well as might be expected." Musgrave had found that he cared about Michael.

"Do you? Really?" Michael was sceptical.

"Yes, I do. Please, Michael? May I call you Michael?" Michael shrugged, but heard the sincerity in Musgrave's voice, and gave a little.

"I manage. I don't need to keep from you what she meant to me." There was no need for Michael to say who he meant. "It has been, it is hard, but the pain lessens." He paused and glanced briefly at Musgrave, "I have just returned from a visit to my Grandfather."

"Ah, yes, General Harcourt's old Chaplain."

"Indeed, and I told him everything." Michael looked squarely at Musgrave, challenging him.

"Everything?" Musgrave was clearly taken aback.

"Yes, everything, and he was a help." He paused. "I think that you may depend upon his discretion."

"Of course, of course, I don't doubt it. And I am glad he helped." Musgrave paused, he needed to get through to Michael, to make an accommodation, if not a peace. "Michael, I can't begin to imagine what you feel, but you should know that I miss her as well." For a moment Michael looked as if he might speak, but stayed silent as Musgrave went on. "She was a great agent, one of the best, I trusted her judgement completely. More than that, I could confide in her, discuss things with her, in complete confidence. Over the years that we worked together we became close, good friends. I haven't just lost a great agent; I lost a great friend. She meant a great deal to me, a very great deal. And I am so very, very sorry that I failed to protect her. Michael, can you forgive me that, please?"

Michael sat silently, staring out of the window without seeing. A minute, perhaps two passed in silence until Michael spoke. "Yes. Yes, I believe I can. She told me about her husband, about his death. She described what she did for you as her small form of revenge, against the French. You enabled her to do that, she knew it was dangerous, but she chose to take the risks. To have kept her safe would have meant denying her that. She wouldn't have wanted that. So, yes, if you want my forgiveness, you have it."

"Thank you." Musgrave's relief was palpable.

Michael turned from the window and looked at Musgrave. "You gave her the chance to fight back, and I believe she was grateful to you for that." The two men stared at each other, and both saw the others pain and understood each other. A strained silence fell, broken by Michael. "And now, do you have any news for me?"

"Yes, I do Michael." Musgrave gathered his thoughts. "It has been difficult, but I think we know who the assassin is. His claim to be from Lisbon was not so far from the truth. He is rumoured to be an officer in one of Buonaparte's cavalry regiments. Oddly enough he is also about the same age as you. As a young man he spent some time in Lisbon, about '03, '04, we think, perhaps even into '05. You left in '05, I recall?" Michael nodded, frowning with the effort of recollection. "His father was a minor official with the French Embassy…"

Realisation struck Michael like a thunderbolt. "Raposa Negra!"

"What?"

"Raposa Negra. That's what we called him."

"You know him? Good God!" Musgrave was amazed at the revelation.

"Oh, I know him." Michael's voice took on an icy tone. "Jean-Paul Renard, Raposa Negra, the Black Fox. And he was a fox, as nasty and as verminous a creature as you would ever meet. His hair was black, and his whole demeanour was dark, so we called him the Black Fox. He would kill just for the pleasure it gave him."

"Renard is the name that we have heard. How well did you know him?"

"Well enough to know that I will have no compunction in killing him." Michael gave a humourless laugh. "I might have killed him once." Musgrave looked rather startled. "We got into a fight; I can't even remember what started it. When he pulled a knife, so did I, it was Lisbon, we all carried them. The other boys stepped in and stopped it before anyone got hurt. His father was transferred back to Paris soon afterwards. I wondered at the time if there was a connection." Michael shrugged. "So, now he has killed the woman I loved. Then I shall kill him, or he shall kill me."

Musgrave sat quiet, stunned by both the revelation and Michael's calm statement.

"Do you know where he is?" asked Michael. "What's his Regiment?"

"I know very little," replied Musgrave, "just what I have told you, but now you have, rather unexpectedly, confirmed a name, we should be able to find out more. We do know that he might have been in Lisbon last spring, with Junot."

"Lisbon?" Michael thought for a moment. "And you will let me know what you learn?" asked Michael.

"Of course. And now I have a confession. That was not the only reason that I came to see you, although the trip was worth it for that information alone. There is something that

I would like you to do in Lisbon, if you would be so kind? It might relate to Renard."

"Of course I will, if I can, and if my duties allow."

"Oh, I rather think that they will." Musgrave gave a little smile. "I think that your command of Portuguese will make you much in demand, but you should have no difficulty escaping your duties for a day or two, which should be long enough for what I need from you. I should also warn you that the Quartermaster General may ask if he can borrow you from your regiment for a little while, from time to time."

"What Quartermaster General?"

"The one who will be appointed by the General being sent out to take command in Portugal. Now don't ask for names, you never know, I might prove to be wrong, and that really wouldn't do." Musgrave chuckled. "Now, I recall that you said you know the Palacio Quintela?"

"Yes, I sometimes went there with my father."

"Did you know that Junot used it as his quarters?"

"No, I didn't."

"What I am rather hoping," Musgrave went on, "is that you might be able to find some Portuguese staff who continued to work there throughout the French occupation. The Palacio has been thoroughly searched, of course, and nothing useful found, as you would expect. What I am interested in is people who might have visited, discreetly. We are concerned that the French have established a network of spies in Lisbon. That's where Renard might have been involved." Michael nodded. "What we need is information about any, shall we say, slightly unusual visitors?"

"It has been a long time since I was there," a thought stirred in Michael's mind, "so I make no promises, but I can only go and enquire. And I may have a good excuse to call."

"Thank you, that is all I ask. If you discover anything, go to the Quartermaster General, you can pass the information to him. If you have any difficulties send him my compliments and he will know who you are. Similarly, if he needs you he will send an officer to give you my compliments. And be assured, if I learn anything about Renard, you will be informed."

Shortly after this the two men parted company, with a handshake that was warm and understanding, if not actually friendly. Both felt better about the other, the air was clearer.

In March the regiment was moved again, to Radipole Barracks, just outside Weymouth. While they were there the news came of the resignation of the Duke of York as Commander in Chief, driven out by financial scandal. News of his replacement by Sir David Dundas, a through and through infantryman nicknamed 'Old Pivot', brought groans from all. The stay at Radipole was brief, at long last they received orders to march to Falmouth and embark for Portugal. It was only on the way they learnt that Sir Arthur Wellesley was to have the command in Portugal. Michael wondered who his Quartermaster General would be,

The regiment moved by squadron to ease accommodation problems. Thus Ashworth's troop, in company with that of Captain Swetenham, marched together into Falmouth from Truro. The two troops rode straight on to the quayside and started the process of loading baggage, horses and men onto the transports waiting for them. The horses were loaded by the simple expedient of having a long sling put under them, hoisting them up, and then down into the hold, where each was placed in a narrow stall, with a sling under the belly, to prevent falls and knocks. Remarkably, all the horses were loaded without incident, except that Lieutenant Tomkinson's horse, a bay called Bob, kicked the mate of his transport over the side of the ship. Unfortunately the tide was out, and the man was severely injured. As one Dragoon was heard to say, "He were lucky, if the tide had been in he might ha' drowned."

Each Dragoon carried his own equipment aboard. But Michael, like all the other officers, had a large trunk of personal belongings, spare clothes and equipment that would stay in store at Lisbon, two saddles and bridles, one smaller trunk for his immediate needs that would be carried on a pack animal that he didn't yet have, along with a tent, a folding bed with its bedding, and baskets containing a canteen, kitchen equipment and supplies. All this was carried on board along with the chests of ammunition and spare uniform and equipment belonging to the Troop.

Jocelyn Roberts came down to the quayside to see Michael, who was fully occupied supervising the loading of the troop onto its transport ships. He asked Michael to dine with him that evening. Michael was reluctant, but his uncle persevered, seemed sincere in his invitation, and that evening, with everyone and everything safely on board, he got permission from Captain Ashworth to visit Jocelyn.

As might have been expected, the conversation over dinner was rather stilted, formal and sporadic. Both men felt uncomfortable, but finally they sat down in the parlour after dinner, to take a glass of port, and Jocelyn asked Michael if he knew when they were sailing. "No, uncle, there are still three more squadrons to come and be embarked. I understand that tomorrow morning our ship will leave the quayside and anchor in the Carrick Roads. I shall be able to see Falmouth, but not to get ashore."

Jocelyn nodded, "I see. So this is your last dinner here for a while." He paused to take a sip of port. "Michael, I do not want us to part on bad terms, which I fear we will be because of a simple misunderstanding." He paused, Michael said nothing, but stared into the fire. "The letter from Mr Rutherford came as a great shock, but it made me realise my carelessness in my letters to you. I also realise now how much you want to do this." He gestured at Michael's uniform. "You won't remember your aunt Jane? No, of course not, how could you, you were a babe when she died. It was a lasting regret of hers and mine that we never had children. I look upon you, Michael, and love you, as the son I never had." He paused. "Michael, I just don't want to lose you, I just want to keep you safe, here, with me, in Falmouth." Still, Michael stared into the fire. Jocelyn took a deep breath. "That's all I can say Michael. I am so very, very sorry. I will, of course continue your allowance, and willingly. And when you are twenty one you shall have everything that you should." Silence fell again. "Michael, please, say something, we should not fall out over a simple misunderstanding."

Michael turned his face towards his uncle, who saw a look of loathing. "Say something, you want me to say something? You want me to forgive you for trying to rob me of my inheritance and the chance to do something that I have found I love? You expect me to forget that instead you tried to bind me to you and Falmouth for the rest of my days? You talk to me about doing me a wrong and about forgiveness? As if you had trod upon my foot? And you dare to call it a simple misunderstanding?" Jocelyn sat, stunned.

Michael felt the burning, ice cold anger consuming him, and went on, "And you speak of love, your avuncular love for me, when, if it had not been for someone who truly loved me, and helped me, you would have had your way, I would have been forced to come crawling back here, subservient to your wishes."

"No, sir, that is no simple misunderstanding. By God, had you been honest with me, had you admitted your greed, your selfishness, your error, then I might have forgiven you. But, no, no, you seek to evade, to dissemble, to play upon my emotions. You seek forgiveness, reconciliation, what for? So you might try again? Well, let me tell you, uncle," he spat the word, "you will pay me what is mine, or I shall set Mr Rutherford upon you, and I shall see you brought down, and destroyed. No, I do not forgive you."

Michael drained his glass, rose from his chair, and left the room, leaving a shocked and speechless Jocelyn. In the hall he calmly buckled on his sword, took up his cloak and helmet, and left the house. As he walked back towards the harbour he smiled grimly, the anger ebbed away, but he felt no regret, no remorse, he had no time for those anymore.

Another three days saw all the regiment embarked, but the time was not without its drama. On the first day of lying at anchor in the Carrick Roads, just after first light, Lloyd approached Michael as he stood on deck, drinking a cup of coffee and looking towards Falmouth.

"Begging your pardon, sir," Lloyd saluted as he spoke, and without waiting went on, "I think you and the Captain should come and look at Price's horse, sir. I think it's got Farcy."

"What? Damn it, Lloyd, are you sure?"

"Yes, sir."

"Damn and blast! That's just what we need. I'll get the Captain, can you find Sar'nt Taylor?"

Ten minutes later Michael, Ashworth, Taylor, and Lloyd were gathered around the horse, while a nervous Price stood by. Ashworth examined the horse by the light of a lantern.

"Hell and damnation, I think it is." He straightened up. "Well done Lloyd. Price, how long has he had these lumps?"

"I just seen them now, sir, they weren't there when we came on the ship, sir, and the Veten'ry looked at him, sir."

"So he did, so he did. I'm sorry, Price, but you know what this means, don't you?"

The young dragoon looked forlorn. "Yes, sir."

"Very good," said Ashworth, "then let's be getting on with it. Taylor, you, Lloyd and Price get him out of the stall and over to the main hatchway. Mr Roberts rouse up the men, we are going to need all of them, make sure they're all in stable dress. I shall go and make arrangements with the Captain."

The ship's captain was well aware of what Farcy could mean, and within another fifteen minutes had a hoist rigged and ready to lift the infected horse out of the hold. Once up on deck the horse was examined again by Ashworth in the early morning light. He turned and looked at Lloyd.

"Have another look, Lloyd, tell me what you think."

Lloyd bent to the horses legs, and peered closely at the small nodules. "I'm sure, sir."

"It's not Glanders?"

Lloyd moved to the horses head and peered at its nostrils. "No, there's no sign that I can see, sir."

"Well, that's something, I suppose." Ashworth turned to the ship's captain. "Can you have your men lift the horse a little, if you would be so good?" He turned to Taylor. "When you are ready, Sar'nt."

The sailors heaved on their line, and the horse was lifted just clear of the deck in its canvas sling. Price turned his back. Taylor stepped up to the horse, placed the muzzle of the pistol against its head, and pulled the trigger. There was a loud report, and the horse dropped in the sling.

The body of the horse was dropped over the side of the ship. The dragoons went to work. Every inch of the stalls, mangers, deck, everywhere was meticulously scrubbed and washed down. Horses were moved out of their stalls in turn so they could be thoroughly cleaned out. Price's horse accoutrements were gathered up, what would burn went in the galley stove. The rest was thoroughly scrubbed, and put aside. The two horses on either side of Price's were swung up, out of the hold, and onto the deck where Ashworth and Lloyd examined them carefully.

"I can't see any signs, what about you, Lloyd?"

"No, sir, nothing, they seem to be alright. If I might make a suggestion, sir?"

"Yes, what is it."

"I think it would be a good thing to put these two in stalls a bit apart from the others, sir. And just under the hatch, if you take my meaning, sir?"

"Good idea Lloyd, thank you. Taylor! Did you hear that?"

It took most of the day to move around the three dozen horses and thoroughly clean everything. Michael and Ashworth both worked alongside their dragoons, helping with their own horses. It was a hard and risky business in the narrow confines of the hold, but, eventually, it was all done.

Michael stood once more, looking out towards Falmouth. This time with a large glass of wine in his hand. The day's business had cleared his head of the events of two nights before. Rather like the ship's hold, he felt cleansed of his connection to his uncle. The anger and resentment had completely passed. There was no remorse, no regret. He had put Falmouth behind him. His was now utterly convinced that his future lay elsewhere.

Chapter 12

Unfavourable winds meant that they did not sail out of Falmouth until the wind shifted on the 7th of April. The small fleet of transports was escorted by the frigate HMS Magicienne, and the new winds were kind, giving them a fast and easy passage to Lisbon. The days and nights were spent caring for the horses, ensuring their wellbeing, keeping them calm, feeding, watering, and cleaning the decks of muck and urine. On the evening of the 15th, Michael saw Lisbon in the distance. Captain Ashworth joined him on deck where he was looking away to the city on the north bank of the Tagus.

Ashworth spoke first. "There's a very welcome sight. It must be like coming home for you, Mr Roberts?"

"Indeed it is, sir. I have missed it."

Ashworth smiled and continued, "I look forward to seeing it, and I shall be damn glad to get ashore. I have to say that I am mightily relieved that we had no more farcy. Lloyd did well there, and I'm glad Price had the sense to ask his opinion."

"He does know a lot about horses." Michael paused thoughtfully. "I cannot but help wonder where he gained his knowledge. And his knack with the horses, it's more than just knowledge, I've seen him with mine, he has a way with them, they will do anything for him."

"I have never heard anything about him. He had just joined in '03 when I did. I have no idea who recruited him, you could ask Barra, he might know more, if you're curious?"

"Thank you, sir, I might do that."

Ashworth was silent for a moment, and then spoke, hesitantly. "I, err, I understand that you have some, err, errands to run? Colonel Anson tells me that you will need, and be allowed, a day or two away from us for some, err, official business?"

Michael was surprised, and a little concerned by what Ashworth said. "You know about that?"

"No, no, not a thing," Ashworth replied hurriedly, "don't want to either, frankly."

Michael heard the antipathy in Ashworth's voice, and felt uneasy. "I hope that my absence will not inconvenience you too much, sir?" He felt the need for some formality.

"No, no, Roberts. I am sure that we will manage for a couple of days, Keating is coming along, and a little extra responsibility won't hurt him, but if, by any chance you should come by some baggage horses?"

"Mules, sir, that's what you need here." Michael smiled at Ashworth, glad to change the subject, and relaxing back into their usual off duty informality. "It's been a few years, and the French were here for almost a year and a half. But I will see what I can do. I imagine that half a dozen would suit us quite well. And I'd suggest a muleteer as well, they can be awkward animals, and it is usual to hire the two together. If the two Georges are agreeable?" Michael referred to Lieutenant George Thompson, and Cornet George Keating. Informally, they were known as Old George and Young George. They were on another transport.

"Yes, of course, we will discuss it once everyone is ashore. There will be a question of grooms and other servants as well. Our dragoons will not have the time to give to us what we are used to at home. I have Brown, of course," this was his English servant and valet, "I don't know if you and the Georges want to hire anyone here, that's rather up to the rest of you. I was rather hoping that with your speaking Portuguese, and having lived out here, that you might take on arranging all that sort of thing for us?"

"Of course, sir."

"Excellent. We will get the men and horses ashore tomorrow, and settled in their billets, and then you shall go about your errands."

The following morning the transport ran in close to the beach, and started ferrying dragoons ashore. Once a couple of dozen were ashore, Michael among them, they started to unload the horses, hoisting them out of the hold and lowering them into the sea. The first few were guided ashore by dragoons holding their reins from the backs of boats. But as soon as the first few were ashore those that followed were keen to join their comrades and swam to the shore without urging. Once all the horses were ashore, the transport unloaded the baggage into large boats that ran ashore to unload.

Michael realised that they were coming ashore at Belem, some four miles from Lisbon. The reason became clear when they were informed that the regiment was going to be billeted in the Royal Palace, the horses in the Royal Stables. The regiment had over six hundred and fifty horses, remounts and officers' chargers. The stables took them all, with marble mangers and huge tanks of fresh water. The dragoons had never seen the like. By the end of the second day all was settled, the officers had their billets on nearby Portuguese families, and the men were spread around the Palace, much to their amusement. Michael's fluency with Portuguese had been called upon continuously, and earned him the gratitude of officers and men alike. He was even thanked by Major Stanhope for sorting out a problem at a local tavern.

Late on the second evening Michael was on duty and going around the stables checking that everything was as it should be, and that the dragoons didn't have too much cheap wine. As he had expected, the following day he was free to go about his 'errands'. Discussions amongst the Troop's officers had concluded that six mules would probably be enough for their baggage, with a muleteer, and two grooms should be sufficient to look after the eight horses that they had between them. There had been delight and gratitude expressed at Michael's offer to help. It also covered the real reason for his absence.

Just after dawn, and taking Lloyd with him, he rode Johnny to Lisbon. It felt good to be back in the familiar city after such a long absence. As they rode Michael saw places that brought back memories, he also saw signs of damage wreaked by the French occupiers, and felt anger at the despoiling of the city he considered to be home. They stabled the horses at a hotel near the Palacio Quintela. Both men removed their valises from their horses, and Michael gave Lloyd his to carry. "Right, Lloyd, first of all, we are going to my home."

"Home, sir," Lloyd was puzzled, "I thought that was in Falmouth?"

"Well, yes, and again, no. That is my uncle's home, although I lived there for, oh, four years, but my real home is here." As he spoke he realised the absolute truth, Falmouth was not home, and never would be, not now. "Come on, this way."

A short walk took them to a narrow street that sloped steeply upwards. About half way along Michel stopped outside an imposing looking house. The whole building was bright, with white stone work. Above a solid looking, double leaf door, flanked by barred windows, a row of five windows with balconies was topped by another row of five windows.

Lloyd looked at Michael, "This is your home, sir?"

Michael grinned at him, "It is indeed, Lloyd," and with that he hammered on the door with his fist.

After a few moments, the door opened a crack and a middle aged woman in a head scarf peered out at them. "Sim?"

Michael smiled at her and replied in Portuguese, "Olá, Babá."

The woman stared at him for a moment, and then threw the door wide open, hands flying to her face. "Senhor Michael! Is it you, is it really you?"

Michael stepped forward, "Yes, Senhora Santiago, I have come home," and he lifted her bodily and swung her around in a bear hug, carrying her into the house before putting her down in the hall way and taking her hands in his. "Senhora Santiago, it is so very, very good to see you."

She held Michael at arm's length, looking at him from head to foot. "You are an English soldier?"

"Yes, Senhora, an officer in a cavalry regiment."

"And your face, what happened?" She reached up and gently touched Michael's cheek.

"Just a silly accident, you know how it is." He pointed to Lloyd, keen to change the subject. "And this is my man, Senhor Lloyd." He switched to English, "Lloyd, this is Senhora Santiago, she was my nanny, and she and her husband are my family's longest serving servants, and the only ones now." And back into Portuguese, "Now, Senhora, do you have some of your wonderful lemonade, and I want to know how things are?"

Lloyd was delighted with his glass of cold lemonade, and listened, uncomprehendingly, while Senhora Santiago rattled away, with only the occasional interjection from his lieutenant. The Senhora, apparently at Michael's insistence, had led them to the kitchen, a large, cool room on a lower floor. There they were joined by a middle aged man who turned out to be Senhor Santiago.

The Santiago's were aware of the loss of Michael's parents, and commiserated with him, but could not hide their obvious delight that he had 'come home'. Michael discovered that during the French occupation of Lisbon half a dozen French infantry officers had been billeted in the house. Some were good, some were not. Anything valuable had been pillaged, quite openly, and there had been nothing they could do to prevent it. The house itself had escaped any serious damage, and what little there had been Senhor Santiago had repaired since the French had left. Recently two British officers had been billeted in the house, but they had marched with Sir John Moore's army. At the moment they kept the house closed and kept quiet.

The story complete, and the lemonade finished, Michael went for a walk around the house. Lloyd, somewhat overwhelmed that this was his lieutenant's home, and the Santiagos followed him. Upstairs on the first floor, the main reception room stretched across the whole back, south side of the house, with a single, long balcony with a view right across the Tagus. From it Michael looked down into the garden that had been his mother's pride and joy. It was showing signs of neglect, and looking rather sad. At the front, smaller rooms gave access to the small balconies visible from the street. The ceilings and walls were covered with ornate, decorative plaster work, and all the rooms were comfortably furnished, if looking a little tired and worn.

Michael took a cursory tour of the top two floors, the first being where the family and guest bedrooms were, pausing momentarily at the doors to his and his parent's bedrooms. The very top, hidden from the street by a low balustrade, was the servants quarters, now occupied solely by the Santiagos. It was nowhere near as bad as Michael had feared. He returned to the entrance hall. To one side was a sort of sitting room, open to the hall, on the other, behind a solid door, was his father's office and study where he dealt with business visitors.

He paused for a moment, his hand on the door knob, then with a deep breath, pushed the door open. His father's desk and chair were where they always had been. But all the book cases were empty. The strong box in the corner of the room stood open, and empty, at least the key was in the lock, he thought. There was clearly nothing there for him, just the portrait of his parents that hung over the fireplace. He stared at it for a minute, and then quietly closed the door.

"Senhora, Senhor Lloyd and I will be staying here tonight, probably tomorrow night as well. Will you prepare two rooms, please? My old room, if you will, and a nearby guest room for Senhor Lloyd." He looked at his watch. "I have business to attend to at the Palacio Quintela. We will not trouble you over dinner; bread, cold meat and wine will be enough, but I am not sure when we will be back." He thought for a moment. "Forgive me, I should have asked sooner, how have you managed for money? Can I give you some now?"

"It is alright, Senhor Michael," Senhor Santiago replied, "your father's lawyer, Senhor Furtado, has been very helpful."

"Old Furtado? I shall have to go and see him." Another thought occurred to Michael, "Is there anything left in the cellar?"

Senhor Santiago beamed at him. "Senhor Michael, when we learned that the French were coming your father had me wall up the entrance to the small cellar, and then whitewash all the walls of the large cellar. It is still sealed up, sadly the large cellar is now empty."

Michael laughed, "The cunning old devil! Well, I think you can open it up again. Is there any of the '97 in there?"

"Of course, Senhor."

"Then dig out a couple of bottles for later."

It was a short walk from Michael's home to the Palacio Quintela, and while they walked he explained to Lloyd what the Santiago's had told him and what the arrangements were for their accommodation. Lloyd grinned at the prospect of Sergeant Taylor's face when he could tell him about Michael's home, and staying in a guest room. To Michael Lisbon was completely familiar. Lloyd, however, found a lot to wonder at. One of the first things that struck him was how filthy the streets were, particularly the side streets. On asking Michael about this, he was informed that it was customary to empty all sorts of filth, rubbish and ordure out of the windows, but only after nine o'clock in the evening. Lloyd's eyes were everywhere, at the fine houses, the inhabitants of Lisbon in their strange costumes, and where he was putting his feet.

The Palacio Quintela was a large and imposing building facing on to a square. Followed by Lloyd, Michael strode into the entrance hall. Inside the huge hall Michael was greeted by a porter. In rapid Portuguese he explained that he was here to see Senhor Rodrigues and that he was here with the authority of Baron Quintela. The porter looked more than a little surprised, asked Michael if he would be so good as to wait for a moment, and rushed off towards the back of the building. He returned moments later and asked Michael to follow him. With no other instructions, Lloyd followed along, passing an archway that gave access to a grand, marble staircase. It was lined with white marble, with a stained glass window at the landing, and wall paintings that were just visible to the awe struck Lloyd. Along with the rest of the regiment he had heard about Michael's retort to Major Stanhope concerning Carlton House. Now he began to understand it better.

The porter lead them along corridors and showed them into a large office. The occupant rose from his chair and came forward to greet Michael, shaking his hand energetically. "Senhor Roberts! I did not believe it could be the young man who used to come here with his father, but I see it is, come, come, please, sit down. Perhaps your man would like some refreshment? Tomas," he called to the porter, "take this gentleman and get him something to eat and drink. And have something sent in for us."

"Senhor Rodrigues, it is good see you after all these years. I did not know if you would remember me." Michael switched to English, "Lloyd, go with Tomas. You'll get fed and watered."

"Right you are, sir."

Once they were alone Senhor Rodrigues took his seat opposite Michael. "The Baron has written to me, instructing me to give you whatever help I can. But I need no instruction, Senhor Roberts. I would help you anyway. Your father was a good man, and your mother a good lady, please, accept my condolences."

"Thank you, Senhor, I appreciate what you say." There was a moments reflective silence before Michael continued. "As it is, there are a few matters that I would appreciate your help with."

"If I can," Rodrigues spread his hands wide, "of course I will."

"First, Senhor, do you know of anyone of my father's acquaintance called Augusto?"

"Augusto, Augusto?" Rodrigues looked thoughtful before shaking his head. "No, I am afraid that no one comes to mind. I am sorry."

Michael nodded, hiding his disappointment. He went on, "When it was known that the French were coming, I understand the Baron helped my father to liquidate his assets, into diamonds?"

"Yes, that is quite right. The Baron was eager to see you father and mother safely out of Portugal, and, fortunately, the Baron's interests in the Brazils meant that we had enough diamonds to hand. And he is a merchant, and he wanted your father to be able to trade, with him of course, from England." Rodrigues laughed. "Of course, your father knew and understood. He and the Baron toasted their future enterprises together, here, in this very room. They looked to the day when the French would be gone." He shook his head. "It would have been a great undertaking, I think."

The two men sat quietly for a moment. "Senhor Rodrigues, if I might ask, do you know how much my father was able to carry away in diamonds?"

Rodrigues looked at Michael, puzzled. "I do, but it will do you no good to know. It is at the bottom of the Bay of Biscay."

Michael hesitated, then decided that he had to trust Rodrigues, he had no choice. He told him about the diamonds sent by the packet, and the mysterious Augusto.

Rodrigues took a deep breath. "Well, that is quite a story. What can I say?"

At that moment there was a knock at the door and a young woman entered carrying a tray of drinks, cold meats and bread. "Thank you, Marina, just put it on the desk."

Rodrigues busied himself pouring drinks. "Please, help yourself, Michael. May I call you Michael, it is how I remember you?"

"Of course, Senhor, it seems strange to hear you call me anything else."

"Then, Michael, first, what you have told me will not pass my lips. If it was known there is a small fortune in diamonds somewhere in Lisbon…" He shrugged. "Your father had diamonds to the value of, let me see, yes, about fifty five thousand pounds."

Michael was staggered. "How much?"

"Fifty five thousand pounds. You did not know this?"

"No, Senhor I did not." Michael drew a deep breath. "That is a lot of money."

"It is not a trifling amount, Michael, even half of it. And there is one asset that was not liquidated."

"There's more?"

"Of course, Michael. There is your parents lovely house. I understand your mother would not allow it to be sold, and, anyway, there wasn't time, or anyone likely to buy it."

Michael smiled. "Yes, of course. I'm staying there at the moment."

Rodrigues returned the smile, but then shrugged. "But as for Augusto, the name means nothing to me."

"The Baron wrote to the same effect."

"Ah, yes, he said he had been in communication with your uncle. I shall give it more thought, and make a few discreet enquiries. I am not hopeful, but it is the least I can do."

"Thank you. And if you would be so kind, might I ask you not to communicate with my uncle? I wish to deal with these matters myself. And perhaps you could pass that wish on to the Baron? I know it will take time, but…"

"Of course, Michael. Now, you said there was another matter that you wished to discuss?"

"Yes, and possibly even more delicate." Rodrigues raised his eyebrows, but said nothing. Michael continued, "This Palacio was used by Junot has his headquarters." Rodrigues nodded, acknowledging the fact. "There are concerns that he may have left behind a network of spies."

"I do not understand, what this might have to do with me?"

"Directly, Senhor, nothing at all. But I have been asked, as someone who speaks Portuguese and knows Lisbon, to make some enquiries. What I am seeking to discover, Senhor, is who, if anyone, visited the Palacio while the French were here, who might be, shall we say, unusual, and forgive me, Senhor, not the patriotic Portuguese that they ought to be?"

For a moment Michael thought Rodrigues was going to take offence at the suggestion, but he took a deep breath. "Michael, it pains me that you ask such a question, it pains me even more to agree that there may be such people. I was not here myself. I took my family across the river and to my wife's family, they have a small farm, and there I became a simple Portuguese peasant." He smiled. "Very simple, Senhor. Most people who could not go to the Brazils left the city. I do not think anyone stayed here to work for the French, Senhor. I am sorry, but there, I really cannot help you."

"I thought it unlikely, but I had to ask, Senhor." Michael took a drink of wine before going on. "Do you remember, senhor, some years ago, about a fight I got into, with a French boy, the son of a diplomat?"

Rodrigues frowned at the apparent, sudden change of subject. "Yes, I do. There was awful trouble about it. I believe that even the Baron became involved."

"And do you remember the French boy? Renard?"

"Vaguely, Michael, vaguely, but why do you ask about that? It was a long time ago."

"It was, Senhor, but it is possible that Renard was back here with Junot, and he might have been involved in setting up a network of spies."

"Ah, I understand!"

"It would be of great assistance if anything can be discovered about what he was doing then, perhaps where he stayed? Who he met with? And if anything is heard of him now."

Rodrigues looked sceptical. "I will see what I can do, I can ask the clerks here, Michael, but it is very unlikely that I will learn anything. Still, if I do, I shall let you know. I think I should be able to get a letter to you."

A thought struck Michael. "There is one other thing, Senhor Rodrigues, do you know where I might obtain six mules and a muleteer?"

Rodrigues smiled. "Now, Michael, you ask for help that I can give."

Rodrigues promised to fulfil Michael's request. As he put it, it would be sad day when the chief clerk of Portugal's most successful merchant couldn't supply six mules and a muleteer. They agreed that the mules and muleteer would be at Belem the day after tomorrow. Half an hour later Michael collected Lloyd from where he had been supplied with wine, bread and meat, and strolled out of the Palacio. It was still only late morning, and the bulk of his errands were already completed, official and personal.

The next stop was the office of Senhor Furtado, who was both astonished and delighted to see Michael. The visit, however, did not take long. Furtado explained that Michael's father had left funds with the lawyer so that the needs of the Santiagos and the house could be taken care of. He showed Michael the accounts, there was enough left for another year. Michael asked the lawyer if he would continue as Michael's lawyer, and when he agreed, readily, Michael told him about Mr Rutherford in London. Furtado said he would write to Rutherford so they were in communication. The lawyer also knew of no one by the name of Augusto.

Outside the lawyer's building Michael checked his watch. "Lloyd, I am going to take you back to my house, we can check on the horses on the way, and then I will leave you in the care of the Santiagos. You can try and pick up some Portuguese from them. I have a call that I need to make."

"Are you sure you don't want me to come with you, sir?"

"Quite sure, Lloyd."

Chapter 13

Twenty minutes later Michael had left Lloyd with the Santiagos and was walking towards a house that had been familiar to him, growing up as a sixteen year old young man in an exciting city, with everything that entailed. He took a quick look around and turned sharply down a narrow side street, deep in shadow. A short walk brought him to a heavy door studded with bolt heads, with a small grill at head height, and set into a towering wall, apparently that of a house, but no windows were visible. He knocked hard, and removed his Tarleton.

A small hatch opened behind the grill, and Michael smiled as he recognised the face. Recognition dawned on the face behind the door, and he quickly put his finger to his lips. "Is the Senhorita at home," he asked quietly. The head nodded, the hatch closed, and the door swung open to reveal a woman in her late twenties. "Hello, Constanca." He gave her a hug and kissed her on the cheek. "Where is your mistress I want to surprise her."

"She is in her bedroom, of course, it is early," the woman replied with a mischievous grin, closing the door behind him. Inside, the hallway was dark and cool.

"Alone?"

Constanca punched him on the arm, "Of course she is Michael, there has been no one since you left, she has been inconsolable."

Michael laughed, "You haven't changed."

He kissed her again, gave her his Tarleton, removed his sabre and belt, and then made his way silently up the narrow stairs to the first floor. Down the corridor ahead of him a door was slightly ajar, and he could hear a voice singing softly. He moved quietly along the corridor, pushed the door open and stood at the threshold. To one side of the room, was a large four poster bed with rich, red velvet hangings. Across the room, in front of the window, a woman in her mid-thirties, dressed in a yellow silk banyan, sat at a mirror, brushing her long, black hair. For a moment she did not see Michael, and he was able to look at her face reflected in the mirror. She had been a great beauty in her youth, and was still an extremely attractive woman. Then she saw him, and her eyes went wide with surprise and the brush froze in mid stroke.

"Hello, Roberta."

For a moment she stared at him in the mirror, and then realisation dawned. "Michael? Is that you Michael?" She spun around on her stool and looked at him. "It is! I don't believe it! How? Why? What are you doing here?" Her surprise changed to something approaching concern. "Oh, Michael, you've grown up."

He smiled. "I have, Roberta, I have." The smile faded, became rueful, "And it hasn't all been good."

"Your face?"

Michael touched the scar on his cheek, still red, but no longer painful. "That's part of it."

Roberta stood. She smiled gently at him. "Come here, Michael, and give me a kiss." She opened her arms to him as he came across the room to her. He put his arms around her waist, she pulled his head down to her, and they kissed. "It is so very good to see you again. So, very good. Let me look at you." She pushed him to arms-length, and looked him up and down. "Oh, Michael, you look so handsome in your uniform. And so very grown up. But what are you doing here, tell me?"

"My regiment landed three days ago, we are out at Belem, and I have two days to spend in Lisbon."

"Two days? Is that all? Oh. Michael, I don't see or hear from you for what? Four years? And then you reappear from nowhere and tell me it's only for two days! I didn't even know you had joined the army! I didn't even know if you were alive!"

"I am sorry, Roberta, there was no way to write to you, and I didn't know if you would want to hear from me."

"Want to hear from you? Want to hear from you?" She smiled at Michael, "Sometimes you are a silly boy! Now, give me another kiss." He stepped towards her, but she stopped him with a hand on his chest. "Michael, you have left the door open."

Michael turned from her and shut the door. When he turned back the banyan was in a heap at her feet. "Now kiss me properly, and later you can tell me everything."

And later, as they lay in each other's arms, Roberta teased him. "You have learnt a few things, Michael, and not from me! Who is she?" She asked, laughing as she did.

"Was, Roberta, was. She died."

The laughter died on her lips. "Oh, Michael, I am so sorry." She looked at him for a moment, she had heard the note in Michael's voice. "You loved her, didn't you?"

"I did, oh, God, I did."

Roberta stroked his cheek and asked, "What happened?"

"Not what, who. Raposa Negra!"

"What? That swine? How? Tell me, Michael, tell me everything."

Michael told her his story, omitting Musgrave and the Aliens Office. He told her about the ball, about his first, overwhelming sight of Elaine, then saving the Duke of York, about Elaine taking care of him. He told her about falling in love with her. Then he told her about her death at the hands of Renard, simply saying a French refugee had recognised him. As he told her the tears ran down his face. When he finished, Roberta pulled him close, cradling him in her arms. "Oh, you poor, poor boy." She stroked his head, running her fingers through his hair. She kissed the tears away from his eyes.

They lay quietly for a while, the mid-afternoon sun streaming in through the open window, the curtains moving in the gentle breeze.

"Michael?"

"Yes?"

"What are you going to do?"

"Find him and kill him." Michael's reply was cold and matter of fact. Roberta lay silent for a moment.

"Do you have any idea where he is?" she asked.

"None at all, but he can't hide for ever, there are people, powerful people, looking for him now." He paused. "Apparently he was back here in Lisbon with Junot."

"Was he? I heard nothing, but I will see what I can discover, I have many friends and contacts, and not just in Lisbon."

"I know," said Michael, "and I have never understood why you choose to live here, so quietly, when you could have…"

She silenced him with a finger on his lips. "Because I choose to, Michael, and there are things we do not talk about."

"You are a mysterious and fascinating woman, Roberta, I have always found that attractive about you."

She laughed. "Oh, yes, I remember you mooning around like a love sick puppy, until I took pity on you."

"Yes, I suppose I did rather. I remember it well." A small smile appeared on Michael's lips.

"I should hope you do! And now you are a serious soldier, with a crusade to fight."

"You're teasing me."

"Perhaps."

"Well, if you do ask questions, be careful, Roberta. He is a ruthless killer. And he could be anywhere."

"I will be Michael, I will be. And if I hear anything I shall let you know at once, but only if you promise me that you will be careful. Will you?"

"I will, of course I will."

"Good." She smiled wickedly. "Now, it has been too long Michael Roberts, far too long." She smiled, and bent her head to kiss him.

Michael and Roberta lunched together in the small courtyard of her house, the high whitewashed walls shading it from the sun. They talked as good friends do, friends and lovers, comfortable with their relationship, neither wanting nor expecting more, it was a perfect friendship, too good to spoil with anything else. They talked of old friends, where they were now, what they were doing, who had married who. When Michael told her about his parents she squeezed his hand in sympathy. He spoke about his life in Falmouth and falling out with his uncle, about the regiment, Stanhope, and Lloyd. He told her he had been to his house, and how it was there. Roberta had never been there, Edward Roberts would not have approved of her and her friendship with Michael, but she knew of the Santiagos. Which gave Michael an idea.

"Roberta, you know everyone in Lisbon?"

She laughed at him, "Perhaps."

"I need two reliable grooms to march with us, and take care of our horses. And I have been thinking that I could do with a servant for myself, perhaps someone who can cook a little, and keep my clothes and things clean. Do you know anyone who might be suitable?"

Roberta thought for a moment. "It is a lot to ask, to leave Lisbon and risk the hardships of war, Michael. You will need to pay a little more than the usual pay in the city."

"I don't think that will be a problem."

She thought for a moment, "Do you remember Juan Moreno?"

"Yes, I think so."

"He now runs a livery stable over near Nossa Senhora da Oliveira, you must remember where that is? Well, I did hear that he and his son had fallen out, something about an unsuitable girl. His son knows horses, he might take a chance with you."

"Can you arrange for me to see him? And ask if he has a friend who knows horses as well?"

"I can do better than that. Constanca's brother can run a message for me, and you can ask him yourself." Roberta called out, "Constanca?"

Constanca appeared almost immediately, "Yes, Senhorita?"

"Is your brother here? Ask him if he will run a message for me?"

Constanca vanished, and they could her calling out, "Francisco! The Senhorita wants you to take a message for her, hurry up!" She reappeared a few minutes later with a young lad of about fourteen. Michael could see the family resemblance. Roberta explained to him what she wanted, and he rushed off.

Half an hour later, Francisco was back at Roberta's house with two Portuguese boys who looked to be aged about sixteen. Constanca brought them into the courtyard and introduced them. "This is Pedro Moreno, and this is his friend, Rafael Martins."

The two boys looked surprised when Michael addressed them in fluent Portuguese. "I understand that you know horses, that you know how to look after and care for them?"

"Yes, Senhor," came the response from both boys. Pedro added, "I have worked with my father at his livery stable for many years, Senhor, and my friend Rafael with me. We are very good with horses, but now we want to do something more."

"How would you feel about coming with me to look after my horses and those of other officers, eight altogether? It will not be easy, we march in all weathers, at all hours, it will be cold and wet at times, hot and dry at others. You will sometimes be hungry, you will sometimes sleep outside, by the horses. There will always be danger from the French. You will be well paid if you do a good job, if you don't, you will be sent packing, wherever that might be. What do you say?"

The boys looked at each other, and then both nodded, "Yes, Senhor, we would like to do that, if the pay is right, of course," added Pedro.

After some haggling a rate of pay was arrived at that the boys thought was good, and Michael thought reasonable if they were good. "Very good. We will go to Belem to join the Regiment the day after tomorrow. Meanwhile, meet me at eight o'clock tomorrow morning at the stables of the hotel on Praca sao Paulo. There are two horses there, you can start by looking after them."

After the boys had gone Roberta said, "Are you really leaving me so soon, Michael?"

"Yes, I'm sorry, but I must, I have to obey orders now," he smiled at her, "but I am sure I will be back in Lisbon from time to time. I will come to see you when I can. You know you are a very dear, and special friend."

"And I am very fond of you, Michael, more than fond, but one day you will find a fine English lady to marry, and you will forget all about me."

Michael reached across to where she sat and took her hand. "Perhaps I will, one day. For a while I thought I might have," she squeezed his hand, "but for now I am here, in Portugal, and even when I do go back to England I will not forget you, Roberta, never!"

She smiled at him. "Who knows? And perhaps I will find myself a rich aristocrat and settle down. Then again, perhaps not."

"You really are a mysterious woman, Roberta. You are well connected, you have money, you have independence, and no one knows anything about you. I know, I tried to find out about you all those years ago."

She laughed. "And that is how I like it. And it is time, I think for a little siesta. Will you keep me company?"

Dark was falling as Michael returned to his house. He thumped on the door, which soon opened to reveal Senhor Santiago, carrying a lantern. "Good evening, Santiago, do you think that your Senhora could bring me something to eat? Just meat, cheese, bread, and bring me a bottle of the '97. In the dining room, I think, better bring me some light as well. How is Senhor Lloyd getting along?"

"Very good, Senhor, He is very well, and has learnt a few words. Do you wish me to bring him to you?"

"Not just now, I'll see him after I have eaten."

Michael found his way up the darkened staircase to the dining room on the first floor. There was just enough light to make out the furniture, and Michael sat down where he always had, to the left hand of where his father always sat, and across from his mother's chair. He wondered if, one day, he would feel able to sit at the head of the table, and who might sit at the table with him? Would he find Roberta's fine English lady? Could he really be so fortunate, twice?

Light flickered from the corridor and the Santiagos brought in a candelabra and plates of food, along with a dark bottle and a glass. After eating, and drinking half the bottle of '97, which really was a rather good year for port, Michael rang the bell, and Santiago and Lloyd both answered the summons. "Thank Senhora Santiago for me, that was just what I wanted." Santiago removed the plates and left.

"Lloyd, I hear that you are learning a little Portuguese?"

Lloyd replied, in Portuguese, but with a distinctive Welsh lilt, "Yes, Senhor, wine, bread, cheese, meat." He beamed at Michael.

Michael laughed, "It's a start, Lloyd, well done. Now, I have been busy as well. I have managed to find two grooms to look after the horses of myself and the other troop officers. They are young lads, both about sixteen, I think, but they come recommended by a good friend. We are meeting them at the stables at eight tomorrow, I have told them they can start by looking after Johnny and your Edward. We should leave here at a quarter to the hour. Can you tell Senhora Santiago…? No, I'll come down to the kitchen myself."

Once the arrangements for the next morning were settled, Michael returned to the dining room and sat in the flickering candlelight. It was quiet, silent even in the house. He suddenly felt very alone. There had always been someone to talk to, nanny Santiago, his parents, his uncle, his fellow officers, even the General, and then Elaine. He poured another glass and took a gulp. It really was very smooth. Elaine. It was still difficult to grasp. Not just that she was dead, but that he had known her at all. It had been so brief, almost over before it began. They had met in the spring, she had died in the autumn, they had spent so little time together over barely six months. It was not enough; it would have to be enough. He recalled again what Roberta had said, about him marrying a fine English lady. Bless Roberta, she had been a good friend and lover to Michael when he had lived in Lisbon. Her welcome today was more than he had hoped for. And it had brought him some solace, even if it also brought a feeling of guilt. Guilt at betraying the memory of Elaine. Although she had released him from any bonds, that was easier said than done, he thought. And guilt at the idea that he had taken advantage of an old friendship with Roberta, which was laughable, really. No one took advantage of Roberta. He poured another glass, emptying the bottle. He could have married Elaine; she was a fine English lady by any measure. She had been his, he hers, and he loved her, still. He realised that he was a little drunk and his thoughts began to slur and slide into the melancholic.

Michael rose from the table, picked up the candlestick and took himself slowly off to bed. Memories came back of creeping up the staircase late at night, hoping not to disturb his parents and thus avoid awkward questions. His father never knew he had a key to the little side entrance, coming in through the kitchen. Or did he? Looking back Michael wondered if he had fooled himself. In his room he found a jug of water and a glass. He smiled at the thoughtfulness of Senhora Santiago, and poured a glassful. She had been looking after him since before he could remember. His room was at the back of the house, with a view across the Tagus, but all he could see in the window was his own reflection, everything beyond was lost in darkness. A bit like him, he thought.

In the morning Lloyd woke him with a jug of hot water for shaving. As he shaved Michael felt a lot better than he had a right to. When he pulled his clean shirt out of his valise he saw the small pouch that contained the key from his father. It reminded him that he hadn't asked Roberta about Augusto. Well, any excuse for a visit, he smiled.

After breakfast Michael and Lloyd walked over to the stables where they had left their horses. Pedro and Rafael were waiting for them. "Boys," he addressed them in Portuguese, "this is my Dragoon servant, Lloyd. He's a good man with horses, very good. Do what he tells you. He will start with teaching you how all our tack goes on, after you have given both horses a good grooming." He switched to English. "Lloyd, that's Pedro on the left, Rafael on the right." Lloyd nodded, "see how their grooming is and then show them how all the tack goes on." Michael pointed across the street, "I'm going over there for a coffee. I'll send some over for you as well."

An hour later Lloyd strolled across to where Michael was sitting. "I think they'll do, sir. They're good lads with horses and they are picking up on the tack pretty quickly."

"Excellent. Do you think that you can find your way back to the house?"

"Yes, sir, I reckon so."

"Right, show the boys where it is, then have the rest of the day to yourself. Don't get drunk, will you, Lloyd? In fact, I think it might be an idea for the boys to show you around Lisbon. How does that sound?"

"Just fine, thank you, sir."

"Right, I'll explain to them. I want to leave early tomorrow. They can get the horses ready for us, we can see how they've done, then they can follow us out to Belem. We will breakfast early, at five thirty, I'll get Senhora Santiago to have hot water for five, and tell the boys to be here at first light, say half past six."

"Very good, sir." Lloyd looked quite happy with the arrangements.

Michael and Lloyd walked across to the stables where the two boys were talking over the tack. Michael found the stable keeper, and paid him in advance so they wouldn't be delayed in the morning. Then, having explained things to the boys he left them to look after Lloyd, and he decided to take a stroll around himself, he didn't want to call on Roberta before eleven.

He called in on Senhor Rodrigues at the Palacio Quintela, and the same porter led him to the office at the back of the Palacio. Rodrigues was pleased to see him.

"Senhor Michael, I am glad that you have called in. I have found you an excellent muleteer, Salvador Gomes. He has six splendid mules. We have used him frequently for smaller consignments, but with the war we do not have so much work for him, and he is glad to go with you. His rate is fair, very fair, he needs the work."

"That is very good news, Senhor, I am grateful. Do you think that it can be arranged for Gomes and his mules to meet us at the stables, the ones just around the corner, across the square, for six thirty? That will be better than meeting him out at Belem."

"Of course, Senhor, that is not a problem."

"I was just wondering, have you had any thoughts about who the mysterious Augusto might be?"

Rodrigues shook his head. "No, Senhor, and I have asked among the other clerks and staff. No one has any idea at all. And no one has even heard of Renard, but I hardly remembered the name myself."

Coming out of the Palacio Michael decided to walk down to Black Horse Square on the river side, and see if anything of interest was happening. There he treated himself to another coffee, and walked back up into the city, arriving at Roberta's house not long before twelve.

Constanca let him in and asked him to take a seat in the courtyard while she let her mistress know that he was there. Michael relaxed in the shade and stretched out his legs. The day was warm, summer was coming. Constanca reappeared with a jug of lemonade and two glasses.

"The Senhora will be down in a few minutes. She was half expecting you, Senhor," she added, with a smile, pouring a drink for Michael.

"Thank you, Constanca." He took a sip of the lemonade. "I am afraid that I must rejoin my regiment tomorrow, and who knows when I might be back in Lisbon. Probably not before the winter."

"That is a shame, Senhor. The Senhorita has been so pleased to see you again." She seemed about to say something more, but hesitated.

"What is it?" Michael asked her.

Constanca paused before answering. "It is my little brother, Francisco, Senhor. He has got it into his head to look for a job with the British army. I think he will just run away, and then I will not know what he is doing, or where he has gone."

"How old is Francisco?"

"Nearly fifteen, Senhor."

"What can he do?"

"He helps me around the Senhorita's house, he helps me clean and take care of the washing, and he helps me in the kitchen, Senhor."

"Do you think you can stop him running off, keep him here?"

"No, Senhor, I don't."

"What is this Michael? Are you seducing my maid now?" Roberta laughed as she walked into the courtyard and poured herself a glass of lemonade.

"Oh, Roberta, how could you think such a thing? Constanca is far too good for a poor cavalry officer!"

Roberta threw a cushion at him. "Michael Roberts, you are an awful man."

Constanca explained, "Senhorita, I was telling him about Francisco wanting to go with the army."

"Ah, yes, this is a serious matter. Michael, do you have any ideas?" Roberta sat down next to Michael and took his hand, all sense of frivolity gone.

"Well, I am not sure. As I told you, I have been thinking about hiring a servant. Perhaps, if he is determined to go, it would be better if he went with someone you know?"

"What do you think of that, Constanca? And he knows Pedro and Rafael."

Constanca's face lit up, "I think that would be wonderful, I would be so much less worried if that was possible?"

"Is he here?" asked Michael, "Let me speak to him, if that's alright, Roberta?"

"Of course. Fetch him here."

While Constanca went to find Francisco, Michael turned to Roberta. "Is that alright with you, I don't want to do anything that you think might be wrong?"

"Michael, if the boy is determined to go, I can't think of anyone I would rather see him go with." She leant across and kissed him. "It is very good of you."

"Does he have any family apart from Constanca?"

"No, there is just the two of them, their mother died when Francisco was born, their father about two years ago, of a fever."

Constanca returned in a few minutes with Francisco, who stood nervously in front of Michael, looking at the ground. "Your sister tells me that you want to have a job and follow the army?"

"Yes, Senhor."

"Do you realise that it could be very dangerous? It would be very hard work, you would go hungry, you would be cold and wet, you would be hot and thirsty. There would be no soft beds."

"Yes, Senhor." He looked up. "But, Senhor, there is nothing for me here, I am only here because Constanca works for the Senhorita, and she is a very kind lady. I must make my own way, Senhor, and I have no trade, only what I learn helping my sister. There is nothing else for me, Senhor."

Michael looked at Constanca standing behind her brother, and he saw a hint of pride in her face at his words.

"Well," he turned to Roberta, "when he puts it like that," he paused, and turned back to look at Francisco, "I suppose I had better take him as my servant!"

Over the next half an hour a rate of pay was agreed, and arrangements made for Francisco to be at the stables for half past six the next morning. It was going to be, thought Michael, quite a caravan that would return to Belem with him.

Michael and Roberta were left alone by Constanca and Francisco, who went off to gather what he needed ready for the morning. They sat in the courtyard, talking about this and that, people Michael used to know in Lisbon, people Roberta still knew, nothing of any consequence. Constanca brought a light lunch out to them, with a carafe of cold, white wine.

Over lunch Michael said, "There's something that I meant to ask you yesterday, but what with everything else, I forgot."

Roberta smiled at him. "Oh, so easily distracted…"

Michael returned the smile. "Yes, well, you are very distracting. But it is talking about people we know, or knew that reminded me." He sipped his wine. "When my parents left Lisbon they had sold everything that they could, and turned it into diamonds, from Baron Quintela. Some, they sent to me with someone they knew and trusted. I can't be sure of the exact amounts, but I think that when they were lost they were carrying about twenty five thousand pounds worth of diamonds. That's about a hundred thousand dollars."

"Oh, Michael, that's so much money."

"Yes, but the thing is, Roberta, they seem to have left a similar amount here in Lisbon."

"But where? Have you recovered it?"

"No, I haven't. All I know is that they left it in the care of someone called Augusto."

"Augusto? Who is that?"

"That's just it, Roberta, I have no idea. I can't remember anyone of that name. My uncle wrote to Baron Quintela in the Brazils, and he had no idea. I have asked the Baron's chief clerk, and he had no idea either. I just wondered if you knew of anyone?"

Roberta was silent for a moment. "No, I'm sorry, no one at all."

"Never mind, I expect I will find him eventually. If my father knew him, and trusted him, I should be able to find him."

The conversation turned back to matters of no consequence. Eventually, the wine was finished and they were sitting in companionable silence. Constanca stretched in her chair. "I think it is time for siesta." She held out her hand to Michael. "Will you spend one last afternoon with me before you go?"

Michael took her hand and smiled at her. "Of course."

Michael had been right. Their return to the Regiment's quarters at Belem cause a bit of a stir. First came Michael, then Salvador leading the six mules with Francisco, Pedro and Rafael perched on their pack saddles. Lloyd brought up the rear.

Ashworth was in the courtyard as they rode in. "My word, Mister Roberts, you seem to have been successful in your errands?"

"Yes, sir," Michael grinned. "I think we have all we need for the troop to take the field. Of course, I can't speak for the other troops, sir."

Ashworth laughed. "I expect they will manage. Now, what and who do we have?"

Within half an hour, with the help of Sergeant Taylor, the mules with Salvador, Pedro and Rafael had been found quarters, and Lloyd was introducing the two boys to the horses they would be caring for. Ashworth's servant, Brown, delighted at the prospect of some help, had disappeared off with Francisco in the direction of the officer's quarters. Ashworth himself had to go and see Colonel Anson. Michael was soon involved in the day to day affairs of the troop.

Chapter 14

The next two days saw the continuation of the preparations for the regiment to march to join the army. The horses were exercised more each day as they regained their fitness, and recovered from almost two weeks confined to stalls on board ship. The officers of Ashworth's troop, like all the others, sorted out their belongings into what could be left in store in Belem, and what they could take with them. Each of the mules could carry a load of three hundred pounds, and each officer tried to limit himself to one small trunk. In addition there were folding beds, tents, canteens, cooking equipment, and private supplies. The grooms and servants would ride on the spare horses with their own baggage. Michael packed his valise, carried behind his saddle, with a change of linen, spare overalls, his forage cap, his dressing case with shaving kit and brushes, a silver half pint mug, a pair of shoes, and some writing equipment. His personal notebook and pencil he carried in his sabretache, along with a knife, fork and spoon. The portrait of Elaine and her letter he carefully wrapped in oilskin, and stowed away at the bottom of the trunk he was leaving in store. Both were far too precious to risk on campaign. The regimental baggage also had to be organised. Wagons for the farrier, mules for ammunition chests, arms chests, and all the other unavoidable impedimenta of a cavalry regiment on campaign.

The regiment received orders to march to Torres Novas, north east up the valley of the Tagus. They marched one squadron each day, and Ashworth's was the second of the four to march out from Belem. At Santarem, the regiment was halted, and the advanced squadron called back from Torres Novas. The Regiment had been used to simple route marches, and during the march and the following week halted at Santarem they got used to the different daily routine of living on campaign with grooms, mules and servants.

Lloyd had more troop duties, and less time for Michael's horses, but he professed himself happy with Pedro and Rafael, and both Johnny and Duke were in good condition, as Michael rode them on alternate days. The officers of the two troops forming the squadron formed themselves into a single mess, and soon discovered that a servant with Captain Swetenham's troop was an excellent cook, and that young Francisco made him a fine assistant. The men of the troops formed themselves into six man messes, some lucky enough to have the services of one of the five wives allowed to follow each troop.

The weather was beginning to warm up, so Colonel Anson had the whole Regiment out drilling early in the day on the plains south of the town. The afternoons were spent quietly, and Michael took the opportunity to explore Santarem. It was an ancient hilltop town, and still retained much of its ancient defensive walls. The narrow streets were barely wide enough to ride in threes, and it had, to Michael's mind, more than its share of churches. In that respect it reminded him a little of Falmouth, but there all similarities ended.

Colonel Anson insisted that proper sentries and pickets were posted, despite the nearest French being several days march away. It was, he said, 'a good habit to get into.' Michael's turn for duty came around, and he was going the rounds in the early hours of the morning. Walking along the old walls towards a sentry post he saw a faint glow as someone drew on a cigar. "Who's there?" he challenged.

"Roberts? It's Anson." The speaker emerged from the shadows. "Just taking a stroll." He drew again on his cigar. "Actually I was hoping to have a chance for a quiet talk, away from the regiment."

"Sir?" Michael wondered what the Colonel could want.

"Did your business in Lisbon go well?"

"Yes, sir, and the mules and grooms have proved to be very good."

"Ah. I was thinking more of your other business?"

"I beg your pardon, sir?"

"Yes." He drew on his cigar again. "You have some interesting friends, Roberts."

"Sir?"

"I had a visitor when we were in Dorchester, I believe he saw you as well. By the name of Musgrave."

Michael maintained a diplomatic silence; he thought it was best to let the Colonel speak until he saw where the conversation was going.

Anson continued, "He told me something of what happened in London, not everything, I don't suppose, not for a moment, chaps like that never do tell you everything, and you'd do well to remember that. It explained a few things. Such as why we have one more lieutenant than is strictly necessary. I was also given to understand that you have certain talents that might be required away from the regiment." Anson paused again to draw on his cigar.

Michael felt he was safe with "Yes, sir."

"Well, I just wanted you to know that I am aware of the situation. If you need to, you can come and speak to me. I can't say it's quite my idea of soldiering, but if your other activities help us to beat Buonaparte, so much the better. In the meantime, you are making a fair fist of things as a regimental officer." He paused. "I hope that there is no conflict. It can be a tricky thing, serving two masters." He took a last draw on his cigar before dropping it on the ground and grinding it out with his boot. "Anyway, you'd better be getting along on your rounds. Don't want the guard turning out to look for you, eh?"

"Thank you, sir, goodnight."

"Goodnight, Roberts."

The rest of the round and the night passed uneventfully. Back in his quarters after another morning of drill, Michael stretched out on his camp bed to try to make up for the lost night's sleep. On reflection, he was relieved by the conversation with Anson. He realised that he might be able to help the fight against Buonaparte in unorthodox ways, but he already felt close bonds to the regiment, his fellow officers, and to the men of his troop. He felt a responsibility, and didn't want to let anyone down. He remembered the slight tone of antipathy when Ashworth had spoken of Michael's errands. He was well aware of Major Stanhope's views. He closed his eyes with a slight sense of unease with his situation.

Whilst at Santarem the regiment learnt that Sir Arthur Wellesley had arrived, on the very day they had left Belem. Along with him had come a Colonel Murray, as Quartermaster General. The news brought to Michael's mind the comment that Musgrave had made when they had met in Dorchester. Michael wondered if he might hear anything, not that he had anything to report. There was also another reorganisation. Captain Cocks was still absent, now on General Cotton's staff, so Captain Swetenham got a squadron of his and Cocks' troops. Ashworth got Captain Lygon and his troop for his squadron. The messing arrangements were easily changed, all the officers were perfectly familiar with each other. One of Lygon's Lieutenants was William Alexander, Michael already knew and liked him. Lygon's other Lieutenant was Henry van Hagen.

At the end of April came word that they were on the move again. This time they were marching northwards, in the direction of Oporto where Marshal Soult was, with his French army. The city had fallen in March, and during its capture thousands had tried to escape the city across the famous bridge of boats. Disaster had followed when the bridge was blocked, or collapsed, reports were unclear, but hundreds had died.

The regiment was ordered to march to Coimbra, about a hundred miles away, an easy five days march. The weather was beginning to warm up, it was already like England in August. They were up before dawn and ready to march at first light, getting as far as possible before the hottest part of the day. Everyone was becoming acclimatised and acquiring tanned faces. The march to Santarem and the stay there had done a lot to pull the regiment together, and the march was embarked on with the minimum of fuss and effort. There was a feeling that at last they were going to do what they had come to Portugal to do, fight the French.

On the last but one day of the march, Michael was sent on ahead to Coimbra with just Lloyd for company, to arrange quarters for the regiment. It meant a ride of some fifty miles, and he decided that he would ride Johnny. They left before dawn, leaving the Regiment while it was still assembling. While it was cool they pushed the horses along, trotting where the going was good, alternating with walking so the horses didn't get too hot. The road took them along the valley of a narrow river, lined with small fields, and they were able to water the horses whenever necessary. Past Pombal the countryside was more wooded, alternating with farms, and the going was still good as they crossed a series of low river valleys. They stopped at rivers to refresh horses and themselves, refill canteens, and then pushed on again.

It was early evening as they rode across the long bridge and up into Coimbra, and it was clear to Michael that the bulk of the army was there. The fields outside the city were covered with tents, and the streets were full of redcoated infantry, gunners and cavalrymen in blue, all was hustle and bustle. Michael saw a young infantry subaltern, and managed to get directions from him for the Quartermaster General's quarters, where he would learn what the arrangements were for the Sixteenth when it arrived.

As Michael neared where he thought he would find the Quartermaster General's he saw an officer in a red coat, a staff officer of some sort, walking down the street towards him. They both stopped as they met, exchanged salutes, and Michael introduced himself.

"Lieutenant Roberts, Sixteenth Light Dragoons, I am looking for the QMG's to get our billets for when the regiment arrives tomorrow. Can you direct me?"

The officer looked a little surprised, "Roberts? By God that's useful!"

"Sir?"

"I'm Captain Scovell, Quartermaster General's. I was rather hoping to see you, but didn't think you'd be here until tomorrow." He paused and looked around before saying, quietly, "Colonel Murray has asked me to pass on Mr Musgrave's compliments."

"I see, sir."

"Yes, well, that's it really. Now we know who each other is." He smiled. "I suppose you had better follow me. Colonel Murray will want to see you." And so saying, he turned and walked back the way he had come, Michael and Lloyd following.

The Quartermaster General's office was situated, along with the rest of headquarters, in a substantial building in the middle of the town. An archway off the street led to a large, cobbled courtyard where Michael and Lloyd wearily dismounted. Leaving Johnny with Lloyd, Michael followed Scovell, who had disappeared down a passageway, and found himself at the doorway to a dimly lit room.

"Come on in, Roberts, come in." Scovell called to him. Michael stepped into the room, Scovell was standing by a table covered with maps and documents and speaking to another man, who Michael realised must be Colonel Murray, the Quartermaster General himself. In the dim light Michael could see that Scovell was in his mid-thirties, a little old to still be a captain, thought Michael. Was that bad luck or incompetence? Probably not the later if he was working for Murray. Scovell's round, open face, framed by large brown sideburns gave the appearance of a friendly disposition.

The Colonel turned from the table to look at Michael. "So, you're the fellow Musgrave speaks so highly of?" He spoke with a soft, Highland brogue.

"Yes, sir."

"Tell me, did you manage to get to the Palacio in Lisbon?"

"Yes, sir, and I spoke to Baron Quintela's chief clerk, but it seems that all the Portuguese made themselves scarce when Junot occupied the Palacio."

"Hmm, can't say I'm surprised." Murray launched into a minor interrogation. "I understand you were born in Lisbon, and speak the language like a native?"

"That's correct, sir."

"Know the country well do you?"

"Around Lisbon, sir, yes."

"Been up to Oporto?"

"Yes, sir, a few times."

"D'ye know the Douro at all?"

"No, sir."

"Hmm. Anyway, good to know you, Mr Roberts. Scovell, take him to see de Lancey, I think he will have the billets for the Sixteenth."

It took a couple of hours for Michael to get the billets sorted out, chalking troop letters and officer's names on doors, and then to find food for himself and Lloyd, but eventually he was confident that he had everything prepared for the arrival of the regiment sometime the following afternoon. With most of the army in Coimbra, billets were at a premium, and it was going to be a tight squeeze. He had managed to secure a reasonable house for the squadron's officers. Its owners, an elderly lawyer and his wife, were none too pleased, but seemed slightly relieved to discover Michael spoke Portuguese and he promised that they would be paid for everything that might be required. A very nice house was identified for the regiment's headquarters, and Colonel Anson should have no cause for complaint.

He was fully determined to enjoy the luxury of a room to himself for the night, he had been forced to share with Keating in Santarem, and the young man snored. With the regiment not due to arrive until the afternoon, he was looking forward to the chance to have a slow morning and a good shave with plenty of hot water. He had already made arrangements with his hosts' maid for that. In the meantime, having settled in, he thought he would take a stroll around the town and see if he could find a drink.

First he wandered down and out to the building where Johnny and Edward were stabled. Lloyd was there, his work done, he was sitting just outside, on an upturned bucket, smoking a pipe. When he saw Michael he got to his feet and saluted.

Michael returned the salute. "At ease, Lloyd. All well here?"

"Yes, sir, but I will sleep here, with the horses tonight, sir, until we can get proper stable guards. Too many light fingers around."

"Very good, Lloyd, I'll see to it that you have no duty tomorrow night, but we should have a quiet day tomorrow. The regiment won't be in until the afternoon."

Lloyd looked over Michael's shoulder and came to attention again. Michael spun round to see Scovell walking towards him. They exchanged salutes.

"Roberts, look, sorry about this, but something has come up, and you're needed at headquarters, immediately."

"Yes, sir. I'll just get my helmet and sword." Michael was wearing his more comfortable forage cap.

"No, no, no need, you'll do fine as you are."

Michael turned to Lloyd, "Carry on Lloyd, I'll call in when I get back," and turning to Scovell, "Right, I'm with you, sir."

Conversation was impossible as they made their way through the streets. Even at this late hour troops were still moving about Coimbra, and the occasional gun team rattled along, the horses kicking sparks off the cobbles. They got back to the headquarters building, but once through the archway Scovell turned away from the passage to the Quartermaster General's office. He stopped and faced Michael.

"Now we can have a quick word before we go in. Don't worry about your appearance. Sir Arthur doesn't much care about a man's appearance, more about what he can do."

"Sir Arthur?" asked Michael in surprise.

"That's right, Roberts, Sir Arthur Wellesley." In the dark of the courtyard, Michael could just make out a smile on Scovell's face. "Oh, and Beresford and Murray."

"Marshal Beresford?"

"Yes, that's the one. The Portuguese Commander-in-Chief."

Scovell turned and led the way down another passage, past a couple of sentries, up a flight of stairs, past more sentries, and into a large room, presumably a dining room from the table in the middle and the chairs scattered around. Sitting around the table were three men. One, Colonel Murray, Michael knew. He had never seen either of the other two. They were both wearing long, plain blue coats. One was a well-built man, with a large, open face, and rather bald, his remaining hair thick and curly. The other man, seated between the others, had a full head of brown hair, and a long chin, but what caught Michael's eye was his large, Roman nose. That, he realised, must be Sir Arthur Wellesley. This was soon confirmed.

Scovell coughed politely, and said, "This is Lieutenant Roberts, Sir Arthur." All three looked up, but it was Sir Arthur who spoke.

"Ah, Roberts. Has Scovell told you why you are here?"

"No, sir."

"Colonel Murray, perhaps you would explain to the young gentleman?"

"Of course, Sir Arthur." Murray paused for a moment to compose his thoughts. "As you know, Roberts, Soult has taken Oporto, and it is our intention to retake it from him, as soon as possible. That presents some difficulties. There is only the one bridge, the bridge of boats, as you know, of course. Once that is destroyed, which we assume Soult will do, the Douro is a major obstacle. Soult is not a fool, and we expect him to have taken precautions to prevent us crossing using boats by seizing or sinking every boat he can lay hands on. The only other route to Oporto is north east, up through Viseu and Lamego to Peso da Regua, and then west down the right bank. That route, however, would take a considerable time, could easily be blocked, and would leave the way open for Soult to advance on Lisbon. No, we must advance directly north against him, and we must have boats to cross the Douro."

Michael wondered where on Earth this was going, and how it could possibly involve him. Murray continued. "We could, of course, ask the navy for help, or requisition fishing boats, but both those approaches are obvious, and Soult will be ready for any amphibious attack from the coast. Indeed, we rather hope that he expects us to do that. Fortunately, we have received intelligence that could provide us with the boats we need. Peso da Regua is being held by part of General Silveira's army, while most of his force is at Lamego, some seven or eight miles to the south. It would appear that at Regua there are a number of large wine barges. Marshal Beresford is marching to Regua, never mind why, but you are to go with him, secure as many barges as you can, and bring them down river to a safe point as close to Oporto as you can get."

Michael's mind reeled at the enormity of what had just been said. Still Murray went on. "You speak fluent Portuguese, and none of Marshal Beresford's Portuguese and English speaking staff can be spared. You leave in the morning. You should arrive in Regua by the ninth, we expect to reach the Douro on the twelfth, it would be ideal if you can be there then. We are reliably informed that it should be possible to sail down the Douro in a day or so."

Murray at last stopped speaking. Then it was Beresford's turn. "One of my staff officers, Major Warre, knows Regua, and the Douro, he was born in Oporto. There will plenty of time for you to talk to him during our march. He can give you more details. We leave at first light. Be here half an hour before then, say half past five."

Sir Arthur had been looking intently at Michael, and now he spoke. "I cannot stress too highly the importance of your mission, Roberts. We must cross the Douro at Oporto, and we must have those barges, nothing else will do. See to it that you are there."

Murray then dismissed Michael with "I think that's all? Yes? Carry on Roberts."

Michael saluted, but the three men had turned their attention back to the papers on the table. Michael felt a hand on his arm, and Scovell whispered, "Come away now."

Outside in the courtyard, Michael paused, leaning with one hand on the wall. Scovell put a friendly hand on his shoulder. "Sorry, that was rather sprung on you, but there was no chance to warn you. Look, I know Warre, he's a good fellow, and you will have plenty of time to learn all you need to know from him. He knows the Douro well, he's one of the Warre port family, you must have heard of them?"

Michael nodded, he had, Warre's was one of the major port houses, but he had never met any of them. They managed their own shipping, and it was two hundred miles from Lisbon to Oporto. Scovell went on. "He would have done it himself if Beresford didn't need him. Fortunately you were on hand." Scovell chuckled, "Cheer up, I've got to meet your Regiment tomorrow, show them their billets, and explain to your Colonel where you are."

On the way back to his billet Michael heard a clock strike midnight. He swore silently to himself. So much for a good night's sleep. The streets were quieter now, just a few patrols, and a handful of officers making their way on various duties. All was quiet at the billet, a dim light showed the entrance to the stables, and Michael found Lloyd by the light of a pierced tin stable lantern. He was sound asleep, wrapped in horse blankets. He hated to do it, but it had to be done.

"Lloyd, Lloyd, wake up man."

"Beth y diafol…" Lloyd thrashed his way out of the blankets and to his feet. "Beg your pardon, sir."

"Bad news, I'm afraid, Lloyd. We need to be up and at headquarters for five thirty, ready to march. We won't be waiting for the regiment. Special orders."

"Is that right, sir? Well, then I better be giving you a call at four, sir."

"And how will you manage that?"

"Sir, there's a blessed clock somewhere that chimes every hour, And I have heard every one of them!"

Michael laughed at Lloyd's rueful explanation. "Very good, Lloyd , four o'clock then." And he took himself off to get what sleep he could.

It might have been early May, the sixth, in fact, but at four in the morning there was a distinct chill. Michael didn't know how he did it, but Lloyd had appeared with a bowl and a jug of hot water. Then, while Michael was shaving, he came back with a mug of tea and a plate of bread rolls and cheese. Michael dressed, and then packed his valise while having what passed for his breakfast. By five o'clock he was clattering down the stairs and out into the cold and dark of the courtyard. Lloyd had both horses ready, and as soon as Michael's valise was secured they rode off towards the army's headquarters. At one junction they were forced to wait while a battalion of Beresford's Portuguese infantry marched by in their dark blue jackets.

"So, that's the Portuguese army, sir?"

"That's right Lloyd, what do you think?"

"Well, 'it's awful dark to tell much, sir, I reckon we'll find out soon enough if they can fight."

"Yes, I suppose we will." Michael replied.

They arrived at headquarters with a few minutes to spare. Passing through the archway Michael found that all was hustle and bustle, with a large, mounted party, and more horses waiting for riders. "I think we'll just sit quietly here, Lloyd."

"Right you are, sir."

A few minutes later Marshal Beresford emerged from a nearby doorway. Catching sight of Michael, Beresford called out to him, "Just follow along, Roberts!" The marshal mounted his horse and was out through the archway and trotting off down the street, followed by all the other riders. With a nod to Lloyd, Michael turned Johnny after them, Lloyd just behind him.

They passed quickly through the streets of Coimbra and emerged onto open ground to the east of the town, where Beresford's small army was drawn up ready to march. In the pre-dawn half-light, Michael was surprised to see a squadron of British Light Dragoons drawn up.

"I think that's a squadron of the Fourteenth, sir."

"I do believe you're right, Lloyd, can't really be anyone else." Michael tried to make out who the officers were, after training with the Fourteenth he knew them quite well, but it was still too dark.

Beresford and his staff passed by the troops towards the road to Vizeu. The bulk of Beresford's force was Portuguese, five battalions of infantry, two batteries of artillery, and three squadrons of cavalry. There was also a brigade of British infantry of two battalions of the line and some companies of riflemen, in addition to the squadron from the Fourteenth.

With Beresford leading, the group of riders pushed on past the assembled troops, with just a small escort of Portuguese cavalry. They soon left the main body of troops behind as Beresford pushed the pace. A few riders ahead of them turned around to look at Michael and Lloyd, but otherwise no notice was taken of them until the first rest halt, two hours or so after sunrise. The route took them along the valley of the Mondego, the river winding gently between wooded slopes falling down to its banks. Lloyd was watering the two horses and Michael was resting, sitting with his back against a tree, eyes closed. Around him he could hear the sounds of the escort, voices calling and laughing, accoutrements clattering, it was beginning to get warm, he started to doze, horses stamping, a voice that seemed quite insistent…

"Lieutenant Roberts?"

Michael's eyes snapped open. "Yes, I'm Roberts."

"I'm Major Warre."

Michael climbed to his feet, and saluted, "I beg your pardon, sir." Warre was a slim, well set up man, in his late twenties, and dressed in a plain long, military pelisse with black frogging, and a peaked forage cap.

"Don't worry about it, Roberts. I'm sorry I wasn't able to meet you last night. I was expecting to have to hang around all day for you, and then ride like the fury to catch up with the Marshal. You did me a favour arriving earlier. Now, the Marshal wants to be in Vizeu tomorrow night, and that's almost sixty miles from Coimbra. So it's going to be a long, hard couple of days. And then we push on to Lamego, that's another forty."

Down on the road orders were being shouted, and Lloyd was hurrying towards them with the horses.

"We can ride along together, and I'll fill you in on the plan. Is this your man?"

"Yes, sir, his name's Lloyd. Lloyd! This is Major Warre." Lloyd saluted Warre, and handed Michael Johnny's reins.

"Lloyd." Warre returned the salute. "We'd better get a move on, that's my man down there, Rankin, with my horse."

Minutes later Michael and Warre were riding side by side to the back of the little cavalcade, Lloyd and Rankin behind them. The pace was being pushed, trotting wherever the going was good, walking where it wasn't. The day gradually got hotter and the riders were grateful for the shade of the trees lining the valley sides.

Warre spoke to Michael in Portuguese, "If we get to Vizeu tomorrow, and Lamego the day after, that's Monday, I think we can get you into Regua early on Tuesday, the ninth. Then, if we can organise the boats, we can get you away at dawn the day after, the tenth."

"I see, sir, but how do you know there will be boats there that will go to Oporto?"

"Ah, yes, that's almost embarrassing. The thing is, my family owns them. They're the rabelos that carry the barrels of wine down to the port house at Vila Nova. It's a matter of persuading the crews."

"I see."

"Actually this whole boat thing was my idea, I'm afraid. It seemed like a good idea, and it would get me to Oporto. Then Beresford decided he couldn't manage without me, needs every Portuguese speaker he can find, which is where you came in. Very useful that."

"So you were going to take your family's boats yourself? Do they know?"

"No, my uncle usually looks after things in Oporto, but he's in London. It's all going to be a bit of a bluff with the crews. I just hope that I know some of them. If they agree, then you just have sit there and enjoy the trip. Until you get near to Oporto."

"Forgive me, sir, but you make it sound easy?"

"Yes, well, it should be," said Warre cheerfully. "The boat crews are very experienced, it's just a matter of timing your arrival. If you leave Regua on the tenth you should be able to arrive just after dawn on the twelfth without any difficulty. You could probably even make it for the eleventh, but then you might be seen and taken by the French."

"That would be awkward."

Warre laughed. "It would, indeed. Sir Arthur would be rather cross."

As they rode on the valley sides became steeper, more wooded, and the valley narrower.

"I gather you were born in Lisbon?" asked Warre.

"Yes, sir."

"Oporto, myself, got sent to England in '03. I understand your father worked for Quintela? I heard what happened, please, accept my condolences."

"Thank you, yes he did. I've been living in England since '05, Falmouth in fact, with my uncle."

"And now here you are, an officer in the Sixteenth and back in Portugal. I imagine that we would both wish it were under different circumstances."

"Yes, sir. I imagine that you would have been involved with the family business?"

Warre roared with laughter. "Oh, dear God, no, not that. My father and my uncle tried. I always wanted to be a soldier, but they put me into the office. I stuck it for a while, and then it all got too much." He chuckled. "My uncle's Portuguese partner, Pedro Alves, nodded off at his desk one day. He has a rather splendid and rather long pigtail. I was engaged in sealing up letters. I sealed his pigtail to his desk, with bright red wax and used the company seal." He laughed again. "There didn't seem to be anything to be gained by waiting for him to wake up, so I made myself scarce for the rest of the day."

Michael couldn't help but smile at the image this conjured up.

"Suffice it to say," Warre continued, "there was the devil of a row, but no more objections to my joining the army."

Michael decided that he rather liked William Warre.

"Now, tell me, Roberts, how did you come to be here?"

Michael told Warre his story, or an edited version, leaving out his dealings with Musgrave. The conversation veered to the general, about growing up in Portugal, life in the army, horses, and the time and the miles passed, the heat almost forgotten. It was late in the afternoon when they halted at Santa Comba Dao, and Warre had to go about his staff duties, although not before ensuring that he and Michael would be billeted together.

Chapter 15

That night Michael was invited to dine with Marshal Beresford. Warre was there, along with Beresford's Quartermaster General, Colonel D'Urban, and a number of other staff officers. After a long hard day, and the promise of another pre-dawn start, it was a quiet gathering that soon broke up. Michael and Warre checked on the horses, Lloyd seemed to have come to an arrangement with Rankin, he would care for the four horses, Rankin would take care of things in the billet. With everything taken care of, it wasn't long before Michael was sound asleep.

They left Santa Combo Dao at first light and then climbed out of the valley of the Mondego on to the uplands. The air was fresher, and the change from the heat of the claustrophobic valley was welcome. A gentle breeze further mitigated the heat of the sun. The road was reasonable, and the Marshal continued to push them along, only stopping where they crossed rivers so that man and horse alike could take water. At Tondela they crossed the Dinha, and the road levelled out somewhat. Then they dropped down to cross the Asnes at Fail. From there another hour saw them entering Viseu.

Viseu was occupied by two British battalions under Sir Robert Wilson. Beresford had orders for them to join his force, which resulted in a burst of activity that went on late into the night as the infantry got ready to march. Consequently Warre was kept busy and Michael was left to his own devices. He was billeted in a small house near the centre of the town, the small courtyard was just large enough for four horses, and Lloyd and Rankin spent some time seeking out forage for them. The horses had had a couple of hard days, with another one ahead, and needed to feed well.

Michael, in the small parlour, and Lloyd and Rankin, in the kitchen, were fed by the householder, a local shopkeeper who was surprised to be addressed by Michael in fluent Portuguese. That, and the gift of a dollar, ensured they were well taken care of, and something saved for Warre when he finally appeared. It also secured a supply of hot water the next morning, enough that all four men managed a shave, as well as enjoying tea and bread for breakfast.

By dawn they were on the road again, and from Viseu the going was good, flat and straight, until they crossed the Vouga. As they rode along together, Warre told Michael everything he could think of about the Douro. He mentioned something about rapids, but seemed to dismiss them. Then the road started to wind into the mountains, curling around to follow the contours, following the wooded valley of a small river. At Castro Daire they dropped down to the valley of the Pavia, and crossed it on a high, narrow bridge. The road snaked up out of the valley and through the village. There was time for a brief halt and some refreshment. Then they were mounted and pushing on again. Once they got up above Castro Daire the road once again started to follow the contours and the day's ride finished with an easy few hours ride into Lamego on a road that snaked its way along a steep valley side.

It was late afternoon when they rode into the town. It was occupied by a brigade of the Portuguese army, and Beresford's arrival caused quite a stir. It was clear that it would be a little while before the local situation became clear, Warre was fully occupied with arranging billets for the troops following along and who would have to be squeezed into the town. Michael found a small tavern where he was able to buy himself dinner and a reasonable bottle of wine. Lloyd was left looking after Johnny and

Edward in the street, but Michael had food and drink sent out to him.

Eventually he saw Rankin talking to Lloyd, and apparently giving him directions, before he rushed off in the direction he had been pointing. Michael paid his bill and strolled out into the street. "Did I see Rankin telling you where our billet is?"

"Yes, sir, it's not far, and he says there's feed there for the horses, his and the Major's are already there."

"Excellent. I think we can walk the horses from here, pass me Johnny's lead rein."

Half an hour later the horses had been watered, and while they were eating Lloyd was busy giving them a wash and rub down where they had got sweaty during the day's ride. Michael was doing the same to himself with a bucket of cold water. He dried himself off with his dirty shirt, and put on his clean spare from his valise. The wet shirt he rinsed through and put to dry, then he finished dressing.

"Lloyd," he called out to the Dragoon who was in the small shed that was serving as stables. "I'm going to find Marshal Beresford's headquarters. Don't go anywhere."

"Right you are, sir."

It didn't take Michael long to find Beresford's headquarters and he soon saw Warre. He was busy giving billet details to some Portuguese officers, but once they moved off Michael approached Warre, who smiled when he saw him coming.

"Hello, Roberts," he returned Michael's salute, "this is very timely. I think I have just issued the last billets. I just need to check with D'Urban, and I think I am finished for the night."

"What about pushing on to Regua tonight?" asked Michael.

"No, I'm sorry, but it's a two hour ride through the mountains, and it will be dark in half an hour. The exact situation is a bit confused at the moment, but should be clearer by tomorrow morning. Look, I'll just be ten minutes, and then we can go and eat and get a drink. I'm just a bit hungry and thirsty."

"Very good, sir."

Warre disappeared into the headquarters building, but was back in less than five minutes. "Right, they know where my billet is, if they need me they'll send an orderly. Now, have you eaten?"

"Yes, sir, in a little tavern near our billet, but I could stand another drink."

"Then lead on, Mr Roberts, lead on!"

The tavern was quite busy, with a good number of Portuguese infantry officers and a few of Warre's fellow staff officers. As the sun dropped the temperature fell with it, and they were glad of the large fire burning in the tavern's hearth. Warre got a large bowl of what they were told was lamb stew, and they shared a bottle of the local wine. Warre took a mouthful.

"A bit rough, this local red, but it will do nicely with this stew."

Michael tried it, and thought it was perfectly alright. "I suppose you know the wine of this region well, sir?"

"Pretty well, although I have been away for a while. Look, it's Michael, isn't it?"

"Yes, sir."

"Well, I think that when we are off duty we can dispense with all the formalities, if you've no objection that is?"

"Err, no, sir, of course not."

"Then, please, call me William."

"Thank you, sir, err, William."

"Now, I hate to talk shop, but needs must. There's a battalion of light infantry in Regua, we have a brigade here, and more infantry due to arrive tomorrow. We think there's a French division at Amarante, that's only a little over twenty miles from Regua, and there is a suspicion that they might try to take Regua in order to stop us crossing. The position at Regua has been fortified, and Beresford intends to put more troops across as they arrive. You and I, however, are crossing over tomorrow to see what we can do about some boats for Sir Arthur. There are boats, they have been ferrying troops across the river, the question will be how many we can persuade to make the trip down to Oporto. At the moment they are relatively safe, but the crews know the French hold Oporto, and their fear is of losing their boats and their livelihood if they are taken by the French."

"I thought you said the boats were owned by your uncle?"

"Some of the boats will be, but not all of them, at the moment I don't know how many there are. But they will still need crews, without them…" Warre left the sentence unfinished. "Anyway, we will find out tomorrow. There's no point in rushing, by the way. It's only a two hour ride, if we arrive at about midday, we should find all the crews and boats that we are going to. They will all be in the main tavern on the quay to get the latest news, which will be us!"

Soon Warre had finished his stew and the bottle was empty. He checked his watch. "Nearly ten o'clock." The two men rose from their table, Warre paid his bill, and they walked back to the billet together. Lloyd and Rankin were sitting outside the stable, sharing a bottle and both smoking a pipe. They started to rise, but Warre waved them down. "At ease. We will be leaving here mid-morning. But Mr Roberts and I need to visit headquarters first, so we will start the day at six o'clock. Hot water and some breakfast."

"Right you are, sir." "Yes, sir."

"All well with the horses?" asked Warre.

"Yes, sir," it was Lloyd who answered, "but they could do with a day or two's rest, sir."

Warre turned to Michael, "There's a thought. What are we going to do with Lloyd and your horses?"

"I suppose either send him back to Coimbra, or down the Douro to Oporto, if we get across and if there's a road?"

"There's a road on both sides, the road on the right bank is the best, if the French are cleared out, but the road on the left bank will be safer. It's a comfortable four day ride, with plenty of places to halt. I suggest you leave them with me, and I'll send Lloyd on his way with appropriate orders?"

"Thank you, sir, that would be very good of you. Lloyd! You're going to be on your own for a while. I'll explain more tomorrow when things are a bit clearer."

Michael lay awake. Apprehension about his mission was causing his mind to race, full of what ifs and maybes. It was all very well for Warre to be dismissive about the journey down the Douro, he had, no doubt, done it many times. And if it was 'a comfortable four day ride', how could he do it in a day and a bit? Did the boats sail on through the night? And were there French troops on the north bank between Regua and Oporto? He imagined a

French artillery piece would make short work any river boat. Eventually he dropped off to sleep, and was very deeply asleep when Lloyd woke him with hot water for shaving and the inevitable bread for breakfast.

Neither shaving nor breakfast took long, and soon he was at the stables where Lloyd had tacked up Edward and Johnny, and was getting Warre's horse ready. There was no sign of Rankin. Warre arrived and asked Lloyd. "Where the devil is Rankin, he should be getting my horse ready."

"Ah, well, sir," replied Lloyd, "you see he got the hot water ready, and arranged the breakfasts for you both, sir, and I said I'd do the horses. He's not one of life's horsemen, sir."

"That's a certainty," said Warre with a frown, "well, he can stay here today and see what supplies he can forage for us for the next few days. I'll tell him before we go. But right now Michael, we'd best be getting along to headquarters."

At headquarters Warre found Colonel D'Urban, but the Colonel had no more intelligence on the situation for them. He simply wished Michael good luck, and sent them on their way. Back at the billet Warre, went off to have 'a quiet word' with Rankin.

"Begging your pardon, sir," Lloyd spoke quietly to Michael, "but that Rankin is a rare one."

"What do you mean by that?"

"Well, a light dragoon as doesn't really like horses? I mean, sir, I think he's a bad one."

"What? Just because he doesn't like horses?"

"Not just that, sir, I caught him a looking in your valise last night, sir."

"Oh, you did, did you? I suppose I could have 'a quiet word' myself, with Major Warre. Rankin's not riding with us today."

"I'd rather you didn't, sir, I think the Major thinks quite high of him, and I can keep an eye on him, I think I've got the measure of him now, sir."

"Very well, Lloyd, we shall just be wary, then."

"Diolch, sir." Michael had become used to the Welsh that peppered Lloyd's speech.

Warre returned a few moments later, and the three men were soon mounted and riding out of Lamego, northwards to the Douro. The road snaked along, more or less following the contours of the hills. The views were stunning, and at one hairpin bend, as they dropped down the hill side, Warre pointed off to a town in the distance. "That's Regua. It's about four miles as the crow flies, another hour should see us to the river."

The road continued to descend steadily towards the river, gradually slipping down the flank of the hills. Then the Douro came into sight, just a small section at first, glimpsed between intervening hills. Gradually more and more became visible, and then the road started to drop steeply, and Michael could see the river bending and disappearing away to the west, towards Oporto. For a little while the river and town were lost to view as they dropped lower. Then, suddenly, they were riding alongside the river.

The crossing point for the ferry was guarded by a picket of Portuguese light infantry. Warre spoke to the sergeant in charge, then turned to Michael and Lloyd. "This is where we leave the horses. Lloyd, I have told the sergeant here that he is to take great care of you and the horses. Just smile and nod a lot. I would expect to be back in three or four hours."

They all dismounted and Lloyd led the horses off to picket them under the shade of some nearby trees. The main ferry could take horse drawn vehicles, and that was moored at the landing stage nearby. A small boat with a two man crew was also available, and Michael and Warre were rowed across the river in that.

As they crossed, Warre pointed out the rabelos to Michael. There were about twenty of them moored against the town, strange looking broad beamed craft, with a single mast towards the stern, pointed at both ends, and a massive, long steering oar that pivoted on the stern and reached up to a high platform just behind the mast. Most important was a large area for cargo, that could take a lot of soldiers instead of barrels of wine. Michael and Warre were soon standing on the wharf, where they were greeted by a young officer in command of a picket. He recognised Warre and saluted him. Warre returned the salute and spoke to him.

"Lieutenant, tell me, where can I find your Colonel?"

The Colonel of the Portuguese light infantry was a British officer on secondment to the Portuguese army. They found him on the western approaches to the town, supervising the construction of breastworks commanding the road along the side of the Douro. Matters were helped along as the Colonel and Warre were acquainted. Another brief conversation finished with the Colonel promising any assistance that he could give. He did warn them that French patrols had been seen in the direction Mesao Frio, six or seven miles away down the Douro, and there were reports that a French division was behind them. That was worrying as such a force could easily blockade the river.

Michael and Warre returned to the wharf, and Warre led the way into a large tavern. As they walked in the loud chatter of the customers died away. It was gloomy inside and it took a few moments for Michael's eyes to adjust. There were about forty men sitting around trestle tables on long benches, the tables covered with bottles and glasses. At the far end of the room a simple counter was presided over by a large man whom Michael assumed to be the landlord.

Warre looked around for a moment, and then spoke. "I am Major Warre. How many of you work for my uncle, William Warre?" Hesitantly, about a dozen hands went up. "Which of you are rabelo captains?" Two of the men got slowly to their feet, one took on the role of spokesperson.

"I am, Senhor Warre."

"It's Senhor Gama, is it not?"

"Yes, Senhor."

"I thought I recognised you. How many of my uncle's rabelos are here?"

"Four, Senhor."

"So few?" Warre sounded disappointed.

"Yes, Senhor, most of them are in Oporto," explained the captain, "held by the French."

"Where are the other two captains?" asked Warre.

"At the chandlers, just down the wharf."

"Then I would be grateful if you would send someone for them." At a nod from the captain one of the men who had raised his hand, got up and disappeared past Warre, out into the sunshine.

Warre addressed the room again. "Are there any other rabelo captains here?" Three hands went slowly up. "Then I would like to invite you to share a drink with me and my fellow officer, Lieutenant Roberts. Senhor," Warre called out to the landlord, "four bottles of good wine and glasses for all, if you please."

There was a long, empty table by a window, looking out across the Douro, and Michael, Warre and the captains sat round it.

Introductions were made and they learnt that the other Warre rabelo captain was called Reis. Warre poured wine, and then the other two Warre rabelo captains, Barreto and Peres, arrived, and further introductions were made. The seven rabelo captains sat in expectant silence as Warre poured wine for everyone.

"Gentlemen," Warre started, "I need your help. The British army is marching on Oporto to take the town back from the French." There was a buzz of excited conversation as this news went around the tavern. "However, the French have seized all the boats they can find, and will probably destroy the bridge. What I am asking you to do is to take your rabelos down river, with this officer," he indicated Michael, "and help the British to cross the river." For a moment there was a stunned silence, and then everyone began talking at once. The captains looked at each other, and Michael could see doubt all over their faces.

Warre spoke again. "I know it is a lot to ask, but I promise you my family, my uncle, will be grateful to you. I can promise you that you will be well rewarded. Every man that sails will be paid a hundred dollars. This is an offer to all the rabelo crews, if you can tell those who are not here. And if Oporto is retaken, then the trade can start again."

Michael chimed in, to the surprise of the captains, who had not realised that he spoke Portuguese. "Gentlemen, please, yes, I speak your language, I was born in Lisbon, my father worked for Baron Quintela." They looked impressed, but still doubtful. "Taking Oporto back from the French is just the first step in expelling them from Portugal completely. But without boats it will not be possible."

One of the captains, Peres, the one who had spoken first to Warre now spoke. "But, Senhor, what difference could our boats make against the French army?" He shook his head. "And we must talk to our crews, and the other captains, they are not all here, and our families, Senhor. This is a dangerous thing that you ask us to do."

"Believe me, captain, your boats could make all the difference. How soon will you have your answer?" asked Warre.

Peres looked at the other captains before he answered. "Tomorrow morning, Senhor, here at ten o'clock."

Warre leant back in his chair. "Very well, gentlemen, until tomorrow." He nodded at Michael, and the two men left, leaving behind a very animated discussion.

Outside the day was warming up, the sun high in a clear, blue sky. "Well, that could have been worse," said Warre as they walked along the wharf. "I was afraid of a blunt no. I suppose we had better stay here until tomorrow. I think we will have to leave Lloyd across the river with the horses. Would you care to cross over and see him, while I see about some accommodation? I think the name Warre ought to get us something reasonable."

"I'll bring our valises back with me," Michael said, and the two men went their separate ways.

When Michael returned from seeing Lloyd, who seemed quite happy to stay with his new friends, the light infantry, Warre was waiting on the wharf.

"I found our local manager, Medeiros, at the warehouse, and he has invited us to stay with him. He's also going to go down to see the crews and add his weight to persuading them. I hope that and the hundred dollars a man will do the trick, along with the gratitude of the Warres."

"I didn't know about the money," said Michael, "how big is a crew?"

"Ten or twelve."

"That's a thousand dollars a boat! And there must be twenty boats here." Michael was shocked at the amount involved.

"A small price to pay to retake Oporto. And there was more if there had been more boats. But I don't expect them all to go. Some of these captains own their own boats, and it would be risking their livelihood. Others can't ask their owners. It's fortunate there are four of my family's boats here. I hope we can depend on them."

Michael and Warre walked slowly through the streets of Regua towards the home of Medeiros. His house lay a little way back from the river, up in the old town, and as they approached Michael saw a figure of a well-dressed gentleman hurrying towards them along a side street.

Warre also saw him, and halted. "Here he comes now, he must have already seen the rabelo crews." The hurrying man stopped before them, slightly out of breath. "Senhor Medeiros, this is Lieutenant Roberts."

"Senhor Warre, Senhor Roberts, it is a pleasure to meet you." He turned to Warre. "Senhor, I have spoken to the crews." He shrugged. "I am afraid that I do not know what they will do, particularly the ones who do not work for us. They have promised an answer in the morning, after they have seen their families and met again. They confirmed that they will meet you in the tavern at ten o'clock."

"Well, that's no worse than they said to us," said Warre, "and if they agree, Michael, then there will still be time for you to get to Oporto."

"Yes, Senhor," added Medeiros, "and while we wait, may I offer you the hospitality of my house?"

Senhor Medeiros and his wife proved themselves to be kind and generous hosts. A splendid dinner was accompanied by good, local wines, and Michael and Warre were given a room each for the night.

They were woken at about six o'clock by servants bringing hot water and tea. A breakfast of bread, cheese, and cold meats followed. There was no rush, and by the time they had finished eating they still had three hours before they were due to meet the crews. With time on their hands, Michael and Warre strolled down to the wharf, but keeping well away from the tavern. They took the ferry across the Douro, and found that Lloyd had passed a quiet night, and that the horses were looking rested after their exertions of the previous few days. They agreed that another day of rest should see them fully recovered.

Warre spoke to the Portuguese sergeant and arranged for forage for the horses. Michael spoke to Lloyd. "Lloyd, the reason we are here is to get hold of some boats and sail them down to Oporto to help the army cross the Douro and retake Oporto." Michael saw the look on Lloyd's face. "Just me Lloyd. You will have to take care of Johnny for me. I'll leave you with Major Warre. If we take Oporto you should be able to rejoin the army by following the roads along this side of the river. Otherwise you had probably best return to Coimbra and look for the regiment from there. Before you do leave, Major Warre will give you a pass that should get you through any Portuguese pickets."

"Right you are, sir. I'll get us all back to the Regiment."

"Thank you, Lloyd." Warre was waiting by the boat. "All being well, I shall see you in Oporto in about six or seven days. Good luck, Emyr." With that Michael hurried away to join Warre.

As they were being rowed across the river, the sound of drums came to them and then the head of a column of infantry appeared from the direction of Lamego. "It looks like Beresford is bringing up the reinforcements to Regua." Warre spoke thoughtfully, as they watched the column marching towards the ferry, whose crew were busy getting it ready.

When they reached the wharf at Regua a Portuguese officer informed them that French patrols had been seen to the west and that an attack was expected. Michael and Warre hurried towards the tavern, but stopped when they saw all the moored rabelos being manned by their crews. Warre saw Gama and shouted to him. "Gama! What's happening?"

Gama looked up for a moment, "Senhor, we have to bring the soldiers across to Regua, the French are coming!" With that he turned to the business of getting his boat ready, the crew readying their oars.

At that moment they were joined by Medeiros. "Senhor Warre!"

"Medeiros, what's the news?"

"Senhor, I was talking to the men when they were ordered to help the soldiers cross the river. Our crews have agreed to go to Oporto, if the money is lodged with me for safekeeping first. I am afraid that the others will not risk their boats."

The first of the rabelos were pushing off from the wharf and rowing hard across the river. Altogether there were about twenty of them, including Warre's four. "It's a shame we can't get them all to sail down to Oporto," said Michael.

"Senhor," Medeiros spoke, "I did speak to the other captains and crews, but without permission from their owners they dare not risk their boats."

"I suppose that's understandable," Warre answered, "although with the way the French sacked this town last year you'd think they might be a bit more interested in helping against the French."

"Please, Senhor, many of these men were with the Ordenança, and fought the French with Silveira. Their lives are their own, but the boats are not."

"My apologies, Senhor Medeiros. It is my frustration that speaks."

The big ferry was approaching the landing stage, and Michael, happy to change the subject, asked, "Isn't that Marshal Beresford? And Lloyd, with our horses!"

Warre turned to look, "Good Lord, it is, we had better report to him. Senhor Medeiros, again, please forgive me."

"Of course, Senhor, now, you must go. I will stay here to see what happens with our rabelos."

The two men hurried along the wharf to where the first infantry were disembarking, along with Beresford, a handful of staff officers, and Lloyd with the three horses. The Marshal saw them coming and walked to meet them.

"Warre, Roberts, glad to have found you so easily. There's no time to waste, there is a report that Loison is advancing with his division to take Regua. Horses will not help in the town, so we left ours across the river, but, Warre, you know this area, I want you, Roberts and your dragoon to patrol up towards Mesão Frio and see if that's true. We can see the road along the river from the other bank, but I need to know if they are coming over the hills. Sharp, now!"

Within minutes Warre was leading the way through Regua, through the defensive lines, and up the steep hills to the west. The way was through the vineyards covering the slopes, taking dirt tracks that zig-zagged up, passing up through the terraced vines. There was not a soul to be seen anywhere, and not a sound save the buzz of insects. The horses struggled up the soft dirt tracks, their hooves hardly making a sound. There was little conversation as they rode in single file, listening out for any noise, eyes sweeping for any movement on the hill above.

Eventually they reached the top of the steepest slope and the going was easier, the landscape opening out in front of them. Half a mile ahead lay a small village of whitewashed houses. "That's Fontelas," Warre spoke quietly, "we should be able to see all we need from the other side of it. I think we had better load."

Michael reached under the flounce over the holsters on the front of Johnny's saddle and pulled out one of his pistols. Reaching into his cartouche box, he pulled out a cartridge and loaded the pistol. He replaced it in its holster and then loaded his second pistol, which he kept in his hand. Warre did likewise. Lloyd unfastened his carbine from his saddle, clipped it to his shoulder belt, took a cartridge from his cartouche box, and loaded the short carbine.

Warre looked around, saw that Michael and Lloyd were ready, and walked his horse on. Cautiously, slowly, they rode towards the village, gradually spreading out as much as the vines allowed. It was now the middle of the day, and the sun shone down remorselessly, Michael wiped the sweat from his face with the cuff of his right sleeve.

They reached a road, and looking to his left Michael could see the valley of the Douro and, in the distance, Regua. He could see boats crisscrossing the river, the big ferry and the smaller Rabelos, still ferrying troops across. Warre slowly led the way into the village, Michael and Lloyd riding a few yards behind him and on opposite sides of the narrow road. There was not a person to be seen, and not a sound except the click of the horses' shoes on the rough street. Then, suddenly, they emerged from the village and the vista of the other side of the hill opened up before them.

They reined in and sat motionless, carefully scanning the roads and distant hills. "Well," said Warre after a few moments, "I don't see any French." He and Michael returned their pistols to their holsters.

At that moment Lloyd spoke out, pointing to their front, "There, sir, look you, on the road!" Less than half a mile away a troop of French light cavalry had suddenly come into view along a road as it curved out from behind a ridge.

"Damn it, time to go!" Warre called out and they turned their horses hard and broke into a trot back the way they had come. Lloyd was on Michael's left, with Warre behind them. As they crossed the road toward the vines, Lloyd suddenly raised his carbine and fired. Looking beyond him Michael saw a small group of French light cavalry, an advance guard for the troop they had just seen. They were just entering the village a mere ten yards away. The shot and the sudden appearance of three British cavalrymen caused them to pull up in surprise. As the smoke from Lloyd's shot cleared he saw that there were five of them, but one was reeling in his saddle, falling from his horse, blood spurting from his chest.

The four remaining Frenchmen looked uncertain, that was enough for Warre. "Charge them!" he screamed, drawing his sabre at the same moment. Michael and Lloyd followed suit, Lloyd dropping his carbine to hang by his side. Michael spun Johnny towards the French, clapped his spurs on, and screamed out, "Charge!" Johnny surged forward down the narrow road, Lloyd next to him, Warre only just behind.

The riderless French horse whinnied in fear, and spun and kicked, causing chaos amongst the other French horses. Two riders were almost unseated as their horses spooked. One of the others, who had been carrying his carbine, managed to get a shot off, Michael had no idea where it went, and then Lloyd crashed into him, driving the point of his sabre into the man's face. Michael's opponent thrust at him with his sabre, he turned the point aside, and as the man tried to disengage, he turned his wrist, dropping the point, and then flicked the blade in a sweeping cut upwards, though the man's jaw, sending him swaying backwards, screaming, blood gushing, losing his grip on his sabre. Then Warre was in with them, riding for the two remaining Frenchmen. Their horses were already half turned around, and now they tried to escape, back the way they had come. One got away, the other fell as Warre thrust into his left shoulder, knocking him off his horse.

Warre pulled up his horse and turned him back around. "Now it's really time to go!" They pushed their horses into a canter through the village, out of the other side and into the vines, riding hard and as fast as they dared down the gentle slope towards the drop back down to Regua. Michael leaned back in his saddle as Johnny pounded down the hillside, one hand on the reins, the other tightly gripping his bloody sabre. As they reached the top of the steeper slope they pulled back to a trot, and Michael risked a look back towards the village. It looked just as peaceful as it had ten minutes before as they approached it, with not an enemy horseman to be seen. Then it disappeared as they started down the steep slope, the horses slipping and slithering their way at a breakneck pace.

At the bottom of the slope they came onto the road into Regua, and pushed the horses into a steady collected canter. Michael could feel the excitement coursing through his veins, and grinned. Warre caught his eye, and grinned back at him. Michael couldn't help but laugh with the exhilaration of it all. In moments, all three were roaring with laughter in sheer relief and excitement.

Chapter 16

They cantered on, steadily, to Regua and as they reached the defensive earthworks they slowed to a trot. Beresford was waiting for them, and Warre gave him an account of what had happened. Beresford nodded thoughtfully. "There are no reports yet from across the river," he said, "If they are advancing we should be ready for them. We have almost got all of Baccelar's Brigade across. And some guns as well."

At that moment, a staff officer interrupted. "I beg your pardon, sir, but the post across the river has signalled a French force is advancing."

Another one broke in, "Look, up there, sir!" He was pointing towards Fontelas. Dark masses could be seen coming down from the crest of the hill.

"Well," said Beresford, "it looks as if there was no need to have sent you up there after all. Roberts, I think it would be best if you make your way to the river and secure your boats once all the infantry are across. Warre, you had best go with him. I don't think we can get you away today, Roberts. You would be sitting ducks out on the river. We shall have to see what happens." With that he strode away calling out instructions as he went.

Michael, Warre, and Lloyd walked their horses down to the wharf, pushing their way through blue and brown coated Portuguese infantry heading to the defensive lines. By the time they got to the river, the last of the Portuguese reinforcements were disembarking. The four Warre rabelos were just mooring up. Once the boats were secured the crews made for the tavern, and Michael and Warre joined them inside, leaving Lloyd with three rather sweaty horses to care for.

Inside the tavern the air was subdued. The rabelo crews had seen the advancing French from the river. Another staff officer was in there, distributing money to the captains for ferrying the troops across the river. Michael went to the bar and got a bottle of wine and two glasses, and sat at a table in the corner. Warre had taken the staff officer aside and was speaking to him quietly. The officer looked a little surprised, and then nodded, before leaving the tavern. After he had left, Warre went over to a table where the four captains of the Warre boats were sitting. After a few words they all nodded.

Warre joined Michael. "He's from the Paymaster General's. I have arranged for four thousand dollars to be lodged with Medeiros. He'll let me know later once that has happened. It will take a little while; all non-essential baggage has been left on the other side of the river. I have told the captains; they still seem happy enough. In the meantime, I suggest we have a drink, and see if we can find some food."

Half an hour later Michael and Warre were enjoying a rich, local stew, which the tavern owners wife had produced for them. With a bottle of red wine and some crusty bread it was, thought Michael, as perfect a meal as you could ask for. A little later Lloyd appeared, and Michael ordered the same for him, Lloyd sitting himself down with some of the Portuguese boatmen, and trying out his Portuguese on them.

"That was quite a bit of excitement, Michael." They had finished their meal and were just enjoying the wine.

The remark took Michael back to those frantic few moments in the small village, he couldn't now even remember its name. He remembered the moment of panic as he parried the Frenchman's thrust, and the shock in his arm as his blade had struck home. It had happened so quickly that there had been no time to think. "Yes, I suppose it was, rather." He paused. "That was my first fight."

"Really? I rather thought…" Warre nodded at the scar on Michael's face.

"What? Oh, no. That was an accident." Michael felt awful, lying to Warre, but believed it was necessary.

At that moment, the crash of cannon came to their ears, and then the sound of distant musketry. Inside the tavern all conversation suddenly stopped and the sounds of battle became clearer. The boatmen silently left the tavern, their faces stern. Within a few minutes only the three cavalrymen remained, along with the landlord and his wife, who had emerged from the kitchen to stand with her husband.

"Lloyd?"

"Yes, sir?"

"How are the horses?"

"I've got them in a little stable a few streets back, sir, they're in good fettle, just a little tired, and I have someone keeping an eye on them. I couldn't get any hard feed for them, though."

"Thank you, Lloyd. William, do you think the Portuguese will hold the French? You know them better than I do."

"Well, we've more than a brigade in a fortified position, and with guns. The French might be able to force the position, but I am not sure they will be willing to pay the cost of that."

"Then we can leave the horses, and perhaps try another bottle?"

It wasn't long before the distant sounds of musketry and artillery faded into silence. Shortly afterwards the staff officer from the paymaster General's came back in. He was smiling.

"Well, that was rather satisfactory."

Warre indicated an empty chair, inviting the officer to join them, and waving at the landlord for another glass. "What happened?"

"I don't think they were expecting the town to be so well defended. They advanced a couple of brigades in column, our guns made good practice and then they got shot up short of the defences. They didn't lose a lot of men, but they must have decided it wasn't worth the candle to push hard. It was all a bit half-hearted. At the moment they are retreating back towards Mesão Frio along the riverside road." He took a large swig from the glass of wine Warre had poured him. "Hmm, that's better. Anyway, I am just off across the river to pick up your money. It should be safe and sound with Medeiros in an hour or two. Depending on the French moving off the riverside there would seem to be no reason why you shouldn't get the boats away at dawn tomorrow." He drained his glass and rose to his feet. "I'll let you know once it's delivered. I suppose you will be here or at Medeiros'? I shall need a receipt."

Warre nodded, and the officer left. Michael and Warre took their time, finished their wine and strolled out onto the wharf, followed by Lloyd. At Michael's suggestion they let Lloyd take them around to where he had the horses stabled. Inside the gloomy building the three horses were chomping away, contentedly, on fresh hay. Michael ran his hands over Johnny, and found nothing to concern him. All the tack was neatly piled behind each horse, and was being watched over by a young Portuguese boy of about twelve.

"This is Emilio, sir, he helped me rub the horses down and feed them. I asked him to keep an eye on them for me."

Michael spoke to the boy, who smiled when he heard Portuguese. "Emilio, is it?" The boy nodded. "Thank you for looking after the horses." He put his hand in his pocket and pulled out a few coins. He threw a couple of vintines to Emilio, who grinned even more.

"Thank you, Senhor."

"Whose stable is this?"

"My father's, Senhor, but he is not here, he is away trying to buy hay."

"Where do you live?"

"Through there, Senhor." The boy pointed to a door at the end of the stables.

"Do you think that my man here," Michael pointed to Lloyd, "could stay here for a night or two? I will pay you."

"Of course, Senhor, we often have grooms stay here, there is a room for them. It is cheaper than a room in a hotel or tavern. Only five vintines a night."

"And food and drink?"

"I can fetch that from the tavern, Senhor."

"That's settled then." He switched to English. "Lloyd, I have arranged quarters here for you with young Emilio, he will get you fed and watered as well. But you had better come with us now so you know where we are billeted."

When they arrived at the Medeiros' house the officer from the Paymaster General's was waiting for them, with the four thousand dollars, and Warre signed a receipt before seeing it locked away in Medeiros' strong box. That done the two men walked back down to the wharf to speak to the rabelo crews, and Lloyd set off to return to the stables. The rabelos were all moored to the wharf with no sign of any crews, so, once again, they took themselves off to the tavern.

It was now late afternoon, and the tavern was quiet, however, the four captains were there, waiting to hear from Warre. As they entered, Gama called out to them, "Senhors, please, join us," and a couple more chairs were pulled up to the table. The landlord appeared with two glasses and Gama poured them a good measure each.

"Thank you, gentlemen, your health." Warre made the toast and he and Michael raised their glasses to the captains. "Now, the money is with Senhor Medeiros, and will be paid to you, by him, when you return from Oporto." The rabelo captains nodded their approval. "Lieutenant Roberts will go with you. You must take your orders from him. Regrettably I cannot travel with you, Marshal Beresford needs me with his army." The captain nodded again at this, and looked a little hard at Michael. "You need have no reservations about the Lieutenant," said Warre, "he loves Portugal as I do."

Michael decided to join in the conversation. "Major Warre, If I may?" Warre gave him the floor. "I cannot claim to know the Douro, like the Major here, but I am as much Portuguese as I am English. I think of Lisbon as my home, I grew up there." The captains listened carefully, and Michael pressed on. "My parents died fleeing Lisbon because of the French. I have as much desire to see them thrown out of Portugal as you do. To do that we must get these boats to Vila Nova," he referred to the town on the south side of the Douro, opposite Oporto itself. "Without them the army cannot cross the river. That means that I will not ask you to take any unnecessary risks with them, or your crews. We just need to be there by the day after tomorrow."

The captains all looked at each other and then Gama spoke. "Lieutenant, we do not doubt you for a moment.

God willing, this is something that we can do, with empty boats we think we can arrange it to arrive soon after dawn. We should leave at first light, six o'clock. We think we can easily reach the ferry at Avintes tomorrow evening, where there is a good mooring. From there it is only a couple of hours to Oporto."

"That sounds perfect," Michael looked at Warre, who nodded. "Then I shall be on the wharf at half past five."

The captains left to ensure that boats and crews would be ready in the morning. Warre left to go and find Marshal Beresford and bring him up to date with events and the plans for the next day. He also wanted any information on where the French had withdrawn to. Michael found himself alone, he could just hear the voices of the landlord and his wife at the back of the tavern somewhere. There was nothing to be done, except wait. He wasn't hungry, he didn't want any more wine. Lloyd was taking care of the horses. He rubbed his chin. He had shaved that morning, and while he wouldn't have time in the morning, and he didn't know when he would next get the chance to shave, it wasn't worth another shave. No, damn it, he would shave, and more than that, he would have a bath and put on his last clean shirt.

He strolled back to his quarters and with the help of the expenditure of a few vintines pressed upon the maid, he arranged for a tub of hot water in his room. He also got some rags from her and cleaned the blood from his sabre. He hadn't long finished his rather leisurely bath and shave, and finished dressing when he heard Warre's voice. Looking out of his room, Warre was just coming up the stairs.

"Ah, there you are, Michael. Senhor Medeiros has invited us to join him and his wife for a bite of supper. I think he's opened something special to mark beating the French today."

Michael laughed, "Well, if you and Senhor Medeiros think it's something special, then I would be foolish to refuse the invitation."

And it was, indeed, something special.

That night Michael lay in his bed, trying to get to sleep. He would have to be up at four o'clock, it was already eleven, and he was wide awake. The events of the day, and in particular the skirmish in the little village, were replaying, again and again in his head. He could still feel the jar in his arm when his sabre had cut through the Frenchman's jaw. He wondered if he had killed him. Killed him? He could have been killed himself if he hadn't caught and turned that thrust. Lloyd had been good, that had been quite a snap shot that he got off, and he had gone for his Frenchman like the very devil. And then the ride back to Regua. He was amazed that none of them had fallen as they had slipped and slithered down the hill. All in all it had been quite a day. Tomorrow promised to be another one. He had to admit to himself that he was more than a bit nervous. It was strange, on one hand it seemed as if the whole success or failure of this campaign hinged on him in the next two days, and there again, it seemed as if all he had to do was enjoy a boat trip down a river. Gradually the last of the excitement ebbed away, and Michael fell asleep.

The next day started well, which lasted for all of an hour. When he got up he found that Warre had already left the house. The cook was up and supplied him with hot coffee and fresh bread rolls. He asked about Senhor Medeiros and was informed that he already gone down to the wharf. Apparently early starts were not uncommon in the wine business. Michael collected his valise from his room and set off. He called in on the horses on the way, Lloyd was busy with them, with the boy, Emilio, helping him. Lloyd assured him that he would take great care of Johnny, and rejoin the regiment as soon as he could, and would be guided by Major Warre in the best course of action. They wished each other luck, and Michael walked the last few hundred yards to the wharf.

A faint glimmer of light was beginning to show above the mountains to the east, but the wharf was empty. He walked quickly to where the rabelos were moored, there was not a sign of anyone. Then he saw light from the windows of the tavern a little further down the quayside. Inside all the rabelo crews were sitting around with coffee and rolls, and Warre was with them.

"There you are, Michael, come and sit down, have some coffee, I'm afraid that you're not going anywhere just yet."

"What? Why not? What's happened?" He took a chair across the table form Warre.

"It seems the French have left a rear guard at the bridge over the Seromenha where it enters the Douro. There is a possibility that there is a gun there. If there is, it will cover the river just as well as the road. Until we can be sure they have gone, it would be madness to try to sail down the river."

Michael groaned and looked at the ceiling, stained brown with tobacco smoke. "When will we know?"

"It's only about four miles to the bridge, but there's a few more miles of road beyond there that command the river, we have to be sure they are clear of that as well. I think it will be another two hours, if the news is good, less if it's bad. The patrol that went out should be almost at the bridge by now. There's nothing we can do but wait."

By half past six it was fully light. Impatient, Michael walked out on the quayside and stared down river. "Here you are, sir." It was Lloyd who had appeared at his side with a mug of coffee.

"Thank you Lloyd. It seems my farewell was a little premature."

"Yes, sir. I did hear."

Michael warmed his hands on the drink, there was still a bit of a chill in the air, with the sun just beginning to show over the hills. The two men stood staring away to the west, watching as the shadow of the hills behind them moved slowly down the western hills towards the river.

Half an hour later a horseman came into view, galloping along the road next to the river. Michael and Lloyd saw him at the same time, and Michael sent Lloyd to get Warre. Within minutes a staff officer was reining in his sweat covered horse next to them. "They've gone, the road's clear as far as I could see, and I went as far as Rede, where the road leaves the river and climbs towards Mesao Frio. Now I need to tell Beresford." And he rode off towards the Marshal's headquarters.

"Right, let's get you off, Mr Roberts." Warre turned to the tavern where Gama was looking out from the doorway, and he shouted to him, "Come on, Gama, get everyone aboard, the river is clear!" Gama waved, and disappeared inside for a moment, to reappear followed by the captains and crews of the four rabelos. The boats were all ready and within minutes Michael was on Gama's boat as they cast off from the wharf. The crews laboured at the oars, pulling the boats out into the current.

The crew stood at the oars, facing forwards. Gama was up on the high platform with two crewmen to help him manage the massive, thick steering oar, almost as long as the boat, that projected out behind. Gama looked down at Michael, and smiled. "Now, Senhor, we will show you how we sail the Douro."

Michael looked back, over the stern, and was surprised to see that they had already moved well out from the wharf, and were moving surprisingly quickly. He could see Warre and Lloyd watching. Then he turned his attention to the right bank, that was where any danger would lie. The river curved around to the left and Regua was lost from view. Another long bend followed, around to the right, and then Michael could see down a long, almost straight stretch of the Douro. "Senhor!" Gama called down to him. "We can see all the way to Rede, once we are past there we should be clear of any French."

Swiftly the boats moved along, carried by the strong current. Soon they passed the bridge across the Seromenha where the French rear guard had been. The riverside road remained empty of any signs of life at all. Then they were passing Rede, with its fields and orchards. A small patrol of Portuguese light infantry were on the river bank, and as they passed them they heard them shout that there were no French in sight. Michael waved back, as did the crews. It was the news he had hoped for. Now it should be a simple matter of cruising down the river and finding a suitable landing place near Oporto.

Gama called down to Michael. "Senhor, you should come and stand by the mast. You can hold on to it while we pass down the rapids."

"Rapids?" Michael suddenly recalled Warre saying something about rapids.

"Yes, Senhor, but do not worry, we have passed over them many times."

Looking ahead Michael could see huge blocks of granite on both shores, some projecting out into the river. Two of the crew were taking up positions in the bow, each with a long pole. The others had stopped rowing and were stowing away their oars. Michael could see white water and spray ahead, and he took a firm hold on the mast. The boat was picking up speed, and now Michael could hear a roaring sound. He heard Gama shout, "Pray!" Then the boat crashed into the white water, spray breaking over the bow, soaking the men there, it scraped along rocks, the men at the bow frantically pushing the boat away from the granite outcrops. On the platform Gama and his helpers heaved at the steering oar.

Then they were through, only for Michael to realise that there were more rapids immediately ahead. Again they crashed through white water. The river swung right and then left around a huge granite outcrop. Half way round, in the middle of a series of rapids, Michael was astounded to see a painting on a flat granite face. Gama saw him looking, and called out to him, "That is Our Lady of the Safe Journey!" He took a hand from the steering oar briefly to cross himself, as did all the crew. Michael felt moved to throw her a quick salute.

The rapids came to an end, the progress of the boat became steadier, and the crew took up the oars again. The vine covered hills had given way to much steeper slopes, covered with wild vegetation. More rapids followed at regular intervals, but much less severe, and the boats sailed swiftly on. Michael checked his watch, they had been sailing for less than two hours, and must have already travelled eight or nine miles.

"Senhor?" It was Gama. "We are approaching the falls at Figueira Velha and Cadao. They are very dangerous. You must hold on very tight." Michael nodded, and tried to smile nonchalantly, he realised that it must be more like a rictus grin. Gama laughed, "Do not worry, Senhor, I have not drowned anyone, yet!"

A massive granite rock marked the beginning of the rapids. The boats crashed down through the gloomy narrows, faster, spray flying higher. Then the river split into two channels, and Gama, followed by the other rabelos, steered for the left hand one. As they emerged from the channel, the boat plummeted dramatically down another set of rapids with an even greater drop. Gama kept the boat to the left of the rapids, and Michael saw on the right of the river a tumble of huge granite rocks, which they steered well clear of. Here and there the rapids turned, and eddied, causing whirlpools, ready to suck down man or boat.

There was a brief respite, with three lesser rapids, and then they were flying down another great rapid, before they were through and passed into relatively calmer waters. For a brief few minutes the rapids continued less fiercely, long enough for Michael to take notice of their surroundings. The steep, granite cliffs on the right bank had given way to gentler slopes with olive woods, chestnut trees and meadows. Then they were in the rapids again. They came, less fiercely, but again and again.

Michael shouted up to Gama, "How many more rapids?"

"Another fifty or so, Senhor, but only three bad ones!"

Michael nodded in reply. It was not what he had expected, this was no gentle cruise.

An hour later and Michael had counted another twenty eight rapids. Gama called down to him, "Senhor, we are coming up to Porto Antigo, there on the left, and Porto Manso opposite. Just past them is the Pass of Escarnicha. One of the bad ones, Senhor."

A few more rapids took them past the two small villages, and into a narrow channel between a large sandbank and a rocky shore. Then they were in the narrow passage of the Escharnicha, the river making a hard turn to the left between high, rocky slopes. Great granite slabs jutted out into the river, the water crashing against them, throwing up sheets of spray. Then they were through the pass, the river straightened, and a few more minor rapids saw them in calm water again.

Michael was feeling battered, exhausted, more than a little damp, and he hadn't been working the boat like Gama and the crew. It would, he thought, be a long time before he forgot the feel of the rough wood of the mast. He gave up trying to count the rapids. One of the crew passed him a skin of rough, red wine and a piece of bread. Michael ate and drank even as they shot down more rapids. They passed a town that Gama pointed out as Lavadouro.

Twenty minutes later they entered a deep gorge amidst a mass of thundering, racing water. The boats fought their way through two sets of rapids before reaching calm water, and there was another painting on a towering granite rock face.

"Senhor," Gama called down to Michael, raising his voice over the roar of the rapids behind them, "it is Our Lady of Cardia, and her Holy Family." Gama and the crew had all removed their hats, the crews in the other boats doing the same, and every man offering a prayer of thanks for their safe journey.

Michael removed his tarleton, and quietly muttered a heartfelt "Amen."

Soon they were passing by the town of Vimiero, and the river had quietened down. The rapids were less frequent now. In the next two hours there were only four, as they passed the towns of Fontelas and then Entre Ambos os Rio, divided in two by the river Tamega that joined the Douro. There the river turned in a huge loop, to turn back on itself, and there lay the very last of the rapids, the notorious Pedras de Linhares. The river carried them, roaring, into the long, straight, narrow, and deep gorge, the water rushing unimpeded, the speed increasing, the bows dipping under waves that crashed over the boat. All four boats scraped through; Michael distinctly felt his drag along the bottom for a few moments. Then they were in a slower current than before, and the crews began to row again.

Michael took a deep breath and calmed himself. He looked at his watch for the first time since leaving Regua. It was a little after two o'clock in the afternoon. He looked up and spoke to Gama. "How much longer before Oporto?"

"Another five hours, Senhor, depending on the tide."

"The tide?"

"Yes, it reaches as far up the river as Melres. Climb up here, Senhor, and we can decide what to do."

The two crewmen who had been helping Gama with the rudder now climbed down and went to help with the rowing. Michael climbed up and stood on the platform, one hand on the massive steering oar.

"It will be dark just after nine 'clock, Senhor, we could be in Oporto for about seven o'clock, but I do not think would be a good idea." Gama smiled.

"No, it wouldn't," Michael laughed, "and we are not expected until tomorrow morning."

"Then, I think we should do as we discussed, moor up at Avintes for tonight, we can leave at dawn, and easily be on the outskirts of Oporto for about eight o'clock. If your army is there, we will find them, if not, perhaps we can get back up river and try again the day after, if the French don't see us."

"Yes, that sounds just right, let's do it."

Four hours later the rabelos pulled cautiously towards the shore at Avintes. Gama suggested that Michael stay out of sight under the steering platform, they had no idea if there might be a French presence there. As they approached they could see that there was a ferry there, but the large boat was half out of the water, one end on the beach, the other almost awash in the waters of the Douro. A large crowd was gathered around it, and it was clear that work was underway to salvage the ferry and refloat it. A few other, smaller boats also lay drawn up on the sandy shore. When the rabelos were spotted three men put off from the beach, two rowing hard towards them.

The crews of the rabelos stopped rowing, and waited while the small boat approached. The man in the stern stood up and shouted. "Don't go any further, the French are in Oporto!"

Michael stepped carefully across to the side of the boat. "I know," he shouted back, "we are here to help get them out of Oporto, and out of Portugal!"

Chapter 17

The four rabelos ran onto the beach next to the ferry, and the crews made them fast with ropes to trees lining the shore. Michael and the four captains were soon seated on the ground under a large chestnut tree with the owner of the ferry, Senhor Costa. It was him who had rowed out to them.

"The French came two days ago, cavalry," Costa explained, "they were looking for boats. The people here had hidden their small boats that they use every day, and the French did not find them, but the ferry was here, and could not be hidden. The French prised a gap in the planking and the ferry sank." He smiled. "Fortunately it was high tide, they did not realise the river is affected by the tides here. After they had gone, the tide went out, the river dropped, and we secured empty wine barrels to the ferry. Then the tide came in, the ferry rose in the water, and we pulled it ashore on logs laid on the sand. We did that twice, and now we can repair the planking. The ferry should be afloat again sometime tomorrow morning."

"Senhor, that is very good news." Michael was impressed. "Will you keep the ferry on this side?"

"Yes, of course, Senhor, until we know it is safe to cross the river again."

"Tomorrow," said Michael, "we are going to sail down towards Oporto, and, hopefully, meet the British army at Vila Nova, or thereabouts. If the army cannot use our boats to cross they will want to know the ferry is working again, especially if the French think it is out of operation. Can you send someone to Vila Nova in the morning to pass that message?"

"Of course, Senhor," replied Costa, "it is less than two leagues. They can be at Vila Nova a couple of hours after dawn."

"Then let us hope that the army is there by then!"

The group broke up, the ferry owner going to continue supervising the repairs, and Michael and the captains walked back to the rabelos, where an evening meal was being prepared on fires on the beach. Michael put his sabre and belt in the bottom of the boat along with his Tarleton. From his valise he took his much more comfortable forage cap, and a silver plated cup, from his sabretache he got out his knife, fork and spoon. He would have to borrow a plate or bowl. Dinner was a spicy pork stew, served with bread and good, red wine. Each rabelo crew sat together, and after they had doffed their hats and given thanks to God for the day's events, they fell to with gusto. Much of the talk was about the days voyage, it was rare for the crews to voyage downstream with empty boats. Usually they were heavily loaded with barrels of wine, bound for the port lodges of Vila Nova.

They asked Michael what he thought of the journey, and some good natured ribbing followed his admission that he had not realised just how many rapids there were, nor how fearsome some of them were. Gama admitted that the boats being empty had made a difference to the way they handled. It had been, "a lively voyage, Senhor, everything had happened a little quicker than usual."

After the dinner was finished, and the wine drunk, Michael took a walk over to where work was continuing on the ferry. Night had fallen, and a large bonfire had been lit to give some illumination for the work. He walked a little further on, out of the light, and sat on the sand, with his back against a tree that lay where it had been washed ashore. He removed his forage cap and tipped his head back against the tree. Looking up the sky was ablaze with stars. It had been quite a day; it had been quite a few days. He would never take a glass of port for granted again. Truth be told, the trip down the river had given him more than a few moments of concern.

Tomorrow would be another day to give him concern. At least, so far, he was in the right place at the right time. His biggest concern was that they would sail down the Douro to find the army hadn't arrived and that they would be captured by the French. He thought of the idea of Renard discovering that he was a prisoner. He shivered. It was getting cool, he told himself, and made his way back the fires by the rabelos.

As the fires died down, the crews made themselves comfortable on the sand, wrapped up in blankets. Gama gave Michael one, and he stretched himself out by the fire. With the noise from the work on the ferry, and the inevitable noise of frogs and other nocturnal creatures, sleep just would not come. Thus it was that Michael was staring up at the stars when the western horizon was lit by a brilliant flash of light, followed a few seconds later by a crashing boom that rolled and echoed down the river valley.

For a moment there was not a sound save the for the fading echo, then everyone was up on their feet and shouting at once. It took Michael another moment to realise what it probably was. The French must have blown up the bridge of boats between the south and north sides of the Douro, between Vila Nova and Oporto. If that was what it was, then it must mean that all the French were on the north side of the river, and that the British army was close to Vila Nova. He smiled to himself in the darkness. If he was right, things were looking promising.

When Michael woke it was still dark, but the crews were up and about, the fires rekindled, coffee being prepared. Over at the ferry there was no sign of any activity. A mug of coffee was pressed into his hands by a dark figure, and he sipped the sharp, hot drink gratefully, feeling it warming his hands and his insides. It was cold in the predawn dark. Slowly, the sky began to lighten, and the scene on the beach became clearer. A crewman handed him a chunk of bread, it was getting a bit stale, but was welcome. A figure stood next to him, and he realised it was Costa, the ferry owner.

"Senhor, we have repaired the ferry, we simply need to bale out the last of the water, and then get it back on the river. Once it is empty of water it should slide down the logs easily enough. We will have a lot of help."

"And the messenger?"

"He will leave when you do Senhor. Do you wish to give him a written message?"

Michael thought about that for a moment. "No, just in case there are French about. They might shoot him as a spy if he is caught with such message. But he can tell any British officer that Lieutenant Roberts is on the river and that Colonel Murray must be told."

"Perhaps you should tell him yourself, Senhor?"

Costa indicated a young lad, barely a teenager, standing nearby. He waved the boy forward.

"This is Ignacio, Senhor. He knows the country between here and Vila Nova very well."

Michael smiled encouragingly at the boy. "Hello, Ignacio. Are you ready to go?"

"Yes, Senhor."

"You must be very careful, you must only speak to the British, look for men in redcoats, and with gold on their shoulders, those are the officers."

"Senhor, you have a blue coat?"

Michael smiled. "Yes, I do. Or if you see someone in a coat exactly like mine, and with a hat with fur, like mine. Follow me, I'll show you." He walked across to the rabelo and asked a crewman aboard to pass him his tarleton. "Here, this is my helmet, and anyone wearing one of these should be on a horse."

"Yes, Senhor."

"Now," continued Michael, "what I want you to tell them is that Lieutenant Roberts sent you, that's me, and tell them that I am on the river, tell them about the rabelos, and tell them about the ferry. Tell them they must pass on your message to Colonel Murray. Can you remember that?"

"Yes, Senhor, you are Lieutenant Roberts, you are on the river, there are four rabelos and the ferry will soon be afloat. And they should tell Colonel Murray."

"Exactly, good lad. And be careful."

There was a shout from the river. The four rabelos were floating just off the beach, and Gama was standing on the steering platform, and waving at Michael to get aboard. "Thank you, Senhor, Costa. I hope we meet again soon." They shook hands and Michael hurried down the beach, splashing through the water until he was hauled bodily aboard the rabelo.

"We have the tide with us this morning," Gama informed Michael, "It will make the journey much easier, but we will go carefully." He looked at Michael in his blue jacket with all the silver braid on it. "Perhaps you should slip on an old cloak, I think there's one in the stern somewhere. You look too much a soldier."

The rabelos slipped quietly along, towards Oporto. The crews rowed very gently; the boats were moving with the current as the tide ebbed. The river was much wider here, and the land sloped down to it much more gently, with cultivated fields on either side, and the hilltops crowned with chestnuts and pines. They had the river entirely to themselves, and nothing was moving on either shore. From Avintes the river swept around to the right and then flowed almost due north.

The tension amongst the crew was palpable. Every eye was turned to the right bank, watching for the slightest hint of French troops. Another mile, or less, and the river widened more as it began a long sweeping turn to the left. Gama began to steer gradually towards the right bank, followed by the other boats.

"Senhor Roberts," Gama was almost whispering, "we must keep to the right bank now. At the next bend the left side of the river is visible from Oporto."

Michael nodded. The left bank was still sloping gently down, but the right now rose steeply and looking ahead he could see a large building that overlooked the Douro on top of the cliff that flanked the river. "What's that building?" Michael asked Gama.

"An old seminary, Senhor, I think it is abandoned now."

"Can you pull in under the cliffs there?"

"Yes, Senhor, and we should be as well-hidden there as anywhere. Let us hope there are no French sentries."

They slowly eased the boats in towards the rocky shoreline under the cliffs below the seminary. Crewmen leapt ashore with mooring ropes and made the rabelos fast to rocks. Michael took out his watch, a few minutes after eight o'clock. Perfect, he hoped. Immediately across the river from them was a narrow beach, and a small quay, then the left bank also rose up to cliffs, and a little way ahead he could make out the roofs of a large building.

"What's that building across the river?" Michael asked Gama.

"It is the Monastery of Serra do Pilar."

At that moment there was a shout from the rearmost of the rabelos. The crew had seized hold of a man who was struggling and swearing. Michael and Gama scrambled along the shoreline towards the commotion. Gama demanded to know what was happening. Barreto, who was the captain of that rabelo explained.

"We caught this fellow sneaking along amongst the rocks. He was armed with this!" He held up a razor.

The man caught sight of Michael, "Is he an English officer?" he asked.

"Yes, I am," Michael replied. "What are you doing?"

"I was hoping to cross the river and find someone, Senhor, to tell them what I can about the French."

"And the razor?"

"I am a barber, Senhor, it is the only weapon I have."

"And how were you going to cross the river?"

"I have a little skiff, Senhor, I hid it from the French who were taking all the boats. They have them all in Oporto."

Michael turned to Gama, "That might be useful, a skiff will attract less notice on the river than one of the rabelos." He turned back to the barber. "The seminary up there, are there any French in it?"

"No, Senhor, it is empty, deserted."

Michael looked up the cliff. There was a steep, narrow path winding up the cliff. "Does that path lead to the seminary?

"Yes, Senhor."

"Gama, I need to see if the seminary is deserted, it completely commands this bend in the river. If it is held by the French it will make any crossing very difficult. Hold on to our friend here. If you see any British over there, take the skiff across and tell them what is happening."

Michael dropped the cloak and his forage cap into Gama's rabelo, and removed his sabre, it would just be a nuisance on the climb. "Senhor, take this." Barreto was offering him a folding stiletto. He nodded his thanks, and slid the knife into the scarlet sash around his waist.

The path was steep, zigzagging up the cliff, and Michael found himself crawling up it on his hands and knees. He was half expecting to hear a challenge in French, followed by the crash of a musket. He paused as he got near the top, listening carefully. Nothing. No murmurs of conversation, no cough or sneeze, no clatter of accoutrements against rocks. Just the buzz of insects. He crawled on and up. The path came up halfway along the side of the seminary overlooking the river. As it reached the top, it broadened out, there were steps, a retaining wall to his left. He peered cautiously over the wall. The seminary was over a hundred yards long, with dozens of windows on three floors. There was no sign of life.

Between Michael and the seminary was a wide courtyard, and then, almost opposite him, an open doorway. He paused a little longer, still listening for the slightest sound. Still nothing. He eased the knife from his sash and opened it. Then he strode up the steps and across the intervening yards to the doorway. Reaching it, he flattened himself against the outer wall to one side, and listened again. Nothing. He took a deep breath, and stepped inside.

Ten minutes later Michael was making his way back down to the river, the seminary was empty. Reaching the boats he eagerly accepted a proffered jug of water. "It's empty, he was telling the truth. This part of the river is completely unguarded." He shook his head. "It beggars belief, but there it is." He took another long drink.

"Senhor!" It was one of the crew. "There is a horseman on the other shore!"

Michael turned and stared across the river. Sure enough, there was a horseman, and wearing a redcoat. He appeared to be studying the rabelos through a telescope. Michael stepped up onto the side of the boat, gripping on the supports for the steering platform, and he waved at the figure.

"Quickly now," he addressed the barber, "where is your skiff?"

"Behind those bushes." He pointed to an area of scrubby growth about fifty yards back upstream.

"Gama, can you send a couple of men to bring the skiff here?"

"Yes, Senhor." And two men were off, scrabbling across the rocks towards the bushes.

Michael looked back to the other bank. For a moment he thought the horseman had gone. Then he reappeared, on foot, from a copse of trees. Michael thought that he must have tied his horse there to be less conspicuous. Well, if there were any French about, now was the time they would be spotted. The skiff was quickly alongside the rabelo, Michael grabbed his sabre and cap, and climbed down into it. "Right, across the river as fast as you can, please." The two men grinned and laid on their oars with a vengeance, sending the small skiff flying across the still waters of the Douro.

The redcoated officer was standing at the shoreline as they approached. The skiff grounded on the small beach and Michael splashed ashore. He saw that the man was a staff officer, and a Colonel. "Lieutenant Roberts, sir, 16th Light Dragoons."

"Waters. Was it you sent the young lad with a message about the ferry at Avintes?"

"Yes, sir."

Waters nodded his approval. "There are troops on the way there now. But these," he pointed at the four rabelos, "are really something. And the crews are ready, they know what the idea is?"

"Yes, sir. And I have been up to the seminary." It was Michael's turn to point, up at the large, imposing edifice on the cliff top. "It's empty."

"Is it, by God!? Right, as there's no sign of any French, you get back across and bring those boats over to here, and keep them safe. Run back upstream if you have to, but keep 'em safe. I'm going to report to Sir Arthur. He's just up at the monastery." He turned away, and then paused, looking back at Michael. "Well done, Roberts, very well done." With that he hurried to his horse, and was soon galloping away.

As they rowed back across to the rabelos, Michael looked at his watch. It was just a quarter past ten. Half an hour later and the four rabelos were lying at the quay on the south bank of the Douro. The slopes up towards the monastery, now hidden from view, were steep and tree covered. As Michael and the rabelo crews waited they became aware of noises from the slopes, getting closer. Then Waters reappeared, with a handful of other horsemen, and behind them the head of a column of British infantry. Michael recognised the 3rd Foot, known as the Buffs, leading.

Waters rode to the quay, dismounting along with two other redcoated senior officers. "Gentlemen, this is Lieutenant

Roberts." Michael came to attention and saluted. "Roberts," Waters completed the introductions, "General Paget, who is going to lead the occupation of the seminary, and General Hill, whose troops these are."

Paget spoke. "Well done, Roberts, now, let's get these men across."

Each of the rabelos was quickly packed with about sixty men, barely leaving room for the rowers, and the crews set to work to ferry them across the river. Michael went across on the first one, to point out the path up to the seminary. A young captain was to lead the first men up. He looked up at the high cliffs and the imposing building. "And you say it's empty?" he asked Michael.

"It was an hour ago, and we've seen no movement up there since."

"Let's hope it still is, it's like a fortress."

Michael stayed on the north bank while the rabelos went back for the next wave of infantry. The first of the Buffs disappeared up the path, and Michael waited, anxiously. There were no shouts, or shots.

As the rabelos returned there was a scattering of stones down the path and a sergeant appeared, grinning. "Still empty, sir, and a right fortress too." The sergeant saw a major on one of the next boats bringing the next infantry across, and he went off to report to him. Michael sat on a rock, took his cap off, and wiped his forehead. The next groups of Buffs went past him and up the cliff with barely a glance at him.

All at once Michael felt very, very weary, and completely at a loss, but also very, very relieved. So far as he could tell, he had done everything that he had been asked to do. Now it was all down to the infantry. He decided that he would just sit quietly for a while, and do nothing except watch events as they unfolded.

On their third trip, the rabelos brought with them General Paget. Just as they were nearing the shore, the sound of firing broke out from the cliffs above. Paget leapt ashore and hurried up the path, followed by the remaining companies of the Buffs. The whole battalion was now across the river, about seven hundred men, so far as Michael could tell.

For a few minutes, the sounds of musket fire continued, and then, with a massive roar, British artillery on the south bank, up around the monastery, opened fire. The top of the cliffs opposite disappeared in clouds of white smoke, and Michael heard the roundshot buzzing across the river, far above him. Then came explosions as the shrapnel shells fired from howitzers burst. It seemed to Michael that there must be three batteries firing, eighteen guns and howitzers. He couldn't be sure from where he was, but he thought they must be firing into the flank of the French attack on the seminary at a range of only six or seven hundred yards.

After a while, the fire slackened, and the rabelos continued to ply back and forth across the Douro. Michael realised that the fire of the British artillery was also preventing the French bringing any of their artillery into play against the boats. General Hill came across with the first of the 48th and the 66th, the other battalions in the brigade. He nodded at Michael as he hurried past to climb up to the seminary.

Infantrymen were helping at the oars as the crews tired. Each round trip was taking about half an hour, it was almost painfully slow, and there was a desperation in the efforts of the crews and the infantry. The artillery roared into life again, as another attack was made on the seminary. If they didn't take it the first time, Michael thought, they weren't going to now, as more and more infantry were added to the garrison of the seminary. Musket fire broke out, and for a few minutes there was a crescendo of firing from infantry and artillery that gradually died away as another attack was driven off.

By the time a couple of hours had passed, the rabelos had brought about a thousand infantry across the river. Another thousand were waiting patiently for their turn on the south bank. Another assault on the seminary came, but the flow of fresh infantry across the river and up to the seminary continued unabated. Again the firing died away, and this time was not renewed.

Then Gama, arriving with another load of infantry, called out to him. "Senhor, there are boats on the river in the city, they are carrying troops across!"

Michael jumped up at scrambled along the shore until he could see around the bend of the river. In the distance he could make out dozens of boats hurrying backwards and forwards across the river, carrying British infantry, visible in their redcoats, across to the wharves of Oporto. It looked as if the French were withdrawing, leaving the citizens of Oporto free to regain their boats and bring the infantry across. He watched for a while, and then made his way back to the crossing point.

The artillery fire from the monastery had stopped, and it sounded as if there was no more fighting up at the seminary, the only musketry he could hear from down on the river seemed to be some considerable distance away. On the river the last of the infantry were crossing, the tired crews taking longer now even with help. At last there were no more infantry to ferry across, and the crews sat wearily in their boats. Wine was passed around and bread shared out.

"What now, Senhor?" It was Gama, who handed Michael a drink and some bread.

"Thank you. To tell the truth, I have no idea." On the far bank Michael could see a handful of figures, with a few riderless horses. He supposed their owners would be back for them at some point. He had not seen Waters since they had started ferrying the Buffs over. It felt as if the tide of war had crashed over them and passed on, leaving them washed up and lost.

"Let's rest for a while, and then I think we should have two boats on each side of the river. I'll cross over and go and see what I can discover." He climbed aboard Gama's rabelo and rescued his valise from where it had been stowed away in the stern. "If you can let me have a length of rope I can sling this across my back." He stuffed his cap in the valise and put his tarleton on.

Once the crews had refreshed themselves, Gama and Barreto took their rabelos across to the south bank. Michael climbed ashore, and buckled on his sabre. "I will try and find out what you should do. We need to be sure you are no longer needed here, and then get you moored up somewhere safe until we can send you off back to Regua."

"Thank you, Senhor," said Gama. "We will stay until it is getting dark, and then we will take the boats around to Vila Nova and moor near the port lodge."

Michael took out his watch. "It's almost half past three. If I can't be back by, say, eight o'clock, I will look for you in Vila Nova."

The climb up from the Douro to the monastery was a steep one, and it was hot despite the shade of the trees covering the hillside. As Michael struggled to the top, half an hour after leaving Gama, the monastery itself came into view, and in the gardens in front of it he came across the artillery. Eighteen guns were still trained across the river at the open ground between Oporto and the seminary.

Gunners were busy cleaning out the barrels and reorganising after their continuous action. As he went by one, the gunners lifted the breech end high, and black, sulphurous water poured out, the gunners laughing as one of their number didn't get out of the way quickly enough. He walked on past them, hoping to see someone who he knew. He trudged on around the back of the monastery, and then found a road down towards the river. He emerged onto the wharves of Vila Nova under the cliffs topped by the monastery. Boats were still plying to and fro across the river and company after company of infantry were formed, waiting their turn to cross. He set off along the waterside. As he passed by the troops he heard the odd jest about 'an 'orseman with no 'orse.'

Eventually he found a harassed staff officer he thought he recognised from Coimbra. From him he learnt that Sir Arthur and Colonel Murray had crossed the river an hour before, he knew not where to. He did, however, get Michael a place on a boat, and before long he was standing on the quayside of Oporto itself. Then he had a stroke of good fortune, he came across Colonel Murray arguing with a prominent looking Portuguese gentleman, neither spoke the others language. As far as he could tell, it was something to do with a hospital. Michael stepped forward.

"Colonel Murray, may I be of assistance?"

Murray turned at this interruption, about to vent his wrath, but his expression changed when he saw who it was. "Roberts? By God, man, glad to see you, very glad to see you. Damned if you didn't pull it off, sir. Damned if you didn't. That was good work. Sir Arthur was pleased when Waters brought the news, I can tell you."

The Portuguese gentleman had stood quiet for a moment, but now burst into a torrent of protest.

Murray looked at Michael. "Can ye tell me what the devil he is on about?"

"Senhor, can I be of assistance? I am afraid that the Colonel doesn't understand Portuguese."

The man's face lit up. "Ah, Senhor, thank you! I am the superintendent at the hospital, and I want to know what to do with the French patients that I have?"

"I see. How many are there?"

"About seven hundred and fifty, Senhor, the hospital is overflowing, we cannot manage."

Michael explained to Murray what the problem was.

"Och!" Murray exclaimed. "Never mind looking after them, we need to do something to keep them alive. There's already been wounded French killed by the locals, although I suppose it's understandable given what has gone on here. Cut along the wharf here, you'll find a Portuguese battalion down there somewhere. Find the colonel, he's English, tell him to give you a company, and go with this fellow to his hospital and see that proper guards are posted. When you've done that, come and find me, I should be at headquarters, Soult's headquarters no less. Apparently it's called Palácio dos Carrancas. Think you can find it?"

"Yes, sir. Just one thing, sir!"

"What's that?" Murray snapped impatient to be off.

"The rabelos that I brought down from Regua. What should they do?"

Murray thought for a moment. "Damned if I know. We don't need 'em at the seminary, Hill's moved on and is in touch with us here. I suppose they might as well go home, if they think it's safe."

"Very good, sir, thank you."

Chapter 18

It took Michael an hour and a half to get the hospital secured. The Portuguese locals were not too happy, but the hospital staff were reassured by the presence of armed guards. And, as it happened, the hospital was only a few minutes' walk from the headquarters. Once past the guards he asked an orderly for directions to the Quartermaster General's department, and walking along a corridor he spied a familiar figure.

"Captain Scovell!" Michael hailed him.

Scovell turned when he heard his name called. "Roberts! Good to see you, I gather you have done rather well?"

"Thank you, sir, I hope so. It's been quite a few days, and the trip down the river was rather exciting." Michael could not help but grin.

"So what are you doing here?" Scovell asked him.

"Colonel Murray told me to meet him here, I don't know why."

"Right, you had best come along with me. He's just down here. He hasn't been in long. He's talking to Sir Arthur."

Moments later Scovell was leading the way into a large salon, the high ceiling decorated with ornate plaster work, and the deeply recessed windows topped with decorative panels. Sir Arthur Wellesley and Colonel Murray were preoccupied with maps and documents scattered over a large table. Sir Arthur was speaking.

"We can afford one days rest, Murray, I know the state the men are in, and all the artillery and cavalry are on the wrong side of the river, except for the two squadrons of the 14th. But we must know which way Soult has gone. Order John Murray to follow up and see where they go."

He looked up and saw Scovell and Michael. "Ah, Roberts, isn't it? You did well, Lieutenant, I'm grateful to you."

"Thank you, Sir Arthur."

Murray chipped in. "Roberts, I need to speak with you. Scovell, can you put him in my office, I shall be there shortly."

The two officers backed out of the room as Wellesley and Murray returned to their perusal of the maps and documents. Scovell showed Michael into another, equally opulent salon. "I must leave you here, I'm afraid, things to do, quarters to arrange, that sort of thing. And keeping the men still across the river out of the port lodges. If they get into those we shall need more than a day's rest. Glad to have seen you."

Left alone in the room, Michael looked at his watch, and wound it up, it was already getting on for half past seven. He wasn't going to get back to Avintes. He would go back across to Vila Nova, if he could, and look for Gama and the others at the wharf. He unslung his valise and sat down in a rather comfortable armchair. He thought he would just close his eyes for a moment.

A hand was shaking his shoulder, a voice was saying "Roberts, Roberts, come on, man, wake up."

Michael forced his eyes open to see Colonel Murray standing in front of him. He started to struggle to his feet. "Sit down, Lieutenant, too late now." He smiled at Michael. "I think you deserve a rest." He looked around the table and finally picked up a letter. "Now, this is what I want to speak with you about. It came to me with the latest despatches from London. It was in code, so I have, I'm afraid, seen what it says, although it's actually addressed to you." He handed the letter to a surprised Michael.

'Lieutenant Roberts, 16th Light Dragoons

As I am sending this in code it will be seen by Colonel Murray, who will decipher it. No matter, and it is as well he knows about this. Your black fox has been seen in Paris. He was there in December, but I have no reports of him since, which doesn't necessarily mean anything. He was in uniform, that of the 22nd Chasseurs, and they are, or were, with Soult in Oporto. Whether or not he is now with them is not known. I would like you, if possible, to look into that. Murray can let me know what you discover, if anything.

Musgrave'

Michael sat staring at the letter, stunned by the implications.

"There's little you can do tonight." Murray broke in on Michael's thoughts. "It will be dark in half an hour. I don't suppose you have a billet, do you?"

"Err, no, sir. I thought I would find my rabelo crews first."

"Are they still at Avintes?"

"They shouldn't be, sir, they planned to moor at Vila Nova before dark."

"Then I suggest you take yourself off across there quickly. There will be plenty of boats. We are still bringing troops across. And while you are over there, find your regiment, they should be bivouacked behind the convent. Tell Anson that I need you in Oporto for a few days. Oh, and tell him the army won't be moving tomorrow, but that we will bring the cavalry and artillery across at Avintes. Find yourself a horse, got any servants with the regiment?"

"Yes, sir."

"Find them, and get yourself back here for midday. I'll give you a billet and your orders then. Stay with your regiment tonight."

"Yes, sir."

"Then get along, and tomorrow we will see about how to comply with Musgrave's request. Goodnight, Roberts."

"Thank you, sir," Michael heaved himself to his feet and picked up his valise, "Goodnight."

It wasn't quite dark when Michael disembarked in Vila Nova. Fortunately, he had caught sight of the rabelos as he was being rowed across the river. A short walk along the wharf took him to the boats. The crews were busy stowing masts and oars and generally tidying up after the day's work. When they saw him he was greeted with smiles and waves. Gama waved to him to come aboard.

"I'm sorry I didn't get back to Avintes," Michael apologised to Gama, "but the news is you can take yourselves off home as soon as you are happy the river is safe. It probably is now, but it might be best to wait for a couple of days."

"That's good news, Senhor. Yes, I think we will stay for a few days, it will take us anything up to seven days to get the boats back upstream to Regua. And it looks like it is going to rain, which will put the river into spate. We will wait that out."

"Then I may see more of you. I am being kept in Oporto for a few days. Tonight I am going to find my regiment, which is up behind the monastery, somewhere."

"Good luck, Senhor. If you can't find them, we can always find you a few planks to lie on!" Gama grinned at him.

Michael slowly climbed back up the road he had come down earlier, and eventually found himself back on the heights overlooking the Douro and Vila Nova. Another half hour passed as he blundered around asking all and sundry if they knew where the Sixteenth was. Eventually a voice from the darkness challenged him to identify himself as a dark lantern was flashed at him.

"Lieutenant Roberts, Sixteenth Light Dragoons."

"Gawd! So it is. 'Ere, Sergeant, it's Mr Roberts."

The Sergeant pointed out a large fire to Michael and told him that was where he could find Colonel Anson. Anson and many of the Regiment's officers were sitting on logs or on the ground around the fire and Michael's sudden appearance out of the dark caused some surprise, and a few jests at his expense. Anson stood and gave him a long look.

"Well, Mr Roberts. Welcome home. Let's take a walk, and you can tell me where you've been."

Anson led the way into the darkness until they were out of earshot of the fire. There, Michael told him all that had happened since he had left the regiment a week before to organise billets in Coimbra. When he had finished, Anson was silent for a moment.

"That's quite a tale, Michael, quite a tale. I knew you had been sent off on some detached duty or other, but nothing more than that. Frankly, I was rather cross about it. Not your fault, of course, but we could have done with you. Cocks is still away somewhere, and Tomkinson has been fearfully wounded. Shot in both arms and the neck. I don't know if he will survive. I expect you will hear the story soon enough. Damned staff officer sent his troop down a lane in single file with French infantry lining the walls. The man was an idiot. But you didn't hear me say that. Anyway, we rather need you back with us, so I'm glad to see you."

Michael hesitated. "I'm sorry, sir, but Colonel Murray wants me in Oporto for a few days. There's something I have to look into."

"Dammit, Roberts!" Anson was clearly angered. He took a deep breath and was quiet. "Very well, I suppose we will manage. And you did a good job with those boats."

"Thank you, sir." Michael remembered what Murray had told him. "I can tell you that there won't be an advance tomorrow, sir, but the Regiment will be moved across the river by the ferry at Avintes. Colonel Murray told me himself."

"I suppose that's something. Well, let's get back to the fire. I think there may be some hot food shortly."

Michael passed a miserable night. He had no cloak, no blanket, they were on Johnny, he just had his valise for a pillow. The regimental baggage had not yet caught up with the regiment, so there was no relief from that quarter. The other officers, just as the men did, rolled themselves up in their cloaks and slept in pairs with one horse blanket under them, and one over them. He kept close to the fire, but in the early hours it died down, and he huddled up as close to the embers as he dare.

Before first light the bivouac began to come to life. The fire was rekindled and coffee put on. Michael at least had a mug in his valise, and was soon warming himself with the fire and the coffee. Captain Ashworth appeared, and Michael had to explain all over again where he had been. And also where he thought Lloyd was. At least Ashworth gave him some breakfast.

Orders arrived for the regiment. As Michel had said, they were to cross the river at Avintes, and make their way into Oporto, where billets had been arranged. Then, just as the Regiment was about to march off, the baggage finally appeared. Anson rode up to Michael.

"Roberts, you had better take charge of the baggage. Give you a chance to get your second horse. And you know where the ferry is. Catch up with us there, I expect we will be a while ferrying across." With that Anson rode off to relieve the officer currently with the baggage.

Michael soon found Francisco, who was delighted to see him, as were Pedro and Rafael, even if it meant that Pedro lost his place on Duke. And he found his baggage on one of Salvador Gomes' mules. Things were starting to look up.

Managing the regimental baggage was not a duty that any officer enjoyed. The officers of each troop had their servants, muleteers and mules, grooms and spare horses, and then there was the official, regimental baggage. The mules with camp kettles, tents, forage, the Surgeon's mule, the Veterinary officer's mule, the farriers' cumbersome two-wheeled carts, and last, but certainly not least, the wives of the dragoons who had been selected to follow the regiment on campaign. Michael had the assistance of a handful of dragoons who were, for various reasons, horseless, Price amongst them, and a few mounted troop quartermasters.

Michael managed to get all the baggage down to the beach at Avintes, just as the last of the Regiment was just crossing. Costa, the ferry owner, was a very happy man, as the British army was happy to pay for the use of his ferry, and all the cavalry and artillery and baggage and wagons and so on, had to cross by the ferry, at least until the bridge in Oporto could be repaired. Young Ignacio was also there, and Michael was able to thank him, and press some coins on him.

From the ferry landing on the north bank of the Douro to the billets in Oporto was some five or six miles. On their way they passed by the Seminary that had been the scene of the fierce fighting the day before. The ground was still littered with corpses, stripped naked by the Portuguese. Michael could see clearly the position occupied by the British artillery on the heights across the river. He could see how any troops crossing the ground from the city to attack would have been completely exposed to the fire of the guns.

It was late morning before the regiment was in its quarters on the east side of the city. Michael persuaded Gomes to let him have the use of one of his mules to carry his baggage, and accompanied by Francisco leading it, he set off on Duke to find Colonel Murray. He arrived at Headquarters just after midday. An orderly NCO directed Francisco around the Palacio to the rear where horses were being stabled. Michael went in and soon discovered that Murray was out in the city somewhere. He wandered through the Palacio and found his way to the Quartermaster Generals office. There he introduced himself, and a harried staff lieutenant found him a billet in the Palacio. Another orderly showed Michael to a small room on the top floor, it was completely empty. Then the orderly led him down to the grounds at the back of the house where Francisco was waiting, and left him there.

A couple of Portuguese grooms were lounging against a wall, and Michael persuaded them, with some choice Portuguese and a few coins, that they wanted to look after Duke and the mule. Together, Michael and Francisco carried Michael's baggage up several flights of stairs and to his room.

"Francisco, take the mule back to the regiment, and then see what you can do to make this place comfortable. For the moment at least you had better sleep here as well." He gave Francisco some of his dwindling supply of coins. "And on the way back see what you can buy in the way of supplies. I don't know how long we will be here."

"Yes, Senhor." Francisco looked around the bare room. "At least there is a roof."

Francisco set off on his errands and Michael made his way back down to Colonel Murray's office. There he found Murray had returned.

"Ah, Roberts, good, good." He looked around and picked up a piece of paper. "It seems that there is an officer of the 22nd Chasseurs in the hospital." He looked at Michael. "I suppose it would be too much to hope it's your man? Anyway, you had best get along and see if he can tell you anything. Got your billet allocated?"

"Yes, sir."

"Good, off you go, let me know if you discover anything. I can pass it on to the, err, relevant authority." He smiled. "We are moving on tomorrow, but Colonel Trant is moving in as Governor. You can help him while you carry out your enquiries." Murray turned to speak to a staff officer, and Michael made his escape.

As Michael left the Palacio it started to rain, lightly at first, but as he covered the short distance to the hospital it turned to a steady downpour. By the time he had walked from the rear of the hospital, which was nearest to the Palacio, around to the front, the rain was dripping off the peak of his helmet, and down the back of his neck, soaking his neckcloth.

Fortunately, at the main entrance, the Portuguese infantry he had posted the day before were still on duty. Their officer was quickly summoned and Michael explained that he was looking for an officer of the 22nd Chasseurs who was reported as being in the hospital. The Portuguese officer looked somewhat surprised, but directed Michael to the first floor, saying he was probably in one of the rooms off the balcony that ran along the rear of the hospital.

A high and wide flight of stairs led up to the first floor, and there a short corridor took Michael out onto the balcony. It stretched away in both directions, high, wide, empty, and, fortunately, in the lee of the hospital, as the rain lashed down. He took a guess, turned to the right and opened the first door. He stepped in, and rapidly back out again as a stench hit him. It was the smell of rotting flesh, ordure, vomit and God knew what else. He closed the door and took a deep breath of the rain scented air outside.

"Can I 'elp you, sir?" Michael turned and saw a small man wearing a blood soaked apron who had emerged from a door further along the balcony. "I wouldn't go in there, sir, they've all got gangrene in there, sir. Not long for this world."

Michael recovered himself. "Yes. I'm looking for a French cavalry officer, 22nd Chasseurs."

"Ah, right you are then, sir, there's only one Frenchie cavalry officer in 'ere, and he's down the other way, sir, sixth room along."

"What's wrong with him?" asked Michael.

"Musket ball smashed his arm, sir. It'll likely have to come off in the morning. If you've any business with him…"

Michael nodded. "Thank you. I'll find him myself; you can carry on." And he turned on his heel and walked away, along the balcony. He heard a door close and glancing back over his shoulder he saw that the balcony was once again deserted. Reaching the sixth door he opened it cautiously and stepped slowly in. The room was not particularly large, except it had a very high ceiling. A single window onto the balcony provided the only illumination.

In the corner of the room was a straw filled palliasse, next to it a jug, an empty bowl, and a mug. A figure lay on the palliasse covered in a blanket, with the remnants of a green jacket, trimmed with a light red piping lying over it. As

Michael approached the figure stirred and a hand, dirty and covered in dried blood, pulled the blanket down to reveal the face of a young man. He was about Michael's age, with a fine moustache and dark hair. He was probably quite handsome, but his hair was lank, his face hollow, unshaven, and streaked with grime, blood and sweat. He blinked in the light.

"Who are you?" He asked, in French.

Michael hadn't spoken French for years, but he spoke it well enough to get by with the occasional French visitor, or seaman down on the docks. He had wondered how to approach this conversation, suddenly it came to him. "I am an old friend of Jean-Paul Renard, I think he is in your regiment, the Twenty-Second?"

A startled look flashed across the man's face, and then he looked away. "No, I think you are mistaken. There is no one of that name."

Michael knelt down next to the man, placing himself in his line of vision, catching his eye, forcing himself to smile. "It's alright, there's nothing to worry about. We were boys together in Lisbon, we grew up together. We were good friends, I heard he was in the Twenty-Second and just wanted to hear some news of him. That's all."

The man returned Michael's look for a moment before he spoke again. "I have heard the name, but I do not know him. His father is a diplomat of some sort, and has kept his son safe in Paris. He has never joined the Regiment out here."

The man coughed, and winced with pain. Michael poured some water into the mug and lifted the man's head so that he could take a drink.

"Thank you."

"Are you quite sure about Jean-Paul, I would be relieved to hear he is safe and that we won't meet on the battlefield."

"Yes, Monsieur, he is quite safe in Paris, not like some of us."

Michael didn't know whether to feel relieved or disappointed. "Is there anything that I can do for you? Anything that you need?"

"Thank you, Monsieur. Another blanket, perhaps? And something to eat? I have seen no one for hours."

"I will see what I can do. Good luck, Monsieur, I hope that you recover."

Michael left the room and went in search of the orderly. A few hard words and some coins extracted a sincere promise to see to the Chasseur officer's needs. Michael had no idea if the man would keep his word, and determined to return when he could. It seemed he would not be seeing Renard any time soon.

When he got back to his billet Michael found that Francisco had worked wonders in his absence. A palliasse was covered with his blankets, a rickety looking chair and a small table had appeared. Michael's trunk had a clean shirt laid out on it, and a clean neckcloth, along with Michaels dressing case. His canteen stood open, and a place was laid on the table. Other plates had bread, cheese and cold meats on them. Another palliasse had Francisco's belongings on it. Best of all, the room had a small fireplace, now with a fire, and his kettle and another pot were on it. Francisco stood by the fireplace, a smile on his face.

"This is very good, Francisco, very good." Michael gave the boy a huge grin.

"Thank you, Senhor. In the pot is some vegetable soup, and there will be tea ready soon. And tomorrow you will have hot water to shave."

After he had eaten, Michael lit a small cigar and sat back in his chair. "Francisco?"

"Yes, Senhor."

"We are probably going to be here for a while. Tomorrow I will see if I can get some more ready money, then you can get in some supplies for us. And I think it would be a good idea to get my own baggage animal, a pony, perhaps, and my own groom as well." Michael thought that he could well afford it, and it would make life a little easier.

"Yes, Senhor."

"But just now," he got to his feet, "I am going to take a look to see how Duke is." He put his forage cap on his head, a welcome change from the tarleton drying by the fire. He had realised that Francisco had not yet eaten, but wouldn't do so in front of him. So, he thought, a gentle stroll and a wander around the Palacio would be a fine way to pass an hour or so. Perhaps he would come across Scovell.

The Portuguese grooms had taken good care of Duke. He was in the Palacio's stables along with all the other horses belonging to the General Officers and their staff. Just as well, he thought, the rain was still pouring down. He hoped the Regiment had a good billet tonight. While he was in the stables he asked the grooms if they knew where he might buy a baggage pony and hire a good groom. They were sympathetic to his request, but could not help him, they were all from Lisbon and had come north with the army. They did say that they would let him know if they heard of a pony or a groom, although the French had apparently stripped the city of any good animals.

Leaving the stables, Michael made a dash through the rain for the nearest door. It took him into a different wing of the Palacio from the one where his billet was. Strolling along a corridor he heard voices ahead, and saw the now familiar figure of Sir Arthur Wellesley appear from a doorway. To Michael's right was a staircase, and he ran up it, feeling that he just wanted to keep out of the way for the rest of the day.

The staircase took him to another corridor with windows on one side, and doors on the other. As he walked along he realised that all the doors had names chalked on them. A closer look revealed that they were French names, presumably, he assumed, of French officers who had been billeted here until their precipitate retreat yesterday. He opened a door marked 'Dupont'. The room certainly gave the impression of having been quickly abandoned. Michael couldn't see anything obviously left behind, but he thought he would get Francisco to have a search tomorrow. The rooms hadn't been allocated to any British officers, and he might turn up something useful.

Suddenly Michael came to halt, frozen, staring disbelievingly at one door. Chalked on it was 'J-P Renard 22Ch'. He thrust the door open hard, and it banged back against the wall. Inside it was just like the first room he had looked into. There was nothing to give any indication of who might have occupied it. Nothing except the name on the door. He spun on his heel and set off for the hospital, heedless of the rain still pouring down.

At the hospital he cursorily returned the salute of the sentries, raced up the stairs, along the corridor, and crashed into the room where the Chasseur officer was. The man was sitting up, his back against the wall. It looked like the orderly had kept his promise. Too bad, thought Michael. The look of surprise on the man's face turned to fear as Michael strode across the room and sent jug, bowl and mug flying with a single kick.

"Now, listen to me, you bastard, and listen carefully." Michael snarled with anger. "I know you lied to me; I know Renard was here. Now tell me everything you know."

"No, Monsieur, I swear to you…"

He got no further. His wounded arm was nearest to Michael, who gave it a savage kick. The man screamed and grabbed at it with his good hand.

"Now," shouted Michael, "tell me everything you know!"

Michael was suddenly aware of movement behind him. Spinning around he saw the orderly standing in the doorway, gaping at the scene before him. "Get out!" Michael screamed at him, shoving him out of the room and slamming the door shut.

He turned back to the French officer. "Now, again, tell me everything you know about Renard."

The man began to protest, and Michael bent down and seized him by his shirt front, rain dripping off his hair onto the man's face. As he did so he felt something dig into his ribs slightly. His free hand went to his sash and found the knife that Barreto had lent him. He let the man drop back, took out the knife, and opened it. The blade was only five or so inches long, but it was slim, and curved to a needle point. Michael seized the man's shirt front again, and held the knife where he could see it.

"Let me make something very clear to you, Monsieur. I know Monsieur Renard, I know him well, and he has done me a great harm, a harm that I will not see go unpunished. He killed the woman I loved, and I am going to kill him, so you had better start speaking, or I will use this on that handsome face of yours."

The man's expression changed from one of fear to one that showed, suddenly, some understanding. "Monsieur, please, I will tell what I know, but please, tell me one thing?"

"What?" snarled Michael.

"Renard, he was drunk one night after dinner, he said something about having killed a fine English Lady. Is that true?"

"Yes."

"I am sorry, Monsieur, we did not believe him, he was not popular with the Regiment. Then he was rarely with us, he just visited a few times when we were near headquarters."

"He was on the staff?"

"We never knew what he did, Monsieur. He just appeared here in Oporto after it was captured. He had come from Paris, but he said he had been in London, we didn't believe him. We thought he was just some spoilt diplomat's son who got an easy duty."

"What do you think he was doing?"

"There were rumours that he had been in Lisbon with Marshal Junot, in the Spring and Summer of last year. His name just appeared on the regimental list last year, but no one knew anything about him."

"So you knew nothing of him until he just turned up here as an officer of the Twenty-Second."

"Yes."

"But he never took the field with you?"

"No."

Michael paused, thinking hard, some of it agreed with what he already knew. Some of it was new. "Where is he now?"

"I don't know. With Marshal Soult's staff, perhaps."

Michael lowered the man back on to his palliasse, closed the knife and put it back in his sash. He looked at the French officer. "Jean-Paul Renard is a very dangerous man, he is a killer, and he takes pleasure in it. I would suggest that it would be good for you if no one, least of all Renard, ever hears about this little conversation. Do you understand?"

The man nodded. "Of course, Monsieur." He paused. "Monsieur, I am sorry about your woman."

Michael nodded his appreciation, turned, and left the room. As he reached the top of the stairs he could see the orderly and a man in a surgeon's uniform hurrying towards him. He hurried down the stairs and out of the hospital into the gloom of the early evening.

He walked slowly through the rain, thinking about what the French officer had told him. He didn't even know the man's name. Michael was surprised when he realised that he felt not the slightest hint of guilt about his treatment of the man. What he did know was that Renard was clearly not a genuine French officer, the uniform was something for him to hide behind while he carried out his work as a spy and an assassin. He also knew that he was somewhere out towards the Spanish border with the rest of Soult's beaten army. With the army, but not really of the army? This, he felt, was Musgrave's world.

Chapter 19

When he returned to the Palacio, Michael lost no time in searching out Colonel Murray. He was in the large salon that passed for his office, where all was hustle and bustle. Murray was in deep conversation with an officer in the uniform of a Colonel of the Portuguese Army. He caught sight of Michael and waved him over.

"Ah, Roberts, glad to see you." He turned to the Portuguese Colonel. "Colonel, this is Lieutenant Roberts of the Sixteenth. He will be staying in Oporto to help you for a while, not sure how long for, it all rather depends on Monsieur Soult. Anyway, he's fluent in Portuguese, grew up in Lisbon. Err, he, ah, also has duties relating to other matters from time to time. Roberts, this is Colonel Trant who has been appointed Governor of Oporto."

Trant looked at Michael with an expression best described as suspicious, and then addressed him, to Michael's surprise, in a strong Irish accent. "Ye're not one of these damned spies are ye?"

"Colonel," Murray waved his arms to hush him, "a little discretion, please. And no, Lieutenant Roberts is not a spy, he is a regular officer. He simply has knowledge and experience that has come in useful from time to time in intelligence matters. Is that not so, Roberts?"

"Yes, sir. In fact, sir, I have gathered some information that needs to go to," Murray raised an eyebrow, "err, to the appropriate authority, sir."

"Very good Roberts." Murray looked around. "Sit yourself down over there and write what you want sent, and then give it to Scovell. He will cypher it and then return the original to you. I suggest you burn that."

"Yes, sir."

"And then report to Colonel Trant."

"Yes, sir." Michael turned away, aware of Trant's curious gaze on his back.

Michael quickly composed a brief letter to Musgrave, laying out what he had discovered, but offering no thoughts on what it all implied. He handed it to Scovell, who read it. "Well, Roberts, that is interesting." He saw a look of concern on Michael's face. "It's alright, I do all Murray's cypher work for him, so I have an idea of what this about. I gather this Renard is a very nasty piece of work?"

"Yes, sir, he is, very."

Scovell tilted his head to one side and peered at Michael. "I get the impression this is personal? No, don't answer that, I don't need to know." He straightened up. "Give me a quarter of an hour and you can have this back. Only one copy for London, I assume?"

"Yes, sir."

"Then I suggest you make yourself scarce for a while before Trant seizes on you." He smiled as he spoke.

Michael took the opportunity to check on his billet and Francisco. Everything was spick and span, but there was no sign of Francisco. Michael went down to the stables and found him there, talking to the grooms. Duke was standing in a stall contentedly chomping on hay. Since all was well, Michael went back to his room and lit another cigar. He stretched out on the chair, feet to the fire, and was soon lost, deep in thought.

Michael's stillness belied the turmoil in his mind. He felt tired, not physically, but emotionally. He was still surprised at his anger and brutality in dealing with the unknown French officer. He examined how he felt. Still angry, wanting to find Renard and kill him. He thought about the way that he had treated the French officer, but still felt no guilt, it had been necessary. He was just sorry that it had come to that, and hoped the man would recover from his wound, but he realised that he would do whatever was necessary to avenge Elaine's death. He finished his cigar and roused himself. In the meantime, he had duties to attend to.

Back in the Quartermaster General's office all was still a hive of activity. Michael found Scovell, who had finished cyphering the letter for Musgrave. It would, Scovell informed him, be on a ship for England in the morning. He handed the original to Michael and watched as Michael held it to a candle and burnt it. He smiled at Scovell, who smiled back and spoke.

"Time for some proper soldiering, I think?"

The next few days were a constant round of bureaucracy, diplomacy and long hours. Sir Arthur, Colonel Murray, and the rest of the army had set off in pursuit of Soult. Michael took advantage of the departure of headquarters from the Palacio to claim another room to add to his quarters. Scovell had been despatched on a reconnaissance to the north, up the coast. Work was pushed ahead on reconstructing the bridge of boats across the Douro. It rained solidly for three days, making everything just that bit harder, depressing the spirits with its interminable persistence. Michael found himself dealing with the citizens of Oporto who had claims for the costs of billeting British troops. He was sent to ride out around the countryside to look for forage, and arrange for it to be sent to the city. He saw at first hand the damage wrought on the city and the surrounding area by the French. They had taken what they wanted, and frequently destroyed what they couldn't take.

He did learn that the French chasseur officer had not lost his arm, but would never swing a sabre again. He saw his name on a list of prisoners, Lieutenant Janvier. Michael sent Francisco to the hospital with food and a little money for him, and a note, 'from the officer looking for Renard'. Francisco said the man had looked surprised, and said something in French, but as he spoke no French, and the man no Portuguese, he had just left.

The day after the rain stopped he found himself across in Vila Nova, and the rabelos from Regua were still there. The river was in flood following the continuous rain. He managed to spend a pleasant half hour with the crews in a tavern on the quayside, and took the opportunity to return Barreto's' knife to him. Barreto also told him where to find the shop in Oporto where the best knives could be bought.

After he left them, he walked further along the quay and saw the Warre family port house. Acting on an impulse he went in and asked for Senhor Alves. He was shown into an office, where an elderly gentleman with a long pigtail greeted him with a puzzled 'Senhor?'

Michael quickly explained who he was, that he had been at Regua with William Warre, and that it was he who had brought the rabelos down river. "I thought I should make sure that everything is alright with regard to the crews. I would not like them to be in any sort of trouble for what they did. Without them the French would probably still be in Oporto."

Alves beamed at him. "Senhor, I am delighted to meet you, and very glad to hear that William is well. Of course, the captains of the boats have been to see me, to explain why they are here. Let me say that I am very happy that our boats were able to play such an important part in liberating our city. Please, take a seat." He rang a small hand bell and when a servant answered he instructed him, "Rodrigo, bring a bottle of the '90 and two glasses."

"Now, Senhor, you must tell me more about how William is, and your trip down the Douro, and how it is that you speak such excellent Portuguese."

As Michael was telling Alves a little of his story, and his connection to Lisbon, the door opened and the servant came in carefully carrying a bottle of port and two glasses. Alves took the bottle from him, and the man placed the glasses on the desk and left. Alves carefully opened the bottle. Handling it gently, and then slowly pouring the rich, dark, red wine into the glasses. Michael had stopped speaking while Alves carried out this operation with an almost reverential air. He handed a glass to Michael.

"Now, Senhor, tell me what you think of that?"

Both men raised their glasses and Michael smelt cherries and grapes, and then felt a smooth, velvety, fruit infused liquid like nothing he had ever experienced slide over his tongue. There was a hint of spice, slightly peppery. He thought he had drunk good wine, but this was something else altogether. Alves smiled at him.

"Senhor Alves, this is just wonderful. I have never tasted better."

"Nor will you, Senhor. That is the 1790 vintage, perhaps the best we have ever made. We have perhaps a few dozen bottles left."

"Senhor, you do me a great honour."

"Senhor, the honour is all mine. You are risking all to liberate my country from the French, in comparison, a bottle of port is nothing."

The two men drank again in silence.

"And now, Senhor," said Alves, "is there any way that I may be of assistance to you. I regret to say that I never knew your father, although I had heard his name, of course. And the name of Quintela is famous."

Michael hesitated. "There is one thing, Senhor."

"Yes?"

"I am embarrassed to ask, but I find myself short of ready cash. If you can help me I can give you an order on Praed's in London, if you would find that acceptable?"

"Praed's? Yes, of course, that would be most acceptable. But, first, let me refill your glass."

When Michael left Warre's an hour later he was feeling much cheered. He had passed a very pleasant time in the company of Alves, it had been good to talk about times before the war, and he now had a very adequate supply of cash. Moreover, Alves had promised to send a case of port over to his quarters, and to look out for a groom for him. All in all it had been a most satisfactory visit.

Two days later, as he was shaving, Francisco came in and announced, "Senhor, there is a man downstairs who is looking for a job as a groom. He says Senhor Alves sent him."

"Excellent." Michael hadn't really expected Alves to produce a groom, clearly he had been being more than just polite when he said he would look. "Take him to see Duke, and I will be down shortly."

Michael walked into the stables and saw Francisco by Duke's stall. With him was a stocky man in breeches, a short jacket over a waistcoat, and a broad brimmed hat. As he approached Michael saw that he was an older man, perhaps in his thirties. Francisco saw Michael, and spoke to the man. He turned, a little awkwardly, Michael thought, and removed his hat. Then the man stepped away from Duke's stall and Michael saw that he had a bad limp.

"Senhor, this is Jose Parra." Francisco introduced him.

Parra offered Michael a letter. "Senhor, this is for you, from Senhor Alves."

The letter informed Michael that Parra was a former rabelo crewman with Warre's boats, but he had crushed his leg between a boat and a rock. Alves assured Michael that he was now recovered, but lacked the necessary agility for the boats. Since the accident he had been working in a livery stable, and found that he had a way with horses. Unfortunately, he had lost his job when the French took all the stable's horses. Alves expressed his confidence that Michael would not be disappointed.

The terms of Parra's employment were soon agreed. Michael thought he was going to like him, he had a bit of a sparkle to his eye, and seemed to have a sense of humour, along with a ready smile.

"Tell me, Parra, you must know the horse dealers around Oporto?"

"Yes, Senhor, they are mostly rogues, but one or two are honest men."

"That sounds like horse dealers everywhere. Do you think you can find me a baggage animal? A pony perhaps?"

Parra frowned, and bit his lip thoughtfully. "Possibly, Senhor, possibly, but it will not be easy, the French took all they could find." He smiled. "But I do not think they found all the horses. How much will you pay, Senhor?"

"For a good pony? I will go up to a hundred dollars for a good one."

Parra grinned. "If you will permit, Senhor, I shall come back tomorrow with a pony for you."

Michael laughed. "And see if you can get a pack saddle for it as well."

Michael's day continued much as the preceding days had. He had managed to find the shop Barreto had recommended, and purchased a wickedly sharp, folding knife, which he now habitually carried in his sash. On an impulse he also bought one for Lloyd, he hoped he would be able to give it to him. Michael's duties were not onerous, but neither were they stimulating, and left him plenty of time for reflection. Colonel Trant was a likeable enough man, if perhaps a little fond of his drink. Michael had found it politic to let him have a bottle of the port Alves sent to him. Still, Trant and his staff were convivial company when they dined together each day. After dinner Michael had got into the habit of taking a walk in the grounds of the Palacio and smoking a cigar or two. That evening he was sitting on a bench near the stables when he heard an unmistakable Welsh voice sing out. "Lieutenant Roberts, sir? I've brought you your horse safe and sound, sir!"

Michael leapt to his feet. A few yards away was a grinning Lloyd, sitting on Edward with Johnny alongside on his lead rein.

"Dammit, Lloyd, but you're a sight for sore eyes."

"Aye, well, I'm quite glad to see you too, sir. Duw, but it's been a long ride."

Michael laughed. "Let's get the horses stabled, and then you can tell me about it."

Lloyd told Michael how he had stayed in Regua until they had learnt that Oporto had been retaken. Since no one quite knew what the French were doing, Lloyd had ridden along the Douro on the south bank. It had taken him four days, riding from first light to dusk, finding feed for the horses where he could. It had been hard on them, but nothing a few days rest and good feed wouldn't put right.

"Well, there's some good news, Lloyd, I have just engaged a groom, he should be here in the morning, with a baggage animal as well, I hope."

"That sounds just fine, sir, particularly if we're going to spend more time away from the regiment on these special missions, sir."

Michael stiffened up and gave Lloyd a hard look.

"Begging your pardon, sir, I didn't mean to give any offence."

"It's alright, Lloyd. I'd rather be with the regiment as well. And while we are on the subject, I appreciate your discretion about what happened in London."

There was an awkward silence. Michael broke it. "Come on, follow me. We've a decent billet for a change. Francisco has been looking after me very well. Hopefully, we will have more time for some proper soldiering when we re-join the regiment. And I've a little something for you as well."

Once up at the billet Michael handed Lloyd his new knife. He was delighted, and thanked Michael profusely, adding with a grin, "Ah, it's a lovely wicked thing, sir, and takes a good edge."

Michael smiled at his delight, and said, "Look upon it as a little thanks for London."

Later, Lloyd, and Francisco were in the other room, and Michael was sitting alone in his room, a cigar lit, and a glass of port in his hand. He thought about Lloyd's comment about 'special missions'. And 'proper soldiering'. Scovell had said that, and now he was off somewhere with a brigade of light cavalry. Proper soldiering. What was he doing? Pushing paper, soothing vexed civilians, chasing supplies and counting forage carts. And apart from that? Interrogating a wounded

French officer in the search for a murdering bastard and a spy. It was the dirty side of the war that he had stumbled into, and now he couldn't get free from it. At least not until Renard was dead. He took a mouthful of port. Meanwhile his Regiment was off chasing the French, proper soldiering. He threw his head back and stared at the ceiling. Elaine had set him free with her letter, but he didn't feel free, not yet, and certainly not while Renard lived. He jumped to his feet, this was getting him nowhere, the same arguments were going around in his head that had bothered him a few nights ago. He had to get things straight in his mind. He finished his port, put on his sabre, stuck his forage cap on his head, and walked out of the Palacio.

He strolled through the darkening streets, going downhill towards the river. He realised that he missed the Regiment, and his fellow officers, he recalled what his Grandfather had said about the bonds that were built in war. He now knew what he had meant. But they had seen action together, and he hadn't been there. He wished he had someone to talk to, but there wasn't anyone, and even if there was, there were things he couldn't talk about, to anyone. He reached the quayside and sat on an abandoned crate. He had to work this out for himself.

Slowly it came to him that so much of what had happened was down to the simple fact that he was practically Portuguese. Perhaps Musgrave had had a point back when they first met, and had asked him if he felt British or Portuguese. He recalled his words to the rabelo captains in Regua. He knew he was British; he loved his mother country without reservation, but he also loved Portugal. Well, he thought, a man can love his mother and his wife. He wanted to help beat the French who had invaded his adopted country, and driven his parents out and to their deaths. Everything else had followed from that as naturally as night followed day. Fighting the dirty war was just as important as proper soldiering. It could even be that he would be better at that than proper soldiering. It did seem that he had found a ruthless streak, that had come as a surprise.

He felt better, everything suddenly seemed clearer. If he was to fight in Musgrave's war, he would. He seemed to be needed. He would be as good a regimental officer as he could, and fight as a proper soldier, but he would also be ready and willing to fight the dirty war. A thought struck him. It was a war Elaine had chosen, and perhaps it was the only war open to her, but if it had been good enough for her, it was good enough for him.

He rose from the crate and turned back the way he had come. A movement in a doorway caught his eye, his hand went to his sword hilt. "Who's there?"

A figure stepped out of the shadows. "It's Lloyd, sir."

"Lloyd? What the devil are you doing there?"

"Begging you pardon, sir, just acting as your covering file. You were away somewhere else, sir, so I thought I should just walk along a bit."

Michael smiled. "Thank you, Lloyd, I was rather lost in thought." And another thought struck Michael. "Actually, I'm glad to see you."

"Sir?"

"Yes. I was thinking about proper soldiering." Lloyd said nothing. "You see, Lloyd, I'm not sure how much of that I will be doing." Michael paused and looked at Lloyd, but his face was hidden in shadow. "You were with me in London." He paused again. "I think there may be more of that sort of thing, in fact, there already has been, here, in Oporto, and I wouldn't want to involve you if you didn't want it. If you like you can return to normal regimental duties. I can manage with Francisco and Parra. I'll put in a word for you, perhaps you'll make corporal again, even sergeant."

There was silence on the quayside. In the distance lights moved, reflecting off the dark water, where work was still going on to reconstruct the bridge of boats, and voices carried to them across the water.

"That's very good of you, sir, and it's a tempting offer. But I never have seen eye to eye with Sergeant Taylor, and I think the Colonel would take some convincing that I've reformed, sir." Lloyd stepped forward into the light, a smile on his face. "So, if you don't mind, I'll just carry on as your covering file, sir. It's a sight more interesting than guard duty anyways."

Michael stepped towards Lloyd and held out his hand. "Thank you, Emyr, that means a lot to me."

Lloyd spat in his hand and held it out. "That's a deal, then, sir?"

Michael spat into his hand and shook Lloyd's. "That it is, Emyr, that it is."

The following morning Parra, as good as his word, was at the Palacio early, accompanied by another man, who was leading a small, shaggy, brown pony with a pack saddle on its back. Together Michael and Lloyd looked over the pony, Lloyd nodded his approval, and the haggling began. Realising he had met his match, the dealer agreed a fair price, eighty dollars, and Parra took charge of the pony. Lloyd suggested that they call it Fred, and Michael agreed. It was only later that he remembered Sergeant Taylor's first name was Frederick.

Word arrived that morning that the pursuit of the French had been called off after Soult and his army crossed into Spain, having abandoned all their artillery and blowing up guns and chests full of coin, scattering it over the surrounding countryside. At once Michael found himself swept up in the work of allocating billets for the returning troops. Sir Arthur returned to the Palacio, and the Sixteenth to the same billets as before. Poor Tomkinson was also brought in from Grijo, where he had been lying in a priest's house since receiving his wounds. Captain Cocks was also back, but still on the staff of General Cotton. With the help of Michael's Portuguese, they managed to find Tomkinson a comfortable billet where he would be well cared for until he could take a ship back to England. Word arrived from England that, following the death of his brother, General Harcourt was now Earl Harcourt. At the end of the month Michael was ordered back to his regiment, leaving the Palacio, moving himself, his servants and horses into a small house on the edge of Oporto, and once more being thrown back into his role as Captain Ashworth's Lieutenant.

About the author

David Blackmore worked for the Royal Armouries Museum for 26 years, for most of them as the Museum's Registrar, and was part of the creative team for the Royal Armouries in Leeds.

He is the author of four non-fiction books;

Arms and Armour of the English Civil Wars.

British Cavalry in the Mid-18th Century.

Destructive and Formidable, British Infantry Firepower, 1642 – 1765, (the published version of his PhD thesis from Nottingham Trent University).

So Bloody a Day, the 16th Light Dragoons in the Waterloo Campaign.

Has written more articles and given more lectures than he can remember, and has appeared in Sean Bean's 'Waterloo', teaching him how to use a sabre.

A re-enactor for forty five years, including being Lord General of the Roundhead Association, and commanding the British Light Dragoons at Waterloo 200. He commanded B Troop, 16th Light Dragons from 2014 to 2019.

David says that he is now definitely retired from re-enacting.

However, he still gets out on a horse two or three times a week, including on Johnny, the model for Michael Roberts' horse in the 'Wellington's Dragoon' series.

Brindle Books Ltd

We hope that you have enjoyed this book. To find out more about Brindle Books Ltd, including news of new releases, please visit our website:

http://www.brindlebooks.co.uk

There is a contact page on the website, should you have any queries, and you can let us know if you would like email updates of news and new releases. We promise that we won't spam you with lots of sales emails, and we will never sell or give your contact details to any third party.

If you purchased this book online, please consider leaving an honest review on the site from which you purchased it. Your feedback is important to us, and may influence future releases from our company.

Also available from Brindle Books Ltd

NORMANBY
BY
P.G. DIXON

Pawns were made to be sacrificed.

When Tom Grant is transferred from the glamour of MI5 to a little-known intelligence department, he begins to think that his career is on the slide.

Then, the investigation into the death of an agent leads him into a plot to strike at the heart of the UK.

But who can he trust?
The Colonel – The loud and overbearing Department head?...
Major Green – The dashing war hero with the dedicated team?...
Or Normanby – The prim bureaucrat with dark secrets in his past?

Also available from Brindle Books Ltd

THE 'LOST' VILLAGE OF LAWERS

BY

MARK BRIDGEMAN

The Lost Village of Lawers tells the story of the haunting and enigmatic abandoned village that nestles besides the shores of Loch Tay. Almost 1,000 years of surprising human history are hidden within its tumbling ruins. Unknown, unseen, and forgotten by many, this new publication reveals the story behind the ruins and attempts to answer the question that has puzzled so many people – just who was its most famous resident – 'The Lady of Lawers'?